Ben Pastor, born in Italy, lived for thirty years in the United States, working as a university professor in Vermont, before returning to her home country. *Liar Moon* is the second in the Martin Bora series and follows on from the success of *Lumen*, also published by Bitter Lemon Press. Ben Pastor is the author of other novels including the highly acclaimed *The Water Thief* and *The Fire Waker*, and is considered one of the most talented writers in the field of historical fiction. In 2008 she won the prestigious Premio Zaragoza for best historical fiction.

Also available from Bitter Lemon Press
by Ben Pastor:

Lumen

LIAR MOON

Ben Pastor

BITTER LEMON PRESS
LONDON

BITTER LEMON PRESS

First published in the United Kingdom in 2012 by
Bitter Lemon Press, 37 Arundel Gardens, London W11 2LW

www.bitterlemonpress.com

A CIP record for this book is available from the British Library
ISBN 978–1–904738–82-4

Typeset by Tetragon

Printed and bound by CPI Group (UK) Ltd, Croydon, CR0 4YY

To those who were in the trucks
bound for the concentration camps

Surely men of low degree are vanity,
and men of high degree are a lie:
to be laid in the balance, they are altogether
lighter than vanity.

(Psalm 62:9)

Luna Mendax

"A Liar Moon" (Latin Proverb)

1

"*Si deve far coraggio, maggiore.*"

Martin Bora was in too much pain to say he understood.

"*Dobbiamo pulire le ferite.*"

In too much pain to say he understood that, also.

Courage. Cleaning the wounds. Blood throbbed in his lids, by quick flickers in the blind glow of eyes tightly shut, and at the back of his mouth, where his teeth clenched hard, another heartbeat scanned frantic time in his head.

"*Coraggio, coraggio.* Try to take heart."

A small pool of saliva rose under his tongue, until he had to swallow. The lifting of the stretcher so exasperated the agony in his left arm, the whole length of his body crumpled with it. All he could gather was a convulsed short breathing at the top of his chest, as in one who must cry, or cry out.

They were laying him on the emergency-room table. Taking off his boots. His left leg seemed to tear open with the removal of the rigid leather, as if they were wrenching the bone from his knee. Lights burst over him, human voices travelled from great distances to him, at him, into him.

Blood sprayed as medics cut and dug through the gore of his clothes, and Bora would not let go but grew hard and grim and desperate, trying to resist the pain. To fight it, as if one could fight this, when his whole left side felt crushed in a giant vice and there was no hope of pulling himself out without shredding arm and leg in the process. His left hand, torn already to filaments and gushing blood, gulped and gulped his life out – lungs, stomach, bones – all seemingly heaving from the severance at the end of his arm, a sick red jumble of what had filled his body until now.

They were undoing his army breeches. Anxious hands reached into the blood-matted fleece of his groin, searched thigh and knee. His neck arched rigid in the strain of his back to rise.

"Hold him down, hold him down," a voice said. "You'll have to hold him down, Nurse."

Joints braced as in a seizure, Bora was fighting pain, not being held down.

He could not swallow nor could he say he could not swallow, and when someone gave him water – he knew his mouth was unclenching because breath surged out of it in spasms – it gurgled back up his throat to the sides of his face.

They would work on his left arm next. He hardened for it, and still a paroxysm of pain wrenched his mouth open and he was racked into a fit of trembling but would not scream. He groped for the edge of the table, would not scream. Neck flexed back, hard, unable to close his mouth – it was hard, hard! – he struggled and butted his head against the hard surface and would not scream.

"Put something under his head, Nurse, he's battering it on the table."

The digging of hands into the meat of arm and groin and thigh accelerated and then halted. It began again slowly. Slowly. Digging, pulling, coming apart. Being born must be like this, a helpless nauseous struggle to get out in the overwhelming smell of blood – a butcher-shop smell – pain jagged immeasurably high in it.

He would break. If he pushed through he would break into aborted flesh, and die if he didn't.

"Hold him down!"

Then someone forcibly pried his right hand from the side of the table and clutched it.

Bora could weep for the comfort that came with the hold, as if the act were his midwifery from death, delivering him from the mandible and womb of death. He stopped fighting, and was suddenly coming out of the vice.

Lights blinded him, he saw blood quilting his stretched-out body and people working into the naked red quilt with shiny tools, wads of cotton.

Out, out. He was coming out.

The clasp wrested him to a threshold of agony, brought him forth, and pain was extreme, unbearable at the passage. Bora cried out only once, when birth from pain tore what remained of his left hand with it.

In the morning, the sky was the battered colour of a bruise. The tall hospital window was made sad and livid by it, and in that bruised light Bora asked, unflinching, "Will there have to be a graft, or was there enough skin left?"

"We were able to repair it with what skin there was, Major. We tried to shield the stump and remove enough nervous terminations so that it will not hurt too much later. I am very sorry."

Bora looked away from the surgeon.

"What about my leg?"

"If gangrene doesn't develop, we hope to save it."

Suddenly Bora felt the need to vomit. Only it had nothing to do with anaesthesia this time, nor with pain. He said he understood, but would not look at his left arm.

The Italian surgeon, who was high-ranking and old enough to speak his mind to a German officer, shook his head. "It didn't help matters that you waited two hours to be evacuated."

"My wounded men came first. I lost two of them as it is."

"You lost three. Anyway, since you must be wondering, the metal fragments in your groin have not injured the genitals."

"I see." Bora did not look up, staring at an indeterminate place on the bed. "Thank you."

The wretched odour of disinfectant and blood filled the room. His body smelled of them. "My wedding ring, where is it?"

"Here."

Beyond the bed, everything was a livid off-white colour. The window had a veined marble sill, like mottled flesh. Small cracks in the wall beneath it drew the eyeless, approximate profile of a horse.

"Will you accept something for the pain?"

Martin Bora moved his head from side to side on the pillow, but was too weak to say that he wouldn't.

Lago, 18.5 miles north-east of Verona
21 November 1943

Two months later, when he opened his eyes in the dark, Bora found himself holding his breath. Thinking, he went up and down his limbs, checking with hesitation the usually aching areas of left arm and leg – regions in the dark, uncertain of boundaries as even one's body is when awakening.

It was seldom that he had no pain, and the grateful lassitude, derived from feeling *nothing*, had become a luxury in the past few months. Face up in bed, he avoided any motion that might endanger the precious, transitory balance, though not feeling was far from feeling well. It would be so, it would have to be so until his body forgave him for what had happened in September.

The grenade attack had been unavoidable, but his flesh rejected it, and the truth of mutilation. He was still ashamed for helplessly lying on the butcher block of the emergency table, sewn in his wounds and bloodied as at birth for the length of his limbs, whose ordure a Sister of Charity sponged. The mortified nakedness of chest and belly and thighs and groin under the patient wipe of her virgin hands stayed with him. Forgiveness to himself would not come from simply surviving the agony of it as a wide-eyed animal, without crying out.

So Bora woke holding his breath so as not to rouse pain, while outside of the room – outside the command post – the wind rode high and pushed ahead a moon thin as an eyebrow.

By seven o'clock that morning, a keen, colder gale had blustered out of the north to empty the streets of Lago, a small town like many others, without a lake despite its name, lost in the fields of the Veneto region. Bora sat in his office minding paperwork, with an ear to the hum of vibrating telephone wires outdoors. He heard, too, the idling and then stopping of a motor car before the command, but had no curiosity to reach the window and find out who it was.

Even when the orderly came to knock on his door, he did not stop writing.

"Yes, what?" he limited himself to saying. After being told of the visitor, he added, "All right, let him in."

The newcomer was dark and wiry, with vivacious black eyes and a moustache like a caterpillar lining his upper lip. The sombre Fascist Republican Party mixture of field-grey and black formed a light-absorbing stain in the dim autumn day. Skulls and bundles of rods on the epaulets identified him as a member of the shock troops.

"*Viva il Duce.*"

Bora did not return the Fascist salute, and stared up in a noncommittal way from his chair. He set his face inexpressively enough, while "How can I assist you?" rolled out of him flatly.

"Centurion Gaetano De Rosa, of the Muti Battalion."

The visitor spoke in the manner of training camp, projecting his voice across the office.

"Major Martin Bora of the *Wehrmacht*," Bora replied. And it took him aback that the little man addressed him in German next, in good German, with a pompous, self-conscious ring to the use of tenses as he introduced his reason for being there.

It had to do with a murder, so at first Bora listened, sitting back in the chair with his left arm low and his right hand calmly fingering a fountain pen over the shiny desktop.

"Why don't you speak Italian?" he asked then, in Italian.

"Why? Well, Major, I thought—"

"There's no need for you to go through any such effort. As you can see, I speak Italian too."

It was obvious that De Rosa was disappointed. Bora knew well enough these Fascists moonstruck with all things Germanic, who patterned themselves after his own people to the extent of sounding obnoxiously servile. He had learned to cut short all attempts to favour him with familiarity with German customs and places. And now he went straight to the core of the matter.

"I appreciate your coming to me, Centurion De Rosa, but I don't see how or even why I should offer assistance. The violent death of a Party notable is serious business. Your Verona police will be much better qualified than myself to conduct the investigation."

De Rosa was not easily outdone this time. "I thought you might answer that way, Major. That's why I brought this along. Please read." He handed an envelope to Bora, who sliced through its side with a penknife and began reading. Against the light from the window, De Rosa seemed to glow with pleasure at the sight of the letterhead, the squarish spread eagle of the German Headquarters in Verona.

There was little arguing with the brief of presentation. Bora put the sheet down, glaring at the little man, and prepared himself to listen.

Twenty minutes down the road from Lago, the few houses of Sagràte were buffeted by the pitiless wind. The naked bushes rattled like tambourines when Police Inspector Guidi got out of his old Fiat service car.

Corporal Turco hastened to reach the door of the police command ahead of him, opened it, stepped aside and let him in. He had the encumbering figure of a Saracen-blooded Sicilian, and when he joined Guidi inside, a wild whiff of clothes worn outdoors came with him.

"*Arsalarma*," he let out in his dialect. "With one shoe missing, Inspector, he can't have gone far."

Guidi did not bother to turn around. He removed from around his neck the bulky scarf his mother had hand-knit for him. "Why, Turco, haven't you ever walked barefoot?"

There wasn't much else for Turco to say, since his first footwear had come with his induction into the army. He brought to Guidi's desk the laceless, worn shoe they had just recovered, careful to place a newspaper under it before laying it down.

"Without a shoe, and crazy, too," he mumbled to himself. "*Marasantissima*."

Guidi had started pencilling lines on a topographic map tacked to his office wall. In a wide semicircle that began and ended at the river, fanning out from its right bank, he enclosed the stretch of flat countryside they had searched the night before. It seemed much larger when one had to slog across it, he thought.

Past the river, long and narrow fields, now mostly bare, ran to the guerrilla-torn piedmont, home to partisan bands. Guidi knew there were no farmhouses there to offer shelter to a fugitive – only fields, and irrigation canals bordering them and intersecting with deep ditches alongside endless hedgerows. His instinct told him he should continue to search this side of the river. Guidi marked with a dot the place where the shoe had been found, nearly halfway between Lago and Sagràte, where groves of willow trees flanked the county road.

"Let's give the men a chance to rest until tomorrow," he told Turco. "Then we'll see what else can be done. The *carabinieri* assured me they'll continue the search on their own until sundown." Guidi nearly laughed saying it, because Turco (who was far from daft, but loved theatrics) stared at the muddy shoe as though he could stare it into giving information.

As for Bora, he sighed deeply to conceal his boredom at De Rosa's narrative. Because the talk gave no sign of ending, "Colonel Habermehl is surely aware that I'm very busy," Bora interjected at last. "I have no free time."

In front of him, Habermehl's letter agreed that it was all a bother, but advised him to please the Verona Fascists. Bora knew the arguments by heart: this was northern Italy, four years into the war, and the Italian allies had become potential enemies. The Americans had landed in Salerno and were inching up the peninsula. Why not please the Verona Fascists, who remained pro-German? Habermehl asked "as a family friend, not out of rank". But the rank was there, of course, and Bora knew better than to fall for the outward courtesy.

"Look," he told De Rosa. "If you wish me to get involved in this case, you must supply me with all information gathered by the Italian police and *carabinieri* to date. When did the murder take place?"

De Rosa frowned. "Day before yesterday. Didn't you read it in the *Arena*? It was the most important piece of news, it took up nearly the whole front page."

Bora had spent all day Friday at the hospital in Verona, where the surgeon was still extracting shrapnel from his left leg. He'd had neither the time nor the inclination to read the Italian newspapers. "I must not have paid attention," he said.

Promptly De Rosa pulled out a newspaper clipping, laying it square on the desk in front of Bora.

Bora read. "Here it says that *Camerata* Vittorio Lisi was the victim of a stroke in his country villa."

"Well." De Rosa gave him an unamused smile, a grimace really. "You understand that when it comes to a man of Lisi's fame and valour, the public must be kept from scandals. Lisi was from Verona. All knew him, all loved him."

"All but one person at least, if he's been done in." Bora gave back the clipping, which De Rosa carefully folded again but left on the desk. "What chances are there that it was a political assassination?"

"None, Major Bora. Lisi was not a controversial man. Solid, with a heart of gold."

"I'm not aware that partisans or political adversaries would be impressed by a Fascist's golden heart."

De Rosa's grimace caused the well-combed caterpillar on his upper lip to tremble. "With all respect, Major, I know the political climate of the region better than you do. I assure you it is *Fascistissimo*."

Bora was tempted to phone Habermehl with an excuse to avoid the incestuous little world of local politics. His urge might have been visible, because De Rosa spoke up.

"Colonel Habermehl informs me that you have already solved difficult cases."

"By accident." Bora minimized the report. "Always by accident."

"Not according to the colonel. He says you distinguished yourself in the case of a murder in Spain, and of a dead nun in Poland. And in Russia..."

The silvery skulls on De Rosa's uniform glinted dully. The angry eagle clutching a *fascio* on his chest pocket, and the fanaticism it stood for, was beginning to annoy Bora. He said, "All right. Tell me all that is known about Lisi's death, and provide me with the dossier as soon as possible."

"May I at least sit down?" De Rosa asked tartly.

"Sit down."

On that Sunday, Guidi's mother was shelling peas into a colander set on her knees, rolling them out of their green casing with swift, hooked strokes of the thumb. These were the last peas of the season; it was amazing how they'd managed to ripen despite the cold nights. But how well they went with pasta sauce, and how Sandro liked them!

Near the kitchen door, she could now barely make out the voices of the men talking in the parlour. Her son had a soft voice as it was. Only a few of the words he spoke to the German were comprehensible to her, and as for the German, he was even more controlled in his speech.

Signora Guidi was curious, but sat shelling peas with the offended dignity of the excluded.

Bora was saying, "No, thank you, I'm in a hurry."

Having refused to take a seat, he stood rigidly by the set dining-room table, opposite a mirrored credenza. On the credenza sat the black-ribboned photograph of Guidi's policeman father, with the date 1924 penned at the bottom, preceded by a cross.

"That's what De Rosa said, Guidi. And although he came under some pretence of secrecy, God knows why, he did not expressly forbid me to talk it over with others, so here I am."

Compared to Bora's impeccable German uniform, Guidi grew aware of his shirt-sleeved frumpiness, perhaps because Bora seemed to be appraising him. He could feel the scrutiny of his own unprepossessing lankiness, his melancholy features drawn under the limp, swept-back wave of his sandy hair. Bora, on the other hand, looked like steel and leather and immaculate cuffs.

Perhaps he ought to feel flattered by the visit. "Major," Guidi said, "is it proven that Lisi's death was not an accident, first of all?"

"It seems so. His wife's sports car has a sizeable dent in the front fender. De Rosa is convinced it resulted from her purposely running into Lisi's wheelchair. As I said, it happened in the grounds of the victim's country place. Unlikely that he was struck by a passing motorist."

Absent-mindedly Guidi nodded. From the kitchen wafted the odour of frying onions, so he went to shut the door. "Are they keeping the widow under surveillance?"

"Virtually house arrest."

"In the country?"

"No, she lives in Verona." Without stepping forward, Bora handed over a slim folder tied with a rubber band. "These are the notes I took after De Rosa's visit."

While Guidi read, Bora took off his cap and placed it under his left arm. Italian officials made little money, he knew. Dated furniture, old school books lovingly arranged on the shelf, a rug brushed threadbare. The punctilious modesty of this room spoke of the ever-losing struggle of the middle class to keep respectable. More importantly, it might speak of Guidi's honesty.

From the credenza's mirror, unbidden, the stern clarity of his own eyes met Bora. The finely drawn paleness of the face his wife called handsome looked to him new and hard, as if Russia and pain had killed him and made him into another. He took a step aside to avoid his reflection.

Guidi said, "We'll need the physician's report and autopsy."

"I requested them."

From where he faced now, Bora noticed how the photograph of Guidi's father occupied the centre of an embroidered doily, between two vases filled with artificial flowers. A regular home altar, complete with lit taper. Memory of his younger brother's death hit him squarely (Kursk, only a few months ago, the crash site in the field of sunflowers, blood lining the cockpit), so that Bora moodily looked down.

"When the housemaid came out after hearing the noise, the victim had been thrown several paces from his wheelchair. According to De Rosa, Lisi had only enough strength left in his arm to trace a 'C' on the gravel, and then lost consciousness. He had already slipped into a coma when help came, and was dead in less than twenty-four hours' time."

Guidi closed the folder. "I don't see how this detail particularly relates to his wife."

"Her name is Clara."

"Ah. But even then, it all remains circumstantial. Were there problems in the Lisi marriage?"

Bora stared at him. "They were living apart, and their separation had been unfriendly. Apparently there were still occasional violent arguments between them. Naturally the widow denies all accusations, and insists she had nothing to do with the matter, although she was reportedly unable to offer an alibi for the afternoon of the killing. Without an eyewitness, there's no way of knowing whether she drove to the country on that day or not. Whoever killed Lisi, though, arrived and left again within a few minutes."

Noise from the kitchen intruded. Guidi stole a look to the door, embarrassed that his mother was banging pots and covers as a not-so-subtle hint that lunch was ready. Bora's dark army crop moved imperceptibly in that direction.

"Well, Major, I have to think about it—"

Bora interrupted him.

"What do you intend by 'thinking'? That you haven't decided whether you'll collaborate with me, or that you need time before offering me suggestions?"

"I need to think of a plan of action. I'll phone you at the command post this evening."

Bora, who had scheduled an anti-partisan night raid and would not be at the post, nevertheless said it was fine.

Over the occasional banging of pots, "We're agreed, then." Guidi rushed to say, "What I meant to pass on, Major, is that an escaped convict is at large between Lago and Sagràte."

Unexpectedly Bora smirked. "Why, thank you. We'll lock our doors at night."

"He was diagnosed by Italian army physicians as criminally insane, and carries a marksman Carcano besides."

"6.5 or 7.35 mm calibre?"

"8 mm."

Bora frowned. "Ah. Those made for the Russian campaign. They have a brutal recoil. Well, for us it's just one more bullet to dodge, Guidi."

"I did my civic duty by informing the German authorities."

After a particularly syncopated rattle of cooking pots, the kitchen became peaceful again. Guidi breathed easily. "Did De Rosa tell you why they want to keep the murder a secret?"

Bora openly grinned this time. "For the same reason why there are no more suicides in Fascist Italy, and people just happen to stumble on the tracks while there's an oncoming train. Perhaps there are no murders in Fascist Italy, either. It seems Lisi was of some importance. A *comrade of the first hour*, in Mussolini's words." Bora swept his army cap from under his arm and put it on, taking a rigid step toward the door. "Colonel Habermehl recommended my name to the Republican Guard because of what he terms *my part* in solving other small matters. It's only natural I should contact you, since you are the professional in the field." He opened the door, through which a field-grey BMW was visible, with driver waiting at attention. "My apologies to your mother for delaying your holiday meal. Goodbye."

Guidi waited until the army car left the kerb before calling out to his mother. "He's gone, Ma." Because she did not answer, he opened the kitchen door and peered in. "He left."

His mother had taken her apron off and was wearing her good shoes. "Gone? Why didn't you ask him to stay for lunch?"

"I thought you didn't want the likes of him in the house, Ma."

"Honestly, Sandro! Now God knows what he's going to think about us Italians, that we didn't even invite him to lunch."

The shot had been fired from a distance, but even so the shutterless window of the hut had been shattered. Bits and wedges of glass spread a kaleidoscope of reflections as Guidi leaned over to examine them. Through the empty window frame, from inside, one of his men handed him the deformed bullet he'd just pried out of the wall.

It seemed the slug had missed the farmer's head by a hair's breath, and only because he'd happened to turn his face away from the raw wind while hauling wood. Now he nervously stood behind Guidi with hands driven deep in his pockets.

"Happened yesterday while I was cutting firewood, Inspector," he explained. "But I couldn't walk back three miles to Sagràte to give you the news right away. See, here's the axe as I left it. I just turn my face a moment, and the bullet flies right past me. First thing I think is,

'It must be the goddamn Germans,' because I've seen them patrolling the fields for the past week. Quick-like, I throw myself on the ground and wait a good ten minutes before getting up again. No German shows up, and since it's getting dark, I crawl indoors and wait wide awake until daytime. By this much, Inspector, it missed me! I haven't been this scared since the Great War."

Guidi only half-listened. He fingered the bullet he'd slipped into his coat's pocket, alongside the daily sand-wich his mother had stuffed in there. By now the marks-man could be anywhere. Unless, of course, he was even now framing his head in the rifle sight from behind a distant hedgerow. Automatically, Guidi hunched his shoulders. It was windy, all right, but dry and without any snow. Trails would be hard to follow.

In order to calculate the direction of the shot, Guidi stood with his back to the hut and faced the pencil-thin poplars studding the edge of the farmland. Down there, Corporal Turco rummaged in the brushwood, bareheaded, with the fatalistic courage of the Sicilian race that centuries of oppression had inured to do what must be done in a near-stolid way.

Guidi sniffed the odourless wind. The army dogs kept at the German command in Lago might come useful, he thought. Since Bora had not offered them, he had to be asked – if he was willing to spare the soldier who went with the dogs.

He could see Turco's stout figure emerging from be-hind the line of poplars and starting back. The urgency of his heavy step made Guidi hope he'd recovered the bullet casing, but it was a far larger object that Turco carried in his hand. Guidi walked up to meet him.

"Another shoe, Inspector," Turco announced, holding the find aloft.

Guidi nodded. "It matches the one we have, all right."

"What in the world is *stu lazzu di furca* doing, dropping shoes as he goes along? It don't make any sense, Inspector."

"It certainly *doesn't*."

Following Turco and his handlebar moustache, Guidi examined the area where the shoe had been found. Invisible from the hut, beyond the row of poplars ran a deep irrigation ditch, which a man could easily straddle. Ice was already forming on its banks of yellow grass.

"Not on the ground, Inspector," Turco pointed out. "Up there." And he showed the fork of a lonesome mulberry tree behind the poplars. "The shoe was wedged in there, as if the madman had been sitting in the tree at some point."

"He might have fired at the farmer from up there, too."

The first shoe had been found nearly two miles away, stuck between two rocks along an overgrown country track. The anchoring of it had seemed significant to Guidi at the time, and now this. "I don't think he *lost* the shoes," he told Turco. "He left them behind for some reason."

"For us to catch him?"

Guidi lifted his shoulders in a shrug, his usual response to uncertainty. "He lets us know he's been there, that's all."

Bora was not at the Lago army post when Guidi called. Lieutenant Wenzel, Bora's second-in-command, understood no Italian. He kept a freckled, unfriendly young face squared at him and would not volunteer any information. When Guidi gave him a scribbled message for the major, he took it and without a word walked to place it on Bora's desk.

On his way out Guidi paused to listen to the threatening growls of dogs from the small fenced yard behind the building. There Bora kept his German shepherds, he knew. A soldier was trimming willow bushes on the side of the command post.

Guidi was careful not to stare, but he noticed that the army BMW parked on the street had a clear bullet hole through its windshield. Dirt was packed in dry clumps around the tyres and under the bumper, as if it had been run off the road. Guidi's quiet observation was cut short by a soldier who eased him away with a whisked motion of his rifle stock.

Bora contacted Guidi only on Tuesday, when he agreed to meet with him within the hour in downtown Verona.

"The dogs, you may have for one day," he said as they shook hands on the city sidewalk. "If your fugitive is still around Lago or Sagràte, they'll find him. As for the shot to my windshield, since you ask, I would be glad to ascribe it to your lunatic. But I'm afraid he has nothing to do with it." This was as close as Bora got to mentioning the partisans. "No one was hurt, but the windshield is going to be damned hard to replace."

In the nine weeks they'd known each other, Guidi had never seen Bora embarrassed or at a loss for words. Not even when he'd come to introduce himself formally on the fateful 8th of September – the day when the King's government armistice with the Allies precipitated a German takeover of Italy. Curiously, the major's first visit had been to Monsignor Lai, head of the local parish, where he'd spent twice as much time as he would at the police station. Less than twelve hours later, a partisan grenade launcher had struck Bora's car while on patrol. They'd met again two weeks after that, when against medical advice Bora had left the hospital, looking like death. Since then they'd spoken occasionally, as their respective positions required. And Guidi still wondered why one as decorated as Bora should be assigned to such an unimportant place in the Venetian plain.

As they stood across the street from the downtown flat where Lisi's widow lived, Guidi felt a provincial's discomfort with the bustling elegance of the neighbourhood. Even a thousand days into the War, rows of canopied store fronts and chic restaurants lent colour to the pale baroque façades of the buildings. The elegant Green Market Square, Lords' Square, the Roman gate known as Porta Borsari were all a stone's throw from where he and Bora stood. But Bora looked perfectly at ease, as he probably would even if Romeo and Juliet were to walk by him to reclaim their city.

Guidi had the unwarranted but distinct impression that he and Bora could never like each other. Whether or not it mattered, he felt self-conscious, because Bora was observant but revealed little about himself. Other than that he attended mass frequently during the week, Guidi had heard he was upper class, Scottish on his mother's side. And married, judging by the wedding ring he wore on his right hand.

Just now Bora was congenially surveying the windshield of his parked BMW, as if the hole in it were a conversation piece. "Why do you look at me that way, Guidi? Rifle shots are my business, and these days it's easier to replace a German major than a German windshield."

"I was actually thinking about Lisi's widow, and what we ought to ask her."

"Well, she lives right there." Bora's gloved hand pointed at the corner of one of the parallel streets feeding into the Corso on one side, and into the avenue leading to the medieval centre on the other. Clara Lisi's wrought-iron balcony occupied the entire second floor of the building. "There, where you see oleanders still in bloom. But we're half an hour early, so – come."

Taking from the car the leather briefcase Guidi had seldom seen him without, Bora instructed the driver to park further down the street, and with his quick limp started toward a nearby café.

Guidi was still looking at Clara's doorstep, where a plain-clothes man stood guard.

"Yes, he does smack of police." Jovially Bora read his mind.

The café had gleaming windows (free of ugly tape and supports despite the air raids), waiters in white frocks and the delightful, unforgettable aroma of real coffee. Guidi could not help asking himself what it would cost to order anything here.

"My treat, of course," Bora was saying. "I don't like waiting in the street." With a soldier's unspoken prudence, not lost on Guidi, he chose a table from which he could keep an eye on the entrance. There he sat, oblivious to the customers' furtive looks at his uniform. "By the by, Guidi, I went to see the widow's car at the city garage. It certainly has a bad dent, which could have been caused by collision with metallic framework such as the invalid's chair. The angle and height of the damage are about right, too. You are of course welcome to inspect it

29

yourself." With a nod Bora called the waiter. "I can also add something to the information I gave you on Sunday."

After they ordered – Guidi would have the luxury of a cappuccino, Bora black coffee – Bora took out a typewritten sheet from his briefcase. "You wanted to know how Lisi lost the use of his legs. According to my sources it happened during the Fascist March on Rome twenty-one years ago. The accident was unrelated to politics, it was a car wreck on the way to the capital, but it attracted Mussolini's interest and was much publicized at the time. Got Lisi started in active politics, in fact."

"Really." Guidi noticed that in his courteous and indifferent manner Bora referred to Mussolini by name and not by title, as he'd not once but twice spoken of "Hitler" and not the *Führer*. And he addressed Guidi with *lei*, not the regime-imposed *voi*. It would seem strange, except that other subtle traits were combining to make him wonder about the German's political orthodoxy. *Watch out*, he told himself. *Maybe he does it on purpose to gauge my loyalty.* "It was a good career choice for Lisi," he observed. "He's done well for himself ever since."

"Bloody well, indeed." Bora sipped coffee, keeping uncommunicative eyes on the few people at the surrounding tables. Guidi felt sure this unafraid wariness clung to him at all times, with perhaps other concerns he chose not to share.

Scanning Bora's notes, he asked, "Were there any children from the marriage?"

"No, but not for the reasons you might surmise." Bora put down the demitasse. He grinned an unkind boyish grin, but it was a veneer on his circumspection. "The old man was insatiable in that regard. 'The Blackshirt Satyr'

30

they called him in Verona. It seems he liked them all, but servant girls were his speciality."

"You don't say." Letting the excellent drink make slow, warm inroads into his system, Guidi found he rather enjoyed being treated. "Traditionally a good reason why the neglected wife should consider doing him in."

"I'm not so sure. I doubt that she didn't know his habits. She was his secretary prior to their marriage five years ago."

"How old is she?"

"Twenty-eight. Thirty years his junior."

Guidi balanced the cup in his hand, inhaling the pleasurable warm scent from it. More and more, Bora's light-hearted talk appeared to belie rising tension, only detectable by the contrast between words and an increased stiffness of neck and shoulders. With a glance Guidi tried to communicate that he was aware of the alarm, but Bora did not acknowledge him, so he gave up the effort. "Is the woman good-looking, Major?"

"We'll find out soon enough. Here's a photo of *him*."

Guidi received the snapshot of a heavy-set man, weighed down by inertia but still maintaining traces of enormous physical vigour. His features were insolent without being brutal.

"A self-indulgent mouth, don't you think?" Bora said the words staring directly at Guidi, though his peripheral vision was no doubt taking in what went on in the section of the room behind Guidi's back.

"Physiognomy can be deceptive."

"Do you think so?"

"I know so. Cruelty and immorality are not reflected on one's face any more than mercy or good mores, Major.

All you have is features. If you are blessed with the *right* ones, you needn't worry about visual detection."

"I disagree, but then you're the expert."

Guidi played with his spoon in the cup, worried by Bora's survey of the place and his unwillingness to give a motive for it. At last, following guardedly the object of Bora's attention, he saw that it rested on a sallow-cheeked young man with a cloth bag on his knees, seated two tables away from them. The young man seemed immersed in a colourful issue of *La Domenica del Corriere.*

"Anyone suspicious?" Guidi leaned forward to ask.

"No, never mind."

"It has to be *something*, Major."

Bora put an American cigarette – a Chesterfield, it seemed to Guidi – in his mouth. "Just tell me what you found out. Cigarette?"

"No, thank you. Well, I've managed to do some checking on Lisi's bank account. He was in fact exceedingly well off, even for one who'd been grubbing in the political trough for years. I can't figure out what his additional sources of income were, but they're undeniable. Real estate, government bonds, investments in the Colonies. No matter what large sums were withdrawn, larger yet deposits were made. No order to them, no apparent connection. Can't tell where the money came from, or where it went. He might have spent some money on women, but who knows how much."

"Perhaps enough to keep their mouths shut." Bora took one more slip of paper from his briefcase. "These are the addresses of two midwives. I'll follow up on them tomorrow or the day after, as I can. Through the Verona *carabinieri*, I ferreted out of a subordinate the titbit that abortions were performed on two underage country girls known to Lisi some time ago. An arrest followed in relation to the second case: the girl was more than five months along, and died of peritonitis after the operation. When the *carabinieri* pressured her, in self-defence the midwife let slip the name of the prospective father, and lost her licence more quickly than she would have otherwise. Lisi's name remained publicly spotless in the process. This was in 1940, and the woman has just got out of jail." Bora let some cigarette smoke out of his lips, as if blowing off an insect flying around him. "I had no idea what leads cleaning women will give you for a price."

The scent of American tobacco wafted temptingly close. Guidi regretted not having accepted a smoke. "So," he said, "it could have been revenge."

"Only if the midwife had a car at her disposal to run Lisi down."

Guidi did not laugh. "We should interrogate the present housemaid. According to my sources, she speaks of Lisi as some sort of a saint. Amiable toward everybody, good-natured, generous. All he lacked was a halo, listening to her. She blames arguments and separation on the wife, whom she heard threatening him."

"Oh?" To Guidi's horror, Bora squashed the expensive cigarette in the ashtray, only half-smoked. Relaxing his shoulders a little, he asked, "Did the wife say she was going to run him over with her Alfa Romeo sports car?"

"No, but close. A couple of weeks ago Clara was reportedly overheard yelling at him that she would make sure he wouldn't be wheeling around much longer. They were arguing about money, but the maid could not eavesdrop closely enough to find out more."

"It seems she eavesdropped well enough. How's the wife's bank account?"

"Good. She's set up, no reason to complain there. Lisi provided her with an ample settlement when they parted ways four months ago. She got to keep jewels, furs, the silver and the car, although he asked her to return his 'beloved late mother's gold brooch'. She was also given the flat we're about to visit."

"I wonder if *she's* got a lover or two." Bora glanced at the wristwatch he wore on his right arm. He motioned to the waiter for the bill, paid it and stood up from the chair.

Guidi resented that glibness. "You're a gossip, Major."

"Why? I'm not passing judgement. I'm just doing Colonel Habermehl's bidding, remember?" Seconds later, Bora, turned elsewhere, was telling him, "Don't move. Stay seated, Guidi, don't move."

Guidi obeyed, but wondered why Bora should leave the table in such haste, and going where. Turning in his chair, he caught sight of the sallow young man walking toward the exit, and of Bora quickly catching up with him. The German held the cloth bag left behind, and now with imperious courtesy was forcing it upon him.

"You forgot this."

Confusion ensued when the young man attempted to get away and Bora prevented him, shoving him against a table full of fine, empty glasses. The fine glasses flew. Guidi got to his feet to avoid an incident and keep Bora from using his gun. But before he could intervene, out of the blue the plain-clothes man joined in from across the street and, unasked, floored the youth with his fist. Customers and waiters stood around, dumb-struck. "Police. No one move," Guidi said. Stepping on broken glass he reached for the bag, and looked inside. Two silver watches emerged and came to rest on the closest table, along with a packet of currency and a kilo of coffee at least. "We have enough here for an arrest."

Within minutes Bora and Guidi were the sole clients in the café, a space of abandoned tables which suddenly seemed much wider. "Thank God black market is all it was, Major."

"Well, I could hardly wait for the bag to be picked up by an accomplice."

Guidi felt the grudging looks of the waiters on them. "It was even more imprudent for you to touch it. Why didn't you just tell me the man was up to something?"

"I only had his suspicious features to go by." Bora levelled his dispassionate eyes on the policeman. "And you don't believe in those."

"What if it'd been explosives instead of black-market goods?"

"I'd have blown myself up, wouldn't I."

"There's no question about that. And then what?"

Bora laughed, with a bland gesture of the right hand summoning the head waiter to pay for the broken glasses. "And then you'd never have convinced Lieutenant Wenzel to lend you the dogs."

They left the café to the clicking noise of shards being swept from under the tables. Guidi couldn't imagine why Bora didn't want to take credit for his courage, or why he seemed amused. He said, "How can you take it so lightly?"

"God knows I don't mean to laugh. And if I had any sense at all, I wouldn't be here chasing murderous young widows either."

2

Clara Lisi, also known as Claretta, had magazines – *Eleganze e Novità, Per Voi Signora* – strewn all across her parlour. Fashion plates showed a wealth of heart-shaped mouths, cork soles, absurd little hats, padded shoulders; elsewhere in the room, a profusion of cushions, rugs, knick-knacks, fresh flowers. The feminine space reminded Bora of the summers at his godmother's in Rome (hot afternoons, day trips, reading forbidden books, the first sins against innocence). He stayed serious, but could have smiled. A drooling, cross-eyed Pomeranian quit chewing on a magazine to snarl against him.

Claretta was a high-breasted, slim girl with an "interesting taste in perfumes", as Bora was amusedly to remark later. Her bleached hair piled up into a nest of ringlets above her forehead, while polished nails and toenails closely matched the pink shades of dressing gown, heeled slippers and wallpaper.

She had been informed of the visit, so liqueur and candies were daintily arranged on a low table by the sofa, as if the circumstances justified sociability. Guidi, who hadn't seen a full bottle of *Vecchia Romagna* in a year, stared at the jolly Bacchus on the label as if it were a sign that cognac production was alive and well somewhere.

When the visitors introduced themselves, she said with a dramatic little wave of her hand, "I hope you gentlemen have come to listen. Please, please. Make yourselves comfortable."

She sat on one end of the sofa with the dog in her lap, and Guidi sat at the other end. Having precariously balanced his army cap among the knick-knacks on the buffet table, Bora went to take a seat in a more distant armchair. When he looked up, he saw Guidi promptly offer a lit match to Claretta, as she took a cigarette out of a mauve mother-of-pearl case.

She was thanking Guidi with a nod. "You don't know what I've been through." She sighed, leaning slightly toward him. "The past two weeks have been a nightmare."

"I understand, *Signora.*"

"How can you?" Claretta turned anxiously from Guidi to Bora, and back. "I believe neither of you can possibly understand. Carabinieri and police have been badgering me so, and that hideous peasant woman—"

"Your husband's maid?" Bora coolly intervened.

"Who else? Naturally you know why she has an interest in accusing me."

"No, why?" Guidi asked.

"No," Bora only said.

After a long, disconcerted look at the German, Claretta faced Guidi again. She hesitated. "You must have heard how Vittorio behaved with women." Her mouth quivered, but even under a lot of lipstick it was a fresh and charming mouth.

Guidi nodded in sympathy. "We heard."

"This maid, this horrible Enrica – she was just the last of a series, Inspector. If it wasn't one woman, it was another. Life with him was impossible. I cannot imagine having wanted to marry him once." Her eyes darted to the safety of her clasped hands, where the cigarette trembled between her fingers.

"So, what was the source of your husband's wealth, outside of his political office?" Bora asked. The question sank like a rock rudely thrown in water, splashing those around it. Guidi was provoked by his lack of sympathy, and – in spite of it – by the way his unfriendly good looks seemed to affect Claretta.

"Why, Major," she said. "I have no idea. Vittorio never discussed business with me."

"Yet you had been his secretary."

With some bitterness Claretta spoke up. "Facility with numbers is hardly what Vittorio sought in a secretary. It was only because I wouldn't give him what he usually got so freely that he married me."

"Had he been married before?" Bora asked.

"No."

"And you?"

"I? I was a *child*!"

"According to my information, you were of age."

Guidi gave a reproaching look at Bora, who paid no attention to him. Then, "*Signora*," he coaxed her, "everything would be much easier, if we knew how your car was damaged."

"I *told* the police!" Claretta's tone rose defensively. "How many times must I repeat it? Only a few days before Vittorio died, I ran into a bicycle parked between two cement posts. It happened as I was driving out of my parking space after shopping here in Verona. Vittorio and I had had a terrible row, and I was always so ragged after arguing with him." She unsteadily put out the cigarette in a pink onyx ashtray. "Vittorio was still paying the bills and always made a big fuss about little things. I know, I realize I should have tried to find out to whom the bicycle belonged, since I had demolished it. But Vittorio would have flown into a rage, the bicycle owner was nowhere to be seen, so I just drove on." A quivering smile curled Claretta's lips when she looked at Guidi. "Had I been more honest that day, I wouldn't find myself in such trouble now."

From the other end of the parlour, there came the click of Bora's lighter.

"You forget the initial in the garden's gravel," he said in his unaccented Italian. "It may be coincidental, but we haven't been able to find any other associate of your husband's whose name begins with 'C'."

The young woman, Bora could tell by the way her eyes focused on it, had just noticed that his gloved left hand was artificial. "It shows how little you know about Vittorio," she replied. "There was much more to his life than appears in his records."

"I thought you said you knew nothing of his affairs." Having lit his cigarette, Bora deftly dropped the lighter into the rigid palm of his left hand, and then slipped it into his pocket. "But I'm sure it's as you say."

Claretta put the Pomeranian down on the magenta flowers of the deep-piled carpet. The gesture of relinquishing the little dog had no pretence, no intended effect. She *was* weak, and afraid. "Gentlemen," she said, "I understand how things are. Vittorio was powerful and had many friends, and I'm just a poor ex-secretary. I know I'm expendable when it comes down to it. But

I did not kill him, though God knows how many times the thought crossed my mind. Especially when he'd grope for somebody new under my very eyes, so shamelessly, so without a care…" Her voice broke down, and she turned away from the men. For a few moments she sobbed, tight-lipped, with her eyes averted. When Guidi offered her his starched handkerchief, she held it against her lips and then dabbed her eyes with it, still weeping, careful not to smear mascara on her cheeks.

Unmoved in his armchair, Bora suffered the Pomeranian to salivate greedily on his well-greased riding boots. Even before finishing his cigarette, he stretched over to smother it in the pink ashtray. "I am certain you have already told the police, *Signora* Lisi, but where were you at the time your husband was killed?"

Claretta sobbed into Guidi's handkerchief, but Bora pressed on.

"What I really mean is, were you alone or do you have witnesses for your alibi?"

"Major," Guidi cut in, "give her time to catch her breath. Can't you see how upset she is?"

Bora gave a discreet kick to the dog, which pulled back from him with a show of teeth. "You ask her, then."

By the time they left Claretta's flat, Guidi had quietly worked up an anger toward Bora, whose energetic limp reached the street ahead of him. Bora made things worse by light-heartedly observing, "No love lost there, eh?"

It was the last straw as far as Guidi was concerned. "It seems to me you were just plain rude."

"Rude? I'm never rude. Straightforward, maybe. She's a murder suspect; why on earth should I be engaging toward her? She means nothing to me, and her tears leave me cold."

"All the same, Major, you could have achieved the same end by being less *straightforward.*"

Bora stopped at the kerb, where driver and BMW waited. He'd removed his right glove to shake hands with Claretta, and now he put it back on, helping himself with his teeth. It was done unaffectedly, but Guidi did not believe that ease, and did not feel sympathy for the self-command behind it.

Bora said, "Frankly I don't think there's much else to find out about this story, but I'll go along with Colonel Habermehl's wishes. I'll give the Fascists a few days of brain work." He turned sharply to face Guidi. "Let's pay a visit to De Rosa at his headquarters before we drive back. Is there petrol in your car?"

"About half a tank. Why?"

"Take this coupon and fill her up. I want to ride with you and chat on the way to De Rosa's. What is it?" He smiled at Guidi's puzzlement. "It's just that there's less chance of getting a grenade in your lap if the licence plate isn't German. Or do you trust your compatriots more than I do?"

Centurion De Rosa didn't know what to make of Guidi when Bora introduced him. That he was displeased by the interference showed only through an occasional convulsion of his upper lip, where the moustache humped and stretched.

"Inspector Guidi is a loyal, card-carrying Party member," Bora mollified him.

With unconcealed contempt, De Rosa ran his eyes down Guidi's civilian garb. "Well, I assume you know what you're doing, Major Bora. What can I do for you?"

"I'd like to hear additional recollections of Vittorio Lisi."

De Rosa walked back to his desk. Behind it, an Italian flag from which the royal crest had been cut out hung on the wall. As the good republican Fascist, he'd replaced the insignia with a patch of white silk. "What more is there to say, Major? Lisi was an excellent man. He had a good mind."

Bora glanced at Guidi, who didn't look back. "A 'good mind'. I don't know what it means in this context, De Rosa."

"An acute mind. A very acute mind, Major. And he was a happy, jovial man. He loved humour and puns and good-natured practical jokes." Intentionally leaving Guidi out of the exchange, De Rosa turned with his tough little body to Bora, who towered in front of him. As if he were reporting to a direct superior, he said, "Lisi found Verona a sleepy place, for instance. So he nicknamed it 'Veronal City'. What a sense of humour, eh?" And because Bora gave no sign of appreciating the pun, "I'll tell you another one," De Rosa continued. "This is the joke that all who call themselves Fascists without being ready to suffer for the ideal ought to keep in mind: Vittorio Lisi said that such people only put up a hypocritical face of political faith, and called them *face-ists*."

"I'm astonished by such fine humour," Bora said.

"And that's not all, Major! Lisi also had an extraordinary memory. Numbers just stuck to him. Every speech he gave was unrehearsed. He could meet you once in a crowded room and perfectly recall your name six months later."

Guidi had done all the silent listening he was going to do. "What about women?" he asked.

As if the inspector had suddenly materialized in the office, De Rosa tossed an over-the-shoulder annoyed glance at him. "Well, what about women?"

"His extramarital affairs," Bora said with a look of uneasiness. "Our inspector is a good Catholic. He means Lisi's lovers."

"Oh, that. There's always gossip when a man is successful. Women flocked to him. Short of fending them off, what should a red-blooded man do? He was quite a fellow, you know."

"All the more, there must have been disappointed fathers and husbands."

De Rosa winked a daringly familiar wink at Bora. "*Wenn die Soldaten,* even the German song says that... Aren't there always, when the army comes to town?"

"I wouldn't know, I'm faithful to my wife. Come, De Rosa, if you have any names of people who would have a personal grudge against him, I wish you'd convey them to us."

"Sorry, I have none."

"Maybe you should try to recollect," Guidi said.

"Sorry. I can't pull them out of a hat, can I? I'll see what I can do. I'll ask around."

Bora sensed Guidi's anger at De Rosa's reticence. He said, "And of course no one knows the source of Lisi's monetary fortune. Am I right?"

"On the contrary, Major. We all knew Lisi invested wisely. Commodities and real estate, like the prudent man he was. Land, houses. He liked beautiful, fine things." With these words, De Rosa hinted at a rigid bow in front of Bora, as if to demonstrate the flexibility of his back. "That's all the time I can spare right now, Major. If you'll excuse me, I have my work to attend to."

At the city garage, where Bora and Guidi drove next, Guidi walked to and carefully busied himself around the dented left fender of Claretta's blue Alfa Romeo. He touched and measured, standing and crouching, until he was satisfied. Yes, the damage could have been caused by striking full force an object anchored between cement posts. Pointing to the noticeable dent, he said, "No traces of varnish on the fender, but *Signora* Lisi did say the bicycle had a simple chrome finish."

At first Bora did not comment. Even before leaving De Rosa's office, he'd started to feel pain in his left arm, and knew it would jag up soon. He stood a few steps from Guidi to keep him from noticing. After a moment, he said, "Her husband's wheelchair had a chrome finish, too."

"You're right." Guidi was scribbling in a notebook. "And what do you think *really* happened to the wheelchair?"

"You heard what De Rosa said as we were leaving. Lisi's inconsolable Party friends took it apart to make it into relics of The March on Rome. You're Italian, you tell me if it's likely or not."

"All I know is that we won't be able to compare its damage to the dent on the car. Let's take a look inside the trunk."

The trunk was unlocked and found to be empty. On the back seat of the car, however, lay a shopping bag from an expensive downtown store. Inside it were a pair of silk stockings. Guidi wrote down the name of the store in his notebook – an exclusive Verona branch of Milan's *La Tessile* – and they called at that address next.

Only Guidi walked into the store. The dimpled salesgirl remembered that a blonde lady in furs had acquired the stockings the previous week.

"Late Friday morning, it was. I recall, because she was looking for a dozen pairs of pink stockings, but we were fresh out. So she only bought one pair of these. Is she sending them back for a refund? I did tell her I thought these were a bit too long. Would you care for a smaller size?"

Looking at the price, Guidi calculated the unlikelihood of impressing a woman like Clara Lisi. He said, "No, thank you," and walked out with the sight of the girl's hand caressing the silk still flashing in front of him.

Back in the car, where Bora had been waiting, he reported the conversation.

"It's no alibi, but at least it tells us that she spoke the truth about shopping on Friday."

Bora said nothing at all. While Guidi was in the store he had gulped three aspirin tablets to dam the rapidly worsening pain, and now his mouth felt dry and bitter. He drove a cigarette between his lips without lighting it, to chase away the medicinal taste and the nausea that accompanied pain. Paleness and the rigidity of his torso might give him away. "While waiting, I was thinking about that crazy convict of yours." He sought to distract Guidi. "Have you any leads, other than his shoes?"

Guidi took his place behind the wheel. He was perfectly aware Bora was in pain, but chose not to remark on it. "No other leads, unfortunately. I wonder how he feeds himself. At this time of year there isn't much left in the fields to dig up."

"Well, now it depends. If your lunatic had military training, he ought to be able to survive on whatever he finds, whatever the time of year. This is nothing! I was in Stalingrad, in the dead of winter. I know how to find food in the garbage."

Guidi started the car. "In any case, if he makes it to the hills and from there to the mountains, we'll never find him."

There might not have been an intended reference to partisan groups in his comment; even that, Bora could have taken in good part had he felt well. "The mountains?" he said instead, hearing the rancour in his own voice. "The damn mountains mean nothing. I know exactly how to search them."

Lisi's funeral was scheduled for 28 November, first Sunday of Advent. While Guidi resumed the search for the convict with the help of the German dogs, Bora put on his dress uniform and travelled to Verona for the ceremony. He'd spent a sleepless night retching in pain over the sink, but Habermehl wanted him to attend.

Lisi's body lay in state at the medieval castle, on the city side of the River Adige's deep meander. The honour guard was composed of fez-capped volunteers in their M-Battalion outfits and a rabble of boys in Party shorts, undisciplined and red-kneed in the cold reception hall.

Colonel Habermehl loomed massive in the grey-blue of his Air Force uniform. Though it was barely eight in the morning, he'd poured himself a few *Fernet* drinks already; he reeked of liquor and looked flushed. Having caught sight of Bora, he came to sit at his side in the row reserved for military guests.

"So," he whispered under his breath, "How's the investigation going, Martin?"

"I'd rather not be involved in it, *Herr Oberst.*"

"Nonsense. You should. You need distractions. Always

having your nose up the partisans' tail is no good. Makes a man melancholy."

De Rosa, who'd led the honour guard with the colours, now took his seat in the row ahead of the Germans, whom he greeted with a dignified nod. Habermehl nodded back, and then leaned over to Bora's ear. "He tattled to me that you didn't reply to the Party salute. Bravo."

Bora blushed. "Really? I must have forgotten."

The ceremony lasted two interminable hours, during which the Party youngsters grew increasingly unruly. Those in the back started to squirm and make faces, while the adults in the room stood stock-still or sat glassy-eyed through the collection of eulogies.

Lisi had no close relatives, and Claretta had been kept away at De Rosa's request. Crusty comrades bearing faded black pennants from the old days took the family's place by the coffin. Grown plump with the years and the good food, their black-shirted backs pulled at the seams.

At one point Bora had to nudge Habermehl, who'd fallen asleep and was beginning to snore. Uninterested as he was, by habit he kept a wary eye on the crowd in the hall. Here a brutal-faced old-timer wiped a tear, there the few women present, wives of officers and Party officials, gathered into a mournful clot of black hats and veils. How many of the men had *loved* Lisi? How many of the women had got into bed with him? They all looked as if tedium would kill them. Bora even caught De Rosa yawning.

Finally, they did come to an end of it.

"Yes. Eh? What time is it?" Habermehl started up and gave a drowsy look at Bora. "Is it time to go?"

The coffin had already been lifted by six robust Republican Guards. Under escort of Beretta muskets and paratrooper sidearms, they were advancing with a swing-ing heavy step toward the door, when a confusion of angry voices rose from the end of the hall. Rustling footfalls caused everyone to look: first of all De Rosa, who was responsible for the good order of the ceremony.

Above the indistinct hubbub a shrill woman's voice cried out.

"Let me in, let me in! I must see him, let me in!"

Habermehl, who spoke no Italian, asked Bora what was up.

"I have no idea," Bora said. Being far taller than the rest, however, he was able to see that the sentinels at the door had halted a black-clad woman and were pushing her back. He was certain it was Clara Lisi. "It must be the widow," he told Habermehl, and started toward the exit. Quickly he elbowed his way through the crowd, brushing past the Guards, who, unable to turn the coffin around, were stuck with it on their six pairs of shoulders.

De Rosa wiggled ahead of Bora, shouting, "Everyone calm down! Back to your places, everyone. Calm down!"

Meanwhile the woman had been dragged back into the anteroom, and Bora pushed his way there past the mass of sentinels. De Rosa tried to do the same, but was too small to succeed.

"Major, is it Lisi's widow?" he fretfully called from behind.

"Why, no," Bora said. "It's an older woman with a wed-ding photo in her hand."

The dogs arrived in front of the Sagràte police station. Held on a long leash by a snub-nosed young soldier Guidi had sometimes seen with Bora, they pulled and growled. Fiercely they smelled Guidi's shoes when he came out. He

49

tried in his minimal German to explain that the search would begin soon. Nodding, the soldier pointed to one of the dogs, and said, "Lola-Lola, and Blitz."

Back in the office, Corporal Turco displayed the threatening scowl of his namesake ancestors, but was really only worried. "*Mara di mia*, Inspector, have we reached the point that we must work alongside *them*?"

"We need the dogs. Run by my house and fetch my heavy coat. And don't start talking to my mother, or I'll never see you again."

Waiting for the Sicilian's return, Guidi looked out of his ground-floor window at the trees across the street, shaking in a low, angry wind. On the pavement and at the street corners, dry leaves coiled up into funnels and spun like tops. The snub-nosed soldier, green like a lizard in his winter uniform, looked at the leaves too. How dense Turco was, Guidi thought, not to realize that he was more vexed than anyone at having to ask Bora for help.

As soon as the coat arrived, Guidi drove his arms into the sleeves Turco held out to him and, after carefully bundling up, he walked outside. Soon men and dogs were piled up in a small truck loaned by the town garage, a clattery piece of junk which brought them all toward the windy banks of the river.

It wanted to snow. Canals and ditches steamed like foundry sluices, while shallow water holes were already sealed by ice. On the hard terrain, Guidi, Turco and two policemen armed with rifles followed the soldier and his dogs past rows of gloomy trees and briars shiny with frost.

In Verona, despite the interruption, De Rosa had succeeded in bringing Lisi's funeral to a close. As soon as the hearse started down the battlement-thick, fortified bridge with its cortege of cars, he turned back to the castle's courtyard, where Bora remained. So had the sentinels and, in their midst, the woman in black.

Bora paid no attention to De Rosa, as he was busy taking leave of Habermehl. Habermehl always gave advice. He now shook his hand and buffeted him hardily on the shoulder, in the friendly and informal Air Force way.

"Don't let the Fascists get your balls, but do us proud."

Bora was embarrassed by the familiarity, especially as there were Italians present. Soberly he said, "At your orders, *Herr Oberst.*" Then, because De Rosa had ordered a chair to be brought out, and had forced the woman to sit on it, he joined in to hear the latest.

"Who are you?" Pacing in front of her, De Rosa was shouting at the woman. "How do you dare cause an incident in the middle of a state funeral?"

Undaunted, the woman lifted the black veil of her hat to wipe her eyes. "Who am I? I'll tell you who I am. I dare, and how. I have more of a right to dare than the lot of you."

Bora stepped in. "De Rosa, you entrusted the investigation to me. Be so good as to let me handle this."

"But, Major!"

"If you prefer, I'll drop the case."

De Rosa seemed to be chewing on something particularly bitter. "No, no," he grumbled. "Go ahead, see if you can find out what this madwoman wants."

Without asking directly for it, Bora stretched his right hand to receive the framed photograph.

The woman handed it over. Careworn and plain, she seemed sixty or so, but might be a few years younger.

She wore a narrow-shouldered black dress buttoned to her chin, and an outmoded black velvet toque, which in the confusion had been knocked sideways on her head. Under her left eye, a fresh bruise bore witness to the roughness of her treatment.

Bora looked at the photograph. "When was this taken?"

"1914," she said. "One year before the last war. You can see Vittorio was already in his *bersaglieri* uniform."

Craning his neck to look, De Rosa cried out. "What? What? Was Lisi already married?"

The woman slumped in the chair. "I had my daughter three months after the picture was taken. Can't you tell? I didn't make her all by myself."

"*What* daughter?"

Bora silenced De Rosa. "We can't continue this conversation here. Centurion, do me the courtesy of having her accompanied to a private room inside. Also, send me a stenographer."

After smelling the convict's shoes, the German shepherds grew restless. Blitz was a young male, long and lean, while Lola-Lola, a stouter, older female, seemed more intelligent and domineering. Both pulled at the leash, and the soldier kept them in check with short, throaty sentences.

Guidi watched the animals, thinking that either of them could snap in one bite the hairy little neck of Claretta's lapdog. Blitz was more easily distracted. The female kept to the appointed task, pulling and jerking the soldier her way. The sudden passage of a dozen loud crows didn't cause her to so much as look up, nor did the friction of dry branches in the wind. She led the group toward the east, in the direction of the nearby town of Lago, only to make a sudden about-face when Blitz started barking.

"She's heading for the mulberry tree," Turco whispered to Guidi. One after the other, even though no danger was apparent, the policemen clasped their weapons.

At the foot of the tree Lola-Lola acknowledged the cooling trail discovered by her mate, but was still restless. The soldier could hardly hold her back. She started in a straight line, crossing a brownish cornfield where meagre stubs were all that remained of the harvest. Here she picked up speed until the men had to keep up with her by jogging.

"Now she'll lead us where the other shoe was found," Turco predicted.

Thus they came to the place where the swinging, leafless tops of the willows along the county road, at first pale like a distant haze, grew more distinct as the men drew closer. Here the river bent into a deep meander, nearly touching the verge. The water's surface, lazy and even sluggish, was deceptive enough. Guidi had heard that deep mud and fast-moving currents lurked below.

Lola-Lola sniffed the spot where the first shoe had been found, wedged between two rocks. She sat on her haunch to be praised by the snub-nosed young soldier. Blitz came to sniff around after her, and sneezed.

"*Da. Da drüben.*" Taking Guidi by the sleeve, the German soldier pointed to the stretch of the road just ahead. Guidi understood he meant to show him the place where the German convoy had been ambushed in September. The first partisan hit had been aimed at Bora's car, which led the convoy. "*Da drüben wurde der Major verwundet.*" With the edge of his right hand, the soldier made a chopping motion on his left wrist, to make Guidi understand that Bora had been wounded here.

Right. As long as the partisans don't get the idea of doing the same to us now.

The wind awoke gloomy sounds in the willows and across the cornfields. Blitz perked up his ears, but Lola-Lola kept busy. Her greying chin quivered. She turned her tawny head against the wind, half-closing her eyes. She smelled the wind. Suddenly she started out again, without haste but assuredly, nose to the ground, while Blitz trotted festively after.

A long march followed across fields mowed so long ago as to seem fallow, beyond unkempt expanses of land and trails cancelled by time. Silently men followed animals, until they came so close to Lola-Lola's goal that she let out a growling call. Blitz echoed her with a menacing howl. Turco, who had until now held his rifle underarm like a vengeful hunter, lowered it to take a better look.

In Verona, Bora said, "I don't understand why you're so irritated, De Rosa. If she's telling tales, it'll be easy to call her bluff, but the photograph is convincing enough."

"I don't believe any of it, Major. Soldiers all look alike. Until I see the priest's marriage certificate, I won't believe it."

"That will be difficult to obtain. Our Lisi did not marry in church. As a good socialist – you knew he was an ardent socialist until the Great War, didn't you? – he kept well away from religious encumbrances. But since there was a child on the way, why, as the golden-hearted fellow he was, he did consent to a civil marriage. The woman says the little girl died of meningitis within one year, by which time Lisi had already cleared out. You heard the rest. He didn't show up again until 1920, when he returned to live off her parents for a year. Other long absences followed, then came the March on Rome, the car accident, politics. For a girl from the backwoods in the Friuli borderland, who can't read or write, it was easy to put up with abuse."

De Rosa quivered like a dart waiting to be released. "And do you believe she just *happens* to be in Verona now that Lisi has been killed?"

Patiently Bora looked down at the Italian. "No. Not by chance. I believe someone told her to come."

"But who? Who'd profit from alerting her?"

Bora controlled the hilarity he felt at De Rosa's frustration. "I don't know yet. But as you say in Italy, every tangle meets the comb sooner or later. We'll just have to keep combing the right way."

Out in the Sagràte fields, Guidi was the first to reach the place after the dogs.

A man lay supine in the ditch, his shoulders nearly encased in the freezing ground. Ice crystals created delicate spider webs in his bloody nostrils. His eyes, wide open and opaque, showed little of the irises, turned back under the upper lids. Stiffly the man's elbows adhered to his hips in the tomb-like narrows of the ditch, though his forearms rose at an angle and his hands clawed upward like the legs of dead chickens on the butcher's counter. A black stain on his chest marked the spot where life had been blasted out of him. Along his left cheek, bristling with unshaven beard, a dark jellied trickle formed a snaking path to his ear, which was filled with dry blood.

The dead man had no shoes on. Stiff in the cloudy, icy water of the ditch, his feet stuck up covered only by army socks of an indefinable colour. The big toe of his left foot peeked from a hole in the wool. A miserable mixture of Italian and German army clothing covered the entire body. Whether a partisan or deserter, the corpse had no visible weapons on or near him.

Guidi ordered the body to be lifted out of the ditch and searched thoroughly.

Turco came up with a piece of mould-blue dry bread, parsimoniously nibbled all around. He showed it to Guidi.

"Wanted to make it last, Inspector."

"What else is there?"

Turco kept rummaging. "Nothing."

Guidi ordered the men to search for weapons in the area, though he expected to find none.

"He's not the man we're after, that's all. The description doesn't even come close. God knows who he is, but I bet the shoes we found were his. The convict probably took them from him after killing him."

Turco assented. "Well, he's been dead a few days. *Santi diavuluni*, but why would anyone?…"

"If I knew, I'd tell you, Turco."

Guidi was annoyed by Blitz's persistent smelling and pawing of the dead man, and stepped away. These were the times when he grew tired of his sad profession, and became unwilling to talk. Behind him the sun had nearly completed its low arc, and had escaped a long bank of clouds enough to draw enormously long shadows under everything that stood. Guidi's shadow reached well past the edge of the field, and the shadows of the corn stubble formed a bluish forest on the bare lay of the land.

"Let's go back to Sagràte," he ordered the group. "I have other things to do before dark."

After the ostentation of Lisi's funeral, Verona's poor side appeared to Bora as something from another world. Darkened by curfew, tenement houses packed tightly beyond the railroad tracks formed a tall maze he had to enter, park in and walk through.

It took him some time to find the midwife's address. Even so, the leprous front of the multi-storeyed house was so dismal, he double-checked his note in the unsteady glint of his lighter. It was here, and no mistake. Bora walked in, closed the door behind him, found the light switch. He looked up the malodorous stairwell, at the ten ramps of steep, worn stairs leading to the fifth floor, and started his climb.

The late Italian supper-time lent smells and sounds to the house. Behind the flimsy front doors, at every landing different voices flowed to Bora. Children whimpering or old people's complaints – each sound, unhappy or irate, mingled with the stench of cabbage soup, latrines and stoves that didn't work properly. Sometimes you *climb* to hell.

Bora had to pause at the third floor, because of the wrenching pain in his left knee. Leaning against the banister, he held his breath to regain control. And if he closed his eyes, the smells and voices could be Spain, or Poland, or Russia, any of the sad places where he'd brought war in the last seven years of his life.

But the pain was Italy, here and now.

"Watch out," the surgeon had warned him (he, too, using the un-Fascistic *lei*), asking that he return to the hospital before Saturday. "It's become infected twice already, do you really want to end up lame? We must get the rest of the shrapnel out of your knee."

The unlit fifth floor seemed as far as the moon.

When Bora limped up the last step, only by the dim glare of the light bulb below could he judge there was a short hallway ahead of him. The lighter was needed again to read name tags, and even so Bora went the wrong way, judging by the stench of stale urine that wafted to him from the end door.

Finally he knocked on the right door. The noise of a chair scraping the floor followed, but the tenant was tardy in answering.

"Who's there?"

Bora didn't know what to say.

"*Öffnen Sie.*" He decided to identify himself as a German.

At once came the clatter of the lock, and the door opened.

The sun had long set, and it was pitch dark when Guidi arrived in Verona. In the blackout, the streets seemed all the same to him. He found himself passing twice under the vast medieval arches of the castle's raised escape route, and twice down the elegant shopping district. By the time he reached Clara Lisi's street behind the Corso, not one but two plain-clothes men watched her flat. Only after much insistence did Guidi convince them to allow him to visit her at this late hour.

She wasn't expecting visitors. It was the first thing she told him, pulling back the ringlets from her face. "That's why you see me like this, Inspector."

But to Guidi her lounging blouse and pantaloons appeared elegant all the same. It was rather the lack of make-up that surprised him. Without powder and rouge, Claretta's face was far from unattractive. Just different. The astonished look of her blue eyes had a nearly childish emptiness under the thinned eyebrows. Guidi couldn't help wondering what Bora might say about this face.

"Good heavens." Walking ahead of him to the parlour, Claretta kept fussing with the ringlets on her temples. "I must be a perfect horror."

"On the contrary, you look very well."

"Thank you for coming to visit." She invited him to sit on the sofa. "Tea? Real coffee?"

"No, thanks."

On the magenta carpet, the Pomeranian slept in a furry ball on the cover of a movie magazine. In the compote at the centre of the coffee table, the golden wrappers of consumed *Talmone* chocolates stood out among untouched candy pieces. Claretta picked them up swiftly. "I wasn't expecting visitors," she repeated. "And I shouldn't be eating any of these. They're bad for the figure."

After they sat down, closer to each other than the first time, she said nothing else. Hands limp in her lap, she seemed to wait for a message from him. But Guidi couldn't think of a real reason why he'd come, other than to see her again. He whipped a pack of cigarettes out of his pocket.

She promptly accepted one. "How nice of you. I finished mine earlier today. They do not let me out, you know."

Gallantly Guidi offered, "You may keep them." He'd bought *Tre Stelle* cigarettes in anticipation of coming to see her, a small luxury for one who always rolled his own.

"Is the German major coming also?"

Her mention of Bora made Guidi stiffen. "No. Why do you ask?"

"Because I don't think he likes me."

"The major has no interest in liking people." Guidi made up the statement, unsure that it wouldn't actually justify Bora's behaviour in her eyes.

Claretta's eyelids stayed low. "I see. In any case, neither you nor the major can help me now."

"How are they treating you?"

"Not badly. They do not let me out, that's all. The baby suffers most from it, because he loves taking walks."

She meant the dog, but Guidi found the sentence artificial, somehow hollow. There was stupidity in it, but in the way stupidity is varnish rather than substance, lacquered on with careful strokes. Women protected themselves that way. He'd seen prostitutes caught in the act, playing dumb, and – worlds away from them – his own mother using that same empty stare. Unlike Bora, he could forgive the ruse. Claretta was telling him, "It doesn't matter to anyone who the culprit really is." A line drew itself between the shaven ridges of her eyebrows. "If they don't find anyone else to pin the murder on, they'll have *me* to pay for it. And no one will care."

Having little encouragement to offer, Guidi leaned over. "The investigation has barely started." He spoke with trite optimism. "It hasn't even started, really. It takes time." How useless words were, when girls sat close by and smelled sweet. Still, he said, "If at least you could give us a clue, a name, anything suggesting a possible assassin – we'd start working on it right away."

"*You* would, maybe. The major couldn't care less." Claretta took in a greedy draught from the cigarette, so that her cheeks sank in. They sat facing one another, and when she crossed her legs the tip of her pink slipper grazed Guidi's calf. But that was all the blandishment he was to receive. "I haven't the faintest idea of who might have killed Vittorio. I told you. He had at least two bachelor flats in Verona, and spent entire days and nights there. I expect he used them to receive friends and associates, not to mention women. All I know, Inspector, is that after making me unhappy in life, he's making me desperate in death. Besides, do you really think anyone would believe me, even if I pointed fingers?"

"I would believe you," Guidi said warmly, louder than he'd planned.

At the foot of the sofa the Pomeranian awoke with a start. Frantically he leaped into Claretta's lap, snarling at Guidi. Claretta petted him, uselessly trying to smile.

After leaving her flat, Guidi drove to Fascist headquarters, where he reread the dossier and the few papers Lisi had left behind. The originals were still in Bora's possession, presumably at the German post in Lago. These were copies, and only because De Rosa had not been in had Guidi been able to secure them.

But De Rosa was not long in arriving at the archive room, skulls and rods and gloomy uniform.

"Does Major Bora know that you're here on your own, Guidi? He didn't mention you would be coming."

Guidi didn't trouble himself with looking up from the papers. "Yes, he knows."

"And when did you inform him?"

"Last night."

De Rosa sneered. "We'll see. I will telephone the major and ask to speak to him directly."

"It's not necessary," Guidi hastened to say. "I mean, what need is there to call?"

61

"Let us say that if you're telling the truth you have nothing to worry about. I'm going to call from my office."

Guidi had carefully kept from Bora his intention to visit Claretta. He anxiously awaited De Rosa's return, ready to justify himself or to argue. But it was apparent from De Rosa's expression that he had got no satisfaction.

"The major isn't in," he grumbled. "They don't know when he'll be back. I regret I can't kick you out of here as I'd like to. But I'm keeping an eye on you. Trust me, Guidi. I'll sit here and keep a hawk's eye on you."

"Please yourself. Considering that this dossier ought to be with the police or the *carabinieri*, you are hardly in the position to point out irregularities."

Bora was then walking out of the tenement house. He breathed the cold night air fully, to cleanse himself somehow from the oppression of the visit.

He wanted to think, *I'm a childless man, what's any of this to me?* But talk of abortion and death by abortion unnerved the soldier in him, because of the fragility of a soldier's life.

The BMW was parked at the end of the street. Walking stiffly toward it, Bora welcomed the darkness and the cold around him, as if they were a dense liquid in which he had to sink in order to escape. From the darkness he looked up at the sky above the street, reduced to a star-studded belt stretching between the eaves. The moon had waned into a worn sickle, but its blade shone exceedingly bright at the edge of a roof. It was the same unemotional, clear moon he'd seen from the balcony of his parents' elegant town house in Leipzig, or through his brother's telescope up in Trakehnen. And, later, from the mortal vastness of Russia. *Liar moon,* he thought. A liar moon. Bora sighed, feeling lonely. He was a soldier, and a childless man.

Unexpectedly, a dance of flashlights criss-crossed at the end of the street.

"Who goes there?" German voices called out.

Bora stepped up and showed his pass. The soldiers snapped to attention, saluted with a clatter of heels. The leading non-com, who was a grey-haired man, escorted him to his car. "*Herr Major,*" he said concernedly, "these aren't the times to walk around alone."

Bora thanked him, and started the engine.

Back in Lago at about midnight, he was too tired to sleep. He sat up to read, and then wrote a long letter to his wife. No mail had come from her in two months. Since the incident, in fact, when Habermehl had sent her a telegram with the news of his wounding.

Bora had last seen Benedikta during a furlough from the Russian front, a few hours in the unmade bed of the Prague hotel where she'd come to meet him like a lover. Hurriedly, because there was no time, they'd undressed each other behind the barely shut door, in a frenzy to touch each other's bodies. The scented wetness of her thighs, he could have died kissing, each hollow and mound, shaven bare or blond. But, as always, talk had sunk into motion, hard muscles and searching hands had been words and sentences between them, and once more there'd been no time to give intellectual shape to love. She remained unknown as an island, the surge and heave of the sheets like surf around her, bringing him to her and yet surrounding her in ultimate safety and unknowableness. So he had her body, each sweet fold of

63

it memorized and surely to be with him at the moment of his death, but her mind eluded him and he stayed hungry and frustrated for that part of love. And, even as they possessed one another physically, death was in the room, kept at bay by lovemaking alone.

In his loneliness he'd hoped – expected, even – that she would become pregnant, but the card just arrived from his mother made it clear it had not happened.

"She's too active, Martin. Riding or in the pool from morning till night, every day. When you return for good you'll calm her down. The babies will come."

Bora couldn't get out of his mind the crude, defensive words he'd heard from the midwife in the squalid tenement room. They were the only thing in the way of unrestrained arousal now. And the soldier's anguished need to leave something of himself before another accident, before anything else happened, rushed at him again, like rising blood. "Dikta, let's make a baby as soon as I get back," he wrote as a postscript to his letter. But then he crumpled the sheet and threw it away.

I don't want to find out. I don't want to be told, no.

As for Guidi, he returned to Sagràte at one thirty in the morning. It had started to snow in squalls of icy pellets across the bare countryside, and it was very cold.

Two hours later, Bora and his men went out on patrol.

3

In the morning the temperature had risen a few degrees. Although a rabid northerly kept up its strength, the snow patches on the fields had melted. Only on the shady side of the streets, powdery white handfuls lingered, but they wouldn't last. In the western sky a consumptive moon looked like the ghost of a pruning knife.

A block away from the Sagràte police command, German soldiers were alighting from a half-track in front of the local post, usually manned by just three men and a sergeant, and occasionally by Wenzel. All answered to Bora in Lago. Guidi recognized the red-haired, lanky Lieutenant Wenzel as the first man out of the half-track. Clearly the Germans had been scouting the hilly piedmont overnight, seeking out partisans in the woods. Shots had rung out for hours. Lining up to enter the Sagràte post, the ten or so soldiers looked for all the world like hungry young farmers, clumsy and rosy-cheeked. Guidi understood that Bora was in the army vehicle that had just pulled in, by the zeal with which Wenzel came to open the car door. But the vehicle only halted for a moment, before continuing on its way to the police command.

Bora was pale with weariness when he walked in from Guidi's doorstep. "I hope you have some coffee ready," he said in lieu of a greeting.

"Turco!" Guidi called out. "Prepare a strong cup for the major." Stepping back, he let Bora in. "Instead of drinking coffee, why don't you get some sleep?"

Bora waved his right hand to dismiss the comment. Without waiting for an invitation he walked into Guidi's office and sat in a chair by the window. After Guidi followed, Bora had taken off his camouflage jacket, and was nestling three hand grenades in the folds of the cloth, right on the floor. "Left over," Bora explained. In the bald morning light he stretched, sat down again. "Holy Christ, what time is it?"

"Eight fifteen."

"Ah, good. I thought it was later than that. My watch stopped." Like many Germans Guidi had seen, despite the darkness of his hair Bora was fair-complected, and only when he turned to the light could one see the blond stubble on his face. "Have you continued working on the Lisi affair?"

Guidi kept mum about last night. "Yes."

"So have I." Bora yawned into his cupped right hand. "But I don't have time to discuss it now." Turco brought the coffee. There was enough chicory in the grains to dilute the stimulating effect of the drink. Its bitterness, on the other hand, would have woken up the dead. Bora gulped it down. "How did it go with the dogs?"

Guidi told him of the shoeless body.

Bora listened leaning back on the chair, with a relaxed air rare in him. He said nothing until Guidi pointed out on the wall map the place where the dead man had been found. Then he reached over to dig out of the army jacket a box of matches, a pipe, a shell casing and a few Italian coins. He went to place everything on Guidi's desk, and returned to his seat. "We ran into a corpse, too." Whether Guidi's surprise tickled him or not, Bora allowed himself a smirk. "I know what you're thinking. But don't you worry, we're not in the habit of claiming bodies we didn't shoot. We didn't kill this one. I even left a couple of men to guard him."

"Who was it, Major, do you know? Where did it happen?"

"We stumbled onto him two hours ago, behind a rubble wall. Two miles to the east of the ditch where you found the first body. Fosso Bandito, is it?"

"Yes."

"Well, this other place is nameless on the topographic map, and just marked as a farmhouse. But the house is long gone. Only a watering trough and the rubble wall are left. From what I could judge, it was an old man. The shot was fired point-blank and it all but blew off his head. There were fragments of brain tissue stuck to the wall all around." Bora waited for Guidi to examine the objects before asking, "Are you sure your lunatic carries an army rifle?"

Guidi took from his desk drawer the two bullets he'd recovered. "That's the report we have. But look how smashed these are."

Closely Bora studied the shapeless bits of lead, running the fingers of his right hand all over them. "That's why I asked, Guidi. Whoever it is, he tampered with the bullets by filing the tips or cutting the casing crosswise. The Russian partisans did the same; I recognize messy butchery. It's not army-rifle butchery."

Guidi kept for himself the clever comment that had risen to his lips. He limited himself to saying, "How long had the man been dead, in your opinion?"

"One hour. Maybe less. There was no *rigor mortis* yet, not even on the neck muscles. Let's say he was killed within thirty minutes of six hundred hours. This is all he had in his pockets, and we found the casing a few feet away. Now, Guidi, do me the favour of sending someone to fetch the body. I need my men back."

Bora was about to add something else, Guidi could tell. The fact that he kept from doing so meant he wanted to be asked directly, and Guidi let him wait for a moment before satisfying him with a question. "Did you notice anything unusual about the body, or around it?"

"I suppose you expect I'll tell you whether he had shoes on."

"Did he?"

"No. He was barefoot. No shoes, no socks. Oh, and there was also a tobacco pouch, but I wasn't about to pick it up from where it had fallen." Bora closed his eyes in the sunlight, uneasily stretching his left leg. "He must have been a beggar, a vagrant. Or a very poor farmer. You might recognize him when you see him, Guidi. As far as I'm concerned, all I know is that I don't want to end up like him. He'd made a little fire of sticks and apparently walked to the wall to take care of a physical need. They killed him in his own excrement."

Guidi shrugged. "It isn't less honourable than any other death, Major."

"No, but it's *unaesthetic.*" Opening his eyes, Bora smiled unaffectedly. "I believe a dignified death is of the greatest importance."

"Maybe." Guidi walked out to dispatch a couple of men to the place indicated by Bora. When he walked back into his office, Bora was standing at the window, slowly massaging his neck.

"About the Lisi affair, Guidi, you ought to know there's another wife to contend with. No, no, don't ask me now. I'll tell you in a moment. I have also met with one of the midwives."

Claretta's lonely pink figure rose in Guidi's mind. "Another wife? Do you mean to tell me that Lisi was also a bigamist?"

"I'll tell you everything. One thing at a time. I have been thinking that the letter 'C' might not stand for a person's name. It could indicate, I don't know, the name of a bank, or a company. It could mean 'communists'. It could be the Latin cipher for one hundred."

"Come, now!" Guidi was so pressed for real news that Bora's interest in word games seemed inopportune. "I doubt Lisi was proficient in Latin, Major Bora. But I do agree the clue in and of itself is not sufficient to incriminate Claretta."

Perhaps because he'd heard him call the widow by her first name, Bora turned to Guidi with a curious stare.

"The circle of suspects," Guidi continued, "is only limited by the fact that a car was used to commit murder. Since he certainly did not hail a taxi for the purpose, the assassin must have used a private vehicle, and have a good reason to drive around. Why are you smiling, Major? Have I said something that amuses you?"

"No. I was trying to imagine the old lecher as he struggled to get away while the car aimed at him. It's not funny, you're right. I'm just tired. The strangest things seem humorous when one is tired."

"At any rate, we should set a date to visit the crime scene and to interrogate the maid."

"I'm glad that's how you see it," Bora said. He took a road map of the Verona province out of a leather case at his belt. "I'm ready."

Guidi was taken aback. He'd hoped to visit Claretta again, and Bora's zeal came at the wrong time. "I didn't mean this morning," he said. "There's no hurry, is there?"

"There is. Life is nothing but hurry."

Under Bora's stern supervision Guidi donned coat, scarf and gloves, instructed Turco to apologize to his mother and to carry on for the day, and followed the German outside.

The army vehicle had already been refuelled. Bora told Guidi, "Come, let's take mine for a change," and dismissed the driver. "Not *mine*, actually. The BMW is being repaired." Despite his mutilation, he promptly started the engine. "Well, which way?" He turned to Guidi, who was unfolding the map.

Guidi told him. And when Bora steered the wheel to leave the kerbside, he saw why his watch had stopped. Half-hidden by the cuff of the army shirt, the watch's face had been shot clean off its metal band. Bora burst out laughing. "Didn't I tell you that the strangest things become humorous after a while?"

The state highway traversed a stretch of land rich in deeply curving brooks and linked chains of low hills. Now and then, tall, svelte belfries signalled distant villages, with bells in their arched top windows like pupils in hooded eyes. At the edge of the fields, much-pruned trees stood guard like wounded bodies, ready to bud again in the spring from their mutilated branches.

Bora looked away from the trees. Alongside the road, a silvery late grass, bowing in the wind, lent metallic splendour to the gravelly shoulders. "I'm telling you what I was able to find out yesterday," he told Guidi. "The first Lisi woman, née Olga Masi, is fifty-six years old. She says she didn't even know he'd married again. Three days ago a clipping with news of his death came to her by post, with no return address. It was the first time she'd heard about him in ten years. I told you she's illiterate, so she brought the clipping to the city hall to have it read. Then she caught the train and travelled to Verona, where she managed to find out where the funeral was being held. Since the clipping mentioned Lisi's present wife, she brought along her wedding picture as proof of her claim."

Guidi was growing used to Bora's fast driving but still clutched the dashboard at the next curve. "She's after money, then."

"On the contrary. She expected they'd give her a hard time and try to prevent her from attending, as in fact did happen. All she wanted was to prove her identity and see the dead man. I drove her to the cemetery in order to speak to her at length."

"Did the anonymous envelope originate in Verona?"

"Yes. I have it in my right pocket. Take it out. It was sent the day after Lisi's death. You see it's a clipping from the evening edition, since Lisi died in the early afternoon." Bora cut across a double curve careless of an oncoming truck, merrily shaving past it. "Now, who would know that Lisi had already been married, if even the second wife was unaware of it?"

The address on the envelope was typewritten. Guidi kept his eyes on the clipping, so as not to look at the road they were devouring. "Well, Major. Likely someone who had known Lisi for years, perhaps a political associate. He might have thought that after his death there was no need to keep the secret, and that informing the Masi woman was just Christian charity."

"Maybe." Bora overtook a truck on a brief stretch of straight road, and barely missed a tractor parked on the verge. "But maybe his intentions were not so charitable."

Guidi began to wonder if it was out of weariness, or whether unsafe driving was one of Bora's German habits. "Why would a 'friend' wait until Lisi's death to acquaint the first wife with all the details?"

"I don't know."

"But you're thinking of blackmail, are you not? Sure, that someone was blackmailing Lisi on account of his bigamy. But what is there to be gained from a posthumous scandal?"

Bora glanced over. "You assume it was Lisi who was blackmailed. What if it was his second wife? Inability or unwillingness to keep paying after Lisi's death might have precipitated the revelation. One thing is certain, by now Lisi's will is a legal nightmare."

"Yet Claretta told us he'd never been married before."

"If you can trust her." Expertly Bora switched gears, and slightly slowed down. "The private road is half a mile ahead, right? It's a good thing I convinced De Rosa to give me the keys to the gate and the front door."

"According to reports, the garden gate was never locked when the master was at home, so virtually anyone could drive in and out at will."

"Yes, including Clara Lisi." Bora said the last words without looking Guidi in the face, suddenly engrossed in the road as if driving carefully had become more interesting to him than what took place inside the car.

Was he just being hostile toward Claretta? It was more than his looking away. Time and again over the past few days Guidi had noticed and resented Bora's tendency to withdraw from the matter at hand, a sudden, introverted abstraction with the excuse of looking outside, elsewhere, refusing to continue the conversation.

Nothing more was said until the private road branched off the highway with a surprisingly sharp curve, which Bora took at excessive speed but managed without losing control. After the first hundred or so yards of black-topped tarmac, the road turned to dirt. It remained dirt for a mile, becoming gravel at last, where two lines of squat mulberry trees kept watch near the gate.

The gate was painted parrot-green. Guidi and Bora stared at it, brash and solid between two pillars of yellow bricks, each of these surmounted by a truncated pyramid of grey granite and a flowering pot. The gate's bars, reinforced by sturdy horizontal belts, ended up in fearfully acute arrow points. A padlocked steel chain bound the lock in a forbidding clasp.

Bora left the army car. "I'd rather not drive in. There must be enough tyre tracks as it is."

He approached the gate. From his seat, Guidi watched him pry padlock and steel chain loose, and then try, one after the other, all the keys De Rosa had supplied. "What is it, Major?" he called. "It doesn't come open?"

Bora was disappointedly shaking the gate. "De Rosa must have forgotten the gate key, or else they changed the lock. None of these fits."

Guidi joined him. "It's hardly possible to scale the wall. Look at the broken glass cemented on top."

"Speak for yourself, Guidi." Bora took off his cap and tunic, which he slid past the bars. "*I* am climbing the gate."

Guidi tried to stop him. "All right, all right. Let me do it. Give me the keys, I'll try to get inside the house and look for another gate key."

But Bora had already placed his spur-clad boot on the first horizontal belt, as if he were mounting on horseback. He heaved himself up with his right hand, nimbly straddling the acuminate arrowheads of the top. "When I need help, I'll ask you for it."

Once they were both inside the gate, they saw how the evidence had been disturbed by the arrival of other cars: perhaps the ambulance, perhaps the police. Luckily no snow had fallen here. Guidi pointed out the interrupted, snaking double trail of the wheelchair in the gravel, and a few traces of dried blood. He uncovered a square piece of tarpaulin, held down by four pebbles, protecting the letter Lisi had traced before dying.

"It's identical to the photograph at headquarters in Verona," Bora commented. "It really looks like a 'C'. I can't see what else you can make of it."

Without touching it, Guidi followed the outline of the letter. "Not even a 'G', it's true. And look, look where the point of impact is, compared to this spot. Lisi must have been thrown ten yards. And there are no traces of braking, none. To gather this kind of speed, the driver must have floored the gas pedal for the last stretch of the road outside the gate."

Bora nodded. He realized the foolishness of his climb when he tried to crouch down beside Guidi, and nearly cried out in pain. Swallowing his discomfort, he limped to the edge of the nearest flower bed, where the gravel was scattered. "The gate is sturdy," he observed, "but far from wide. Either the driver had a good sense of dimension, or he was familiar with the entrance. See here, Guidi? It seems the killer's car backed up right here before leaving the garden."

Eventually they walked to the house. Beyond a rose garden terracing up from the gate, it was a stuccoed country residence pompously marked *Villa Clara* above the door. From all sides, zigzagging paths led to it among flower beds currently devoid of blooms. The walls, shutters and steps were different shades of pink. The type of wall finish, Guidi thought, that readily absorbs moisture. The kind of house that seems to blush after rain. He halted in front of the main entrance, where juniper bushes clipped to a minimum curved in, bordering straw-covered dirt beds ready for spring planting.

"We know from what the maid told police that she fell asleep after lunch in the pantry at the back of the house. After she heard the crash, it took her 'some time' to reach this door. As we know, driver and car had already vanished. Surely if she'd caught a glimpse of Claretta she'd have promptly accused her."

In pain though he was, Bora struggled to keep from smiling.

Guidi saw it, and grew impatient. "I must really seem ridiculous to you today, Major. It's the second time you've laughed at me."

"I'm not laughing, but I think you like the widow."

"While you despise her. Is that it?"

Bora leaned against the door frame with his shoulder. "I don't despise her. I'm indifferent to her. And as long as your feelings do not interfere with your good judgement, you can like the widow all you want."

"As if it were your privilege to permit it, Major!"

"Maybe not. But at least I do not grow sentimental when it comes to murder."

"Unless, of course, you have something to gain from accusing Clara Lisi." Guidi didn't know why he said the words, but that Bora should then openly laugh provoked him beyond politeness. "You said yourself that the will is a nightmare and will probably be impugned. The Verona Fascists might find it very useful if Clara Lisi is thrown in jail."

Bora stopped smiling. "The Verona Fascists? And what have I to share with them? Why would they come all the way to Lago to seek the help of a German officer? Dirty dealings are best done without adding outside witnesses."

"Or with the help of favourable witnesses."

"You carry a Fascist Party card. I don't."

"I'm sure you carry your own card, Major."

"Not at all. I'm a soldier, and don't dabble in politics. For a police inspector you presume a great deal."

Just then the lock of the front door clicked under Guidi's pressure. He entered first, flipped the light on and let Bora in. It rankled with him that he was reluctant to argue, when Bora seemed to have no trouble speaking his mind. Within moments he overheard Bora's cool comment from the next room, "Holy Christ. What a tasteless place. A regular circus. I wonder where they keep the elephants."

On the second floor, Claretta's quarters were easily recognizable by the profusion of vases, shawls and knick-knacks. *Misticum* brand lipstick jars marked *Persia* and *Capri* lined the dresser. The Lenci doll sitting on her bed was as large as a four-year-old child, dressed in a rose-patterned voile frock and with a straw hat on her head. Stuck behind the bevelled edges of the dresser mirror, postcards from vacation spots formed a garland of sea and mountain views. Bora looked at Guidi in the rose-hued warmth of the bedroom. "I feel like I'm inside a uterus. Don't you?"

"No."

"Hm. Did you notice the single bed? They slept in separate rooms."

"What else would you expect, Major? It's logical that a paralysed man should have a room on the first floor."

"Especially if the maid's room is there too, yes."

When they inspected the parlour, an overwhelming crowd of souvenirs confronted them: silver, pewter, ceramics, gondolas of gilded celluloid and paperweights full of water, with Saint Peter's and the Colosseum inside. Women's magazines and movie magazines were everywhere, scattered on every available horizontal surface. Paper flowers, wax flowers, feather flowers and silk flowers filled a series of crystal pitchers. Soccer trophies Lisi had won in his youth lined the fireplace mantel, watching over a solitary book on architecture.

After this, Lisi's room at the end of the hallway seemed Spartan. It was a simple study with a bed. At once Bora became absorbed in a fine Piranesi print, but then Guidi called his attention to a colour photograph of Lisi shaking hands with *Il Duce*. Mussolini looked pasty, and Lisi – holding a pennant that read *SEMPRE OVUNQUE* – had a mouthful of gold teeth. Bora stared at the photo, too, for a good long time, with an indefinable expression on his face.

It was in Lisi's room that it became apparent to Guidi the Verona authorities had chosen to limit the extent of their search. Save for the removal of a few papers already in the dossier, the premises were virtually untouched. The calendar had not been detached from the wall, even though initials were scribbled all through the pages alongside certain dates. A stack of banknotes still lay in the right-hand drawer of Lisi's mahogany desk, where powerful painkillers and a shot glass kept company with a ream of Pelikan carbon paper. Silver fountain pens – the expected gift from underlings – formed a thick bundle, bound by an elastic band.

Bora recognized the medicines from his hospital stay. "This is powerful stuff to take with liquor."

Guidi rummaged for and found a half-empty bottle in the left drawer. "Cognac," he said. The lower desk drawer had been emptied, but when Guidi tried to close it, he met unexpected resistance from the back. Only after pulling the drawer completely out by the brasses did he realize that a number of magazines had slipped behind it, and become stuck to the back of the cavity.

"What is it?" Bora asked.

"Pornographic magazines."

"Imagine that."

Guidi tossed the magazines on the bed, where Bora sat leafing through a manual on interior decoration found on the night table. "When you're done, Guidi," he said, "take a look at the initials on the calendar."

"Why, did you find the letter 'C'?"

"No. There's a 'B', an 'S', an 'M' and an 'E'. No 'C'. But they seem abbreviated notes, reminders of some sort. Whatever his other businesses, Lisi knew how to keep a lid on them. Thinking of it, why should he write 'C' for Clara on his calendar? With his famous gift of memory, surely he'd remember if he owed her a monthly cheque."

Guidi thought Bora was trying to pacify him, but when he looked, Bora was sneering. He noticed that he'd picked up one of the pornographic magazines.

"Anyway, Guidi, whether De Rosa was right about Lisi's impeccable memory or not, we found no telephone directory anywhere. And if Lisi dealt in cash, good luck with finding any written records."

"Right."

A crumple of paper signalled Bora's sudden tossing of the magazine on the floor. He joined Guidi at the desk and stood there, watching him. "Contrary to what you think, Guidi, I have no interest in proving Clara Lisi's guilt, any more than I care to prove she dyes her hair. Neither issue is of interest to me."

"How do you know she dyes her hair?"

"My wife is a real blonde. Do you suppose I can't tell the difference?" With the side of his boot, swiftly, Bora kicked the pornographic magazine to the other side of the small room. "What amazes me is that Lisi could read about architecture and interior decoration, and still have such atrocious taste."

The last room they visited was the kitchen. Hanging from a hook by the stove, Guidi found a key with a pencilled paper disk reading *garden gate*. They went outside to try it, and it worked. After Guidi unlocked the gate, Bora pushed the swinging leaf until it yawned wide open.

"I don't understand how your colleagues from Verona could be so dim-witted as to confuse the tracks on the gravel. And look at the paint job on the gate, here. How long ago would you say it was done?"

Guidi squatted to release the stationary leaf of the gate from its ground lock, and opened it. "Probably since the legal separation. If you notice, old sprinkles on the pillars indicate it used to be pink."

Unduly interested in the bar that served as a pivot to the gate by the right-hand pillar, Bora said, "There are traces of side-swiping here."

Guidi looked. Undeniably it was the mark left by a large object that had come through the open gate. The green paint was lifted right off, and beneath it showed a fleshy pink hue, and even the bare metal of the gate. "Push on the pillar, Major. Does it give?"

"Not enough to fall on our heads when we climbed over the gate, but it does give a little."

"Well, the left one does not give at all. It must have been quite a shake. It seems our motorized killer didn't know the dimensions of the gate too well."

"Yes, or else the speed was such that the driver lost control."

Guidi thought Bora knew what he spoke about. Glancing at the damaged bar, he said, "Unfortunately, the green paint is still rather fresh. It just peeled off, without leaving behind colour traces of the object that struck it."

Bora nodded. "But if it's a car, it must have got quite a green stripe on its right or left side, according to whether it struck the gate coming or going."

"Remember, there were no traces of green paint on Claretta's Alfa Romeo."

"Except that we were concentrating on the front fender." Bora tossed the bundle of keys to Guidi, and climbed into the army vehicle. "I trust your memory. But all the same I'd like to take another look for myself."

In Verona, Bora visited Fascist headquarters over the noon hour, with the pretext of returning the keys to De Rosa. He spent more time inside than Guidi expected, and when he emerged from the gloomy portals he was in a foul mood.

"Why did you review the dossier without my permission?"

At once Guidi's defences went up. "'Your permission'? You asked me to collaborate. Since when do I need your permission to carry out my police duties?"

"De Rosa said you assured him you had discussed it with me, and it isn't so!"

"What of it, Major? And since you put such trust in De Rosa, did you ask him why he gave us the wrong keys?"

"I couldn't give a damn about the keys. I want to know why you didn't consult me."

Straddling the sidewalk, Guidi felt emboldened. "I've done even worse, Major. I went to see Claretta without telling you."

Bora let something angry escape him in German. "I'm beginning to have enough of you, Guidi. You have decided to thwart this investigation for motives of your own, and if you don't change tack, I want you out of it."

"So that *for motives of your own* you can continue to treat Clara Lisi like a suspect?"

"She is such until I prove the contrary!"

Arguing, they'd approached Bora's parked vehicle, and were now shouting at each other across the canvas hood.

"Did you ever stop to think, Major, that 'C' could stand for *camerati*? How long would it take for a GNR truck to ride from Verona and kill the old man? Of course they'd want an outsider to look into the matter then. What do you know about De Rosa's real intentions? 'Centurion' and 'Captain' both begin with a 'C', no more and no less than 'Claretta'!"

"Don't you speak bloody nonsense!" Bora had opened the door to enter, but now slammed it shut again. "And just what did you discuss, Clara Lisi and yourself?"

"I asked about any possible motive for her husband's murder."

"Other than *her* motives? And I wager you found out nothing. No one knows anything about Lisi's business. How can a man spend years in a town this size, take two wives and make a fortune without anyone noticing?"

Surprisingly, Guidi cooled down at Bora's frustrated words. He said, "If you're bent on arguing, Major, we can continue to do so on our way to the city garage."

As it was, they did not argue during the drive, nor after reaching the garage.

Claretta's Alfa Romeo was still parked near the end wall, but something about it had changed. "Did they wash it?"

Guidi wondered out loud. But now that they were close, both saw that the front fender had been repaired, and a freshly washed and waxed metal body sat like a sleek blue fish under the electric lamp.

Bora was too astonished for a nasty comment. He halted some three feet from the car, while Guidi walked right up to it and then all around, looking inside and trying the doors one by one. He was in the process of squeezing his arm into the partially lowered front window, when a brassy, sonorous woman's voice filled the garage.

"*What do you think you're doing?*"

What, indeed?

Both Guidi and Bora recognized Marla Bruni, the soprano who'd made the papers two years earlier by unexpectedly baring her bosom in the second act of *Otello.* Smashingly appointed and with that glorious portion of her anatomy well sustained by girdle and brassiere, she heel-tapped from the entrance in flashes of red and purple.

"Stop at once, little man!"

She had none of Desdemona's meekness as she flung her foxes in Guidi's face. "You!" she stormed at him. "Will you step back from my car, or should I call the police?"

Ten minutes, several threats and a stormy explanation later, what most burned Guidi was being called "little man" by *La* Bruni.

"First the wheelchair to the comrades, now the car to a bigwig's lover!" he stammered in his anger. "No doubt De Rosa has another fine tale for you, Major Bora!"

Bora kept ominously silent. But it was with an enviable sense of timing that Centurion De Rosa had left headquarters when the German descended on it like a thundercloud.

At half-past one, during a despondent lunch in a Piazza restaurant crowded with German officers, Guidi could not even enjoy the first veal he'd had in years. Across from him, Bora's fork had not touched what lay on his plate.

Bora spoke first, with an uncritical plainness that in him might indicate fatigue, or a worsening of physical pain. "We could hardly expect they'd tamper with evidence to score points with a prima donna." And, having said the words, he looked up from his intact cutlet. "On the other hand, cars are scarce, and lovers plentiful. Losing her car to an opera singer is probably as close as Clara Lisi is going to get to the world of the stage."

No matter how hard he tried, Guidi could detect no humour in Bora's comment. As for himself, he was still smarting at the "little man" matter, and the way Marla Bruni hadn't let out a peep of complaint against Bora. "I hope you will not tell me De Rosa isn't trying to set Claretta up, Major."

"Either that, or he hopes to lay the opera singer."

The expression, so out of place in Bora's otherwise restrained speech, surprised Guidi. Certain now that the German was unwell, he let the issue fall until coffee was served. Even then, all he said was, "Are you by any chance good at maths?"

Pushing the brimming demitasse away from himself, Bora stared at Guidi. "It depends. Why do you ask?"

"At headquarters I saw two of Lisi's bank accounts, dating back a couple of years."

"I know. I saw them too."

"It might be worthwhile to study them more closely. To look for connections between deposits and withdrawals and the dates marked on the calendar at his country house."

"I don't see what good it'll do."

"I'm not sure. But we have little else to go by."

Bora asked the waiter for the bill. "I disagree. We haven't yet spoken with the physician who drafted the post-mortem. Then there's first wife Olga Masi, not to mention any details Clara Lisi might have kept from us. What do I care how Lisi made his money? His killer is what I'm after." With a tired sweep of his hand across the chin, Bora seemed to discover the bristle on his face. "Holy Christ, I haven't even shaved." He groped into his right breast pocket, from which emerged a security razor. "Fortunately I always carry this along. Here, Guidi, leave the tip. I'll be back in five minutes."

When they left the restaurant the sky had grown hazy with feathery clouds, and the temperature was dropping again. Bora, white-faced and clean-shaven, wanted to go directly to the hospital to discuss Lisi's autopsy, but Guidi resisted. "I *must* drive back to Sagràte, Major. I haven't yet seen the body of the old man you found shot by the wall."

"Very well, I'll see the physician on my own. But just to make sure you go right back to Sagràte; I'll have you driven there courtesy of the *Wehrmacht*."

"As you like. Promise that you will take a close look at Lisi's bank accounts."

Bora neither said yes nor no, but before entrusting Guidi to an army driver he stopped by Fascist headquarters and demanded to be given the copy of the dossier kept there.

"I'll examine the accounts when I have time," he briefly informed Guidi. "I'll call your home number if I find out anything worth repeating."

"You have the original. Why did you take the copy as well?"

"Because I want to be able to control everything from now on."

The old Verona hospital on Via Lombroso smelled like all old hospitals. Phenol, old wood, soap, decay. Bora distinguished each odour while walking down the high-ceilinged corridor, as distinctly as when they had rushed him in on a stretcher, and mangled raw flesh was all he ought to have been able to smell. But that was north of here, in the new hospital complex, and the odour of oiled wainscoting had been missing then.

As soon as he entered the office and introduced himself, an intern stared vacuously at him from behind thick glasses. He resembled a young owl, an Italian Trotsky, and the impression was accentuated by the wiry halo of precociously greying hair on top of his head.

"Yes, yes." Having heard Bora's reasons for coming, he leafed through a pale green folder. "Vittorio Lisi, I remember perfectly. Here we are. In a few words, death was caused by cerebral haemorrhage, following the fracture of three vertebrae: the seventh cervical, and the fifth and sixth thoracic. We attempted to intervene, but it was too late even for trephining. As for the rest, there was the old fracture of the lumbar vertebrae from twenty years past."

"No sign of other trauma?"

Pushing back the glasses on his nose, the intern took a passing glance at Bora's left arm, as if to evaluate by habit the extent and type of his mutilation. "Only those consistent with the blow received and the fall. I personally examined every part of the deceased's body to make sure the head wounds were not due to other causes: puncture or slashing wounds, for example, or crushing blows." When Bora asked for the folder, he readily handed it to him. "While cleaning Lisi's face, I noticed a discoloration of skin on his left temple. Not a wound, but rather an abrasion. There had been no break of the epidermis, no loss of blood. I remember not believing the bruise was caused by striking his head against the gravel, because, no matter how superficial, those lesions contained dirt and were recognizable. I thought at the time that it looked like someone had kicked him. But then I understood the mechanics of the rescue. It had nothing to do with premeditation. Medics were not the first on the scene. In the confusion of policemen and volunteers, there was apparently much activity around the supine body. It's evident that, even with the best of intentions, one of the volunteers stumbled on the wounded man." The owlish face knit into a frown, such as Bora had seen in army physicians when death robbed them of success. "In any case, Lisi was as good as gone. I assure you that from the moment the victim was struck, there was no hope whatever to save him."

Bora laid the folder on the physician's desk. "Other than the accident that killed him, would you be able to tell me what Lisi's general state of health was?"

"Yes. Here is the addendum to the autopsy, required by law in such cases. As you see, it was drafted in full compliance with articles 34 and 35 of police mortuary regulations, as by Royal Decree of 21 December 1942. I assume you are interested in the victim's pathological story."

"His epicrisis, yes."

The bespectacled round eyes sought Bora's face. "Did you study medicine?"

"No, philosophy."

"Well, here. You can see for yourself. The internal organs were generally in good shape for a man of Lisi's age, especially given his immobility the past two decades. Small calcium crystals were starting to form stones in the urethra, nothing to speak of. The prostate on the other hand did show a suspicious hyperplastic mass, but the size of it was still small. Had he not been run over, Vittorio Lisi wouldn't have dropped dead any time soon."

4

In Lago, enough snow had fallen overnight to cushion outside sounds, and only because of his vigilance did Bora hear the crunch of tyres under his office window.

Suddenly, it was one of those times when his habit of being unafraid failed him. Ever since Spain, Bora had taken inordinate care in the practice of storing anxiety deeply within, as safely as an army trunk was organized, with the heaviest objects at the bottom, tucked away in the corners. This morning he watched the ugly mottled green of the SS vehicle pulling in, and was for a moment at risk of giving in to fear.

Everything became sharper at once. Images took on the quality of an acid-etched silhouette. He remembered each instance of great fear as a precise scenario comprised of layers, circumscribed horizons, dimensions unforgiving and eternally set. The room where he stood was instantly transformed into a paradigm of itself, so that for ever – in the moment it took an SS officer to dismount from his vehicle – this wall and doorway, that slice of winter light across the desk and flaws in the tiled floor would be associated with fear. Composing himself grew more difficult with the passing years. But the gathering of courage had to happen quickly, and Bora had accomplished it by the time the visitor, like death, appeared on his doorstep.

It took Bora all of three seconds, having heard the question, to answer, yes.

The rest was a matter of details. Called in for consultation, *Oberfeldwebel* Nagel evaded Bora's glance. A family man who'd been with him since Russia, he stared at the SS colonel even as he answered Bora. "The road through Schio is not advisable, *Herr Major.*"

"And why not?" the SS officer cut in. "We have no reports of enemy activity in that area."

"Begging the *Standartenführer*'s pardon, I led patrols through there twice in the last month, and it's not a safe itinerary. I wouldn't drive a truckload of prisoners that way."

Bora lowered his eyes to the map spread on his desk, visibly pondering the alternatives. The map faced him like the world. How well he knew the hazy green and brown shadings, hills and rivers and plains – in his hundred days here he'd committed them to memory until he owned them all. He said, pointing at the rugged brown piedmont, "This is what I suggest."

The SS officer glanced over. "Is it a shorter route?"

"No, it's not shorter. It is safer."

Nagel nodded in assent, with the same detached mien. Had he not known Bora at all, he could not have ignored him more.

The SS officer's attention went from one to the other of them. A pitted scar on his lower lip, like a pinch in the flesh, made his mouth look oddly feminine. "Well," he told Bora at last, "do whatever you goddamn decide, you're the one who's been here. It's on your head if anything goes wrong."

"I anticipate nothing will go wrong."

"The truck will be here tomorrow. It's your job now."

Guidi's men had recovered the dead vagrant's body. It lay now in the mortuary chapel of Sagràte, a miserable sight, next to which Guidi sat with hands on his knees. Bora was right, he recognized the victim. It was a poor old widower who lived as best he could, sometimes begging on the church steps on Sundays. There were no relatives to contact, no property to dispose of, no preparations to make, if not for a pauper's burial. Simple enough.

Simplicity followed death, at least for this man.

"If you could only tell me something." Guidi actually said the words under his breath. "You'd make *my* job easy if you could speak. Or if that Lisi son-of-a-slut could." Then he was ashamed of sounding weak to his own ears.

What had Bora said about a dignified death? In his profession, Guidi was yet to see one. Painlessly he called to mind the snapshots taken of his father after the Mafia had ambushed him in Licata, the snapshots his mother had never been allowed to see. His father lying belly up in the sun-gorged square, legs and arms spread like a marionette pulled every which way, with a bloody puddle on his crotch that in the black-and-white print looked like he'd shit himself.

He'd probably done that, too. Guidi groaned. How wrong Bora was, in squaring his jaw against pain, hoping that it would guarantee him the *beautiful death*. In the face of death, it was easy for Guidi to feel indulgent toward everyone. Not only Claretta, who played stupid because she had to. Toward everyone else. Even the mad-man who killed and took the shoes off the dead, or De Rosa, the likes of whom the mob would surely lynch as soon as the war was over and lost. Guidi was even able to dredge up some understanding for Lisi, who made up for paralysis with whores, and – this was the easiest of all – for the ragged man shot in the ditch, with stale bread in his pocket. Guidi felt mercy for himself too, but less than for others.

He realized Turco was standing behind him by the odour of cheap army cigarettes. Without turning from his bench, Guidi said, "That's all right, Turco. Start the car, I'm coming."

Ignoring his mother's insistence that he be home early for once, he stayed in his office until late at night.

She was still up when he returned. Guidi tried to ignore her, answering her questions in monosyllables. Finally he said, "Ma, it's late. You're tired, and so am I. Why don't you go to bed?"

"Because civilized people have supper before they go to bed, and if you get home late I have to stay up to serve you."

"Can't I help myself? I'm not hungry anyway."

She poured soup into his bowl. "Nonsense, Sandro. Why shouldn't you be hungry? Have you had supper somewhere?"

"I've been dealing with dead bodies, Ma. *I'm not hungry*. And where else would I be having supper, anyway?"

"You tell me. You're the man of the house."

Until now her mood had made no sense. Now from a remote, well-visited corner of his memory, Guidi fished up the image of Claretta wiping her eyes and lips with his handkerchief. So, *that* was the matter. Damn. He had meant to rinse it himself in the bathroom sink, but then he'd forgotten all about it. So, his mother had noticed the lipstick, and now wanted to find out more.

Without removing his attention from the much-laundered tablecloth, Guidi could sense that his mother had the handkerchief in the pocket of her apron. Standing by the wood stove, she'd use the handkerchief as a weapon. Whether she pulled it out or not, the challenge was on.

"God forbid I should ask what you do in your free time," she said. But her words were planted like segments of a stockade against him.

"I told you I'm tired, Ma."

"Go ahead then, go to sleep. We have plenty of time to talk during the day, don't we! Every time I see you, you're either chewing your food or getting ready to leave. I see Turco more than I see you."

"Ma." Guidi put his hands on the table, palms down. "Ma, if you have something to tell me, tell me right away. If you have something to show me, out with it."

"What should I show you? I have nothing to say."

"Good." Guidi stood up from his chair and walked toward the door of the kitchen. "I'll see you tomorrow, then."

Reaching over, his mother took him by the arm. "No, no, no. Wait, Sandro. Let's not argue. You know all I want is for you to be happy." Her hand slid up to his shoulder, with the concerned, kind touch he seldom resisted. "Let me put my heart at ease. Tell me who she is."

Guidi felt he could cry out, like someone who's been forced to his knees, to an uncomfortable place where he does not want to be held down. He slowly freed himself from her hand and walked to the dining room. "I'm turning the radio on, Ma. Do you mind?"

"Who is she, Sandro?"

A froth of spite brimmed in him as he spoke the lie out loud. "She's a street-walker. Would you believe they use handkerchiefs like the rest of us?"

From the radio, there came the grave, neutral voice of the nine-o'clock news announcer. "Following the 14 November *Carta di Verona*, Article Seven, according to which 'All belonging to the Jewish race are foreigners, and in times of war they belong to an enemy nationality', His Excellency the Minister of the Interior has issued Police Order Number Five. As by Order Number Five, all those belonging to the Jewish race are to be arrested and interned in concentration camps."

Guidi heard the news, and – because there were no Jews in Sagràte – reacted to it with a glum lack of interest. His mother watched him from the door, hands clasped. "That isn't true, Sandro, is it?" She, too, not referring to the Jews at all.

Bora's radio was on at that same time. He heard the news by accident, having walked into his office for the first time since that morning. Instantly he found himself in a cold sweat. The errands of the day – run in solitude, as he'd learned in Poland and Russia – took frightful proportion as he listened to the announcer's words. What dinner the men had readied for him had to wait now for the most important task of the evening. He sat at the desk, rearranging his duties with unerring haste. Two phone calls followed, in Italian – a few words each. "Let's go," he then told Nagel, who waited outside his door. With him, he drove to the church, where, in the presence of the bewildered sexton, he arrested Monsignor Lai.

By the time he telephoned Guidi, it was well past midnight. He made no mention of the arrest, or the radio news. "You asked me to go through Lisi's bank accounts," he said. "I have done so."

Guidi was just as cagey. "Anything of use, Major?"

"No. They don't help us in any way. Even rounding up the sums here and there I cannot find any consistency, any meaning to them. I gathered the amounts in temporary groupings, drew means among the intervals of time between deposits and withdrawals. I calculated interest rates. There's no order, no logic to them."

Late as it was, Guidi heard the shuffle of his mother's slippers outside his door. "Maybe it's because you calculated the official interest rates," he said.

"Well? What else should I calculate?"

Flop, flop. Outside the door, Guidi's mother had probably realized that he wasn't speaking to a woman, and was returning to her room. "I can tell you've never been poor, Major Bora."

"I have never been poor."

"And you never had to borrow money in a pinch."

Bora didn't reply to the obvious. "As for the rest, yesterday I spoke to the intern who performed the autopsy, as well as to the medics who assisted Lisi. More about it when we meet. I also found someone for Olga Masi to stay with in Verona for the time being, and caught De Rosa right in front of headquarters. I first secured a time for us to interrogate Lisi's maid, and then gave him a dressing-down he'll remember for the rest of his Fascist life. I know the sentinels will, and likely the tenants of the house next door. Look, even without my watch I know it's bloody late. I haven't slept a wink in more than forty hours, and doing maths has never been my favourite entertainment. I'll see you tomorrow or whenever."

"Sleep well, then."

Bora put the receiver down. Sleep well? He hadn't slept well in over a year. There was no chance of sleeping at all tonight. Monsignor Lai, the well-educated, bright cleric who'd heard his confession every week, was under guard in the room at the end of the hallway. In the morning, Fascist guardsmen would bring a truckload of Italian Jews bound for the South Tyrol. The SS officer, who hadn't so much as given his name, had said on his way out of the command post, "Don't I know you from somewhere, Major?"

Somewhere was the Russian district of Homyel.

Bora went to wash up. He was still tempted to use both his hands for these simple tasks, and his surprise at being unable to do so angered him anew. What had been a given – loosening his collar, clasping the buttons of his braces, undoing his breeches – now required a retraining so basic that his sense of worth was bruised. Doing better at it day by day was not enough. Tonight he felt his injury more than ever, and not just because the harness holding the prosthesis chafed the skin. It was the intimacy of the loss, what it meant to his relationship with Dikta, how he would go back and face her, face his mother. Only his general-rank stepfather would understand, and that was not saying much.

His troubled reflection stared back from the mirror. Unlike so many, he'd consciously chosen soldiering. Yet medals and ribbons gave the lie to the fact that for five out of his seven years in the service, he'd betrayed his soldier's oath. How well the SS knew this, and could come asking him to escort Jews to a concentration camp, and expect him to say yes.

In his bedroom, Dikta's photograph stood for all he might yet lose. Bora took out pen and stationery, but did nothing with them. He could not write to his wife, or to his mother, or anyone else. It repelled him to put thoughts on paper for others to see. Even today's entry in the diary he'd kept ever since Spain, bulky and soiled, and written in minute Gothic script, required an effort. Still fully dressed, he sat on his bed. No, not *his* bed – but the bed he'd requisitioned as he'd requisitioned this building and so many of the objects he used now, scraps of receipts signed and distributed as if any of the debts would be honoured any time soon.

He managed at last to pray, although those mental words, too, disgusted him, to the extent that he sat in complete stillness. Guilt made him intolerably clear-minded, as risk made him drunk. *How do I, as a soldier, justify… There is no justification. I may invoke whatever authority I choose, it still doesn't help. It doesn't help. I can't get out of it, and there's no one I can talk to.*

After turning the light off, his recollection wandered. Places, people. Actions taken and not taken. Dismal seasons. Dismal days. He recalled the impalpable, breath-thin wraiths of Russian snow snatched by the wind off the tops of trees and bushes. Had it been at Shumyachi? Two years earlier, already. The shots at Shumyachi had reverberated under the hospital's vaults as far as the tree-lined expanse across the street, where his car was idling. A dazzling spray had trembled off the bare branches then. The sight of wind-borne minutiae had remained with him ever since, as the flash of sunlight on one of the hospital windows, opening and closing in the icy breeze. No one remembered his name at Shumyachi, if anyone had ever even known it. Why should he think of it? It did no good. But the godforsaken town was a wound he carried around no differently from his other injuries.

Snow was melting on the roof of the command post, and all around the eaves dripping water created a necklace of sound in the dark. Bora had made up his mind hours ago. This was the agony that always followed such decisions. These were the times when he felt most distant from his wife, nearly lost to her and to any hope they would ever reunite. Time collapsed onto itself until their days together – few, so comparatively few – were a kaleidoscope that at will could be reconfigured, but in the end remained nothing but bits of bright foil and coloured paper. He had stood in the face of imminent death, and had not feared it as he struggled through these endless moments between choice and action. Lost, lost. He was lost to Dikta, to his mother, to everyone who'd ever loved him. Of him, as in the stark black-rimmed death notices, it would be said, "He will return to us no more." He'd given himself up for dead long ago, so why was he so tempted to expect a different end? He'd said yes, meaning it as much as he meant anything these days. The answer was immense, a world in itself. Hell could not be larger than the gulf contained in saying yes.

Nagel came and went, without rapping on his door. Bora recognized his step, his refraining from the knock on the door. The room was cold and no longer identifiable by shape. Only the limned strip under the door marked the existence of reality. Bora bent over from where he sat, feeling around for the bootjack. After taking off his boots, he began to undress, until he was naked, and, without prosthesis, he lay motionless under the covers.

There had been a season, still fresh in Bora's memory, when the fastidiousness of German uniforms would have put to shame the Italian Militia. This late morning of 1 December 1943, it was all washed-out field-grey. Everywhere. He could look at the truck pulling into the place in the street where yesterday the SS car had sat, and judge vehicle and men alighting from it as no shabbier than his own soldiers. *I've done this before,* he thought, *I've done it before and know how to manage it; there's no great expenditure of emotions once one has done it the first time.*

He went downstairs and into the street, where the truck rattled in idle. The driver saw him through the window and hopped out, baggy trousers and ankle boots mud-spattered. He gave the Fascist salute, and presented a piece of paper signed by one high official or another. Bora no longer looked at names; it made no difference what the alphabet combination might be – it was all power about to slip away, and not even history's footnotes would pick up those names tomorrow.

"These prisoners are to be delivered to Gries," the driver said. "So we need an escort."

"I've been informed." Bora walked around the truck. The guardsman who was in the back had also alighted and was standing at cramped attention, his black fez impossibly stuck to the back of his head, as if nailed in. Without a word, Bora indicated by a short wave that he wished to have the canvas flaps lifted. When it was done, he looked in from where he stood. "How long have you been riding?" he asked the guardsman, as if the information were no more than a formality.

"Ten hours, *signor maggiore*, with eight more to go."

Bora was in full sight of those sitting in the truck. Indistinct faces were within, people he had no desire to get to know. In the frigid morning it made him unusually comfortable and secure to be warmly dressed, well dressed, to appear every inch authoritative. "Jews, all?"

"All of 'em."

Bora turned on his heel and went indoors. When he returned outside, Nagel was with him. The guardsmen had got *Sondermischung* cigarettes from the German soldiers. The driver, resuming the at-attention stance, said, "*Signor maggiore*, we haven't had anything to eat since last night."

"That happens, at war."

"We could use something to eat, if you could spare some." And, because Bora didn't answer, "The prisoners haven't had anything in forty-eight hours."

"What's that to me? You have a schedule to keep. It is already an imposition for me to give you two of my men as an escort. You should have organized yourselves better, and brought provisions." But even as he said so, Bora ordered a soldier to get some food ready. "Go inside," he said in Italian to the guardsmen. "It will be charged to your command. So will the petrol for your vehicle, since undoubtedly you carry no extra fuel."

The guardsmen wasted no time going indoors, while Nagel drove the truck to the back of the building for refuelling. Bora followed him there. He commanded the flaps of the truck to be lowered again. How many times had this happened, with small variations? A vehicle bringing prisoners from somewhere to somewhere, his part in it. "Take care of everything, Nagel," he said. "You know how. When you're done, go upstairs, and get Colonel Habermehl's cognac from my room. Open it and give it to the Italian guardsmen. Monsignor Lai is to join the prisoners – no special treatment."

Turco, who happened to be in Lago on an errand for Guidi's mother, had caught the last moments of the transfer from the German command post.

"*Gesummaria*, Inspector, it was a terrible sight. You wouldn't expect it of our major," he reported to Guidi at midmorning.

"*Our* major? Since when is he *our* major?" It irritated Guidi that the Sicilian should imply that he trusted Bora. "He'd do the same thing to you or me if he were ordered. It's a good thing he didn't ask us to participate, given what came over the radio last night."

"*Cosi di cani. Di cani!* He wined and dined the guardsmen until two o'clock, but he wouldn't give the prisoners the time to get a sip of water, or do what nature commands."

Guidi slammed his hand on the desk. "It won't make much difference to them, going where they're going." But it bothered him. Not because he trusted Bora. Because it confirmed what he suspected about him. "Do you think it's the first time he does this? Partisans, Jews, priests – it's all the same to him."

"The sexton says the Germans dragged Monsignor Lai out of church right after the broadcast. Charged with having a good radio, as far as anyone can tell. To think the old women bragged about the major being so devout, spending all that time in confession every Sunday! *Cosi di cani.*"

"Goes to prove he needs confession more than most, Turco. Speaking of which, I'm off to Verona to meet Bora. If he doesn't mention the Jews, I'm not about to bring them up. We don't need to give him any ideas. Tell my mother I'll get back when I get back, not to stay up, and while you're at it, remind her I don't want you to go grocery shopping for her."

"A man as good as he, a master like him? I'll never find the likes of him again."

Had Bora's taste run to dark women, Lisi's last maid would have been a remarkable specimen. De Rosa, who'd arranged the meeting in his office to be forgiven the impoundment of Claretta's car, watched him watch her now. "Not bad, uh?" he whispered to him in German. "Wasn't Lisi a connoisseur?"

Bora replied in Italian. "I wish to wait for Inspector Guidi before the interrogation."

"As you like."

The woman was thirtyish, long-legged, shapely, with the tragic face of a Greek heroine. She dressed in modest mourning clothes, but Bora noticed she was wearing silk stockings.

He said, "Please tell me your name, and your age."

"Enrica Salviati. I'll be thirty-two next month."

"Why are you wearing black?"

"For my brother. He was a soldier. He was killed in Africa last year."

"Are you married?"

"No."

A knock on the door was followed by the dopey face of a guardsman, who said something to De Rosa. "Well, what are you standing there for?" De Rosa said irritably. "Show him in, we've been waiting for him."

Flustered, Guidi walked into the office. "Sorry I'm late. A military column blocked us for twenty minutes just outside Verona."

Bora pointed out to him the empty armchair behind De Rosa's desk. "Take a seat, Guidi. You don't mind, Centurion, do you?"

De Rosa said he did not, but immediately took his leave. Then Bora went to sit on a corner of the desk, resting his right foot on the floor. "Do the asking, Inspector."

Guidi didn't expect the title, or the offer. He'd been so certain Bora would take over that he hadn't prepared a questionnaire. "Fine, sure." He tried to take time. "I think we ought to begin with a detailed account of the accident. Tell us – Enrica, is it? – what happened from the moment when you left Vittorio Lisi alive in the garden to the time you found him mortally wounded."

She stood in front of the desk like a sad schoolgirl about to recite a lesson, hands clasping a small pocketbook of cheap, balding leather. "Should I repeat what I told the *carabinieri?*"

"If you told the truth, yes."

"I'd just finished clearing the table after lunch, and since it was fine weather the master asked me to accompany him out into the garden for a breath of fresh air. You must go out from the back with the wheelchair, because there are three steps in front of the main door.

So we came out the back of the house, by the garage. I pushed the chair until we reached the gravel just inside the gate, because from there the master could wheel himself out onto the private road. He liked to take his 'exercise', as he called it, back and forth along the length of the mulberry rows. I've seen him do it up to ten times, back and forth. He said it strengthened his lungs."

Guidi began to take notes. "What time was it when you walked back in?"

"Two o'clock, maybe two fifteen. The master would finish eating at twenty to two, and then smoke a cigarette at the table."

Guidi stole a quick look at Bora, but all he could see of him from the armchair was the severe, bony side of his face. He took notice, too, of his uncharacteristic silence.

"All right," he went on. "Describe everything you did after going back into the house."

"Well, first I washed my hands. I had noticed a weed by the door of the garage, and pulled it. Then I placed a bottle of mineral water in the refrigerator. I had forgotten to do it right after lunch, and the master liked cold water summer and winter. I washed the dishes, and then did some reading. There were always magazines in the house, even though the *signora* no longer stayed at the villa. She had so many subscriptions, the magazines kept coming every week. The master said I could read them, if I wanted to. One of them has been running a love-story serial by Liala, and I'd started clipping the instalments."

"So you read. And then?"

"This chapter was longer than the others, more complicated. I'm not a fast reader, and I must have fallen asleep." Framed by the light of day, Enrica's sullen face seemed modelled in wax, as if by an experienced, powerful hand. The schoolgirl had given way to a disconsolate, perhaps more reticent adult.

Guidi said, "Major, would you like to continue?"

Bora did not turn, or stir. "No."

"Well, then. How long did you sleep, Enrica?"

"To tell you the truth, I don't know how long I slept. But it couldn't have been more than a few minutes, because I'd put the tea kettle to boil, and when the noise woke me up it was just starting to bubble up."

"Describe the noise."

Enrica swallowed. She spoke in her faulty, rough Italian, a self-conscious peasant speech. "A *noise*, I didn't know what kind, because I heard it in my sleep. A thud-like noise, like something hitting something hard. It startled me, and right away I heard a car speeding on the gravel, spinning the gravel under its tyres. I thought it was the *signora*, because she always drove in and out of the gate at full speed."

"What do you think now?"

She did not answer, and Guidi repeated the question in the same calm tone.

"If you must know, Inspector, I still think the same."

"That *Signora* Lisi killed your master?"

"I told you what I think. Just the day before they'd had the biggest shouting match, and she'd driven out of the place like a cat with her tail on fire. She almost hit the gate that time."

Once more Guidi flashed a glance at Bora's profile, whose immobility was complete. He seemed to listen intently to what the woman said, yet to be lost in thought. Was he by any chance attracted to her? Guidi couldn't make it out. What else was the matter with him, otherwise? It wasn't like Bora to play second fiddle.

"Tell us the rest of the story," he encouraged Enrica.

"Well, you know how it is when you first wake up. Your mind races and you can't move. I decided, I don't know for sure why, to go and look. Maybe because I was afraid that if she'd come to the villa there would be another scene."

"And why should you care about what took place between your employers?"

It was the first question Bora asked, and as always he went straight for it. Guidi saw by the way Enrica chewed on her bloodless lip that she was inwardly debating an answer.

"I know it was none of my business," she said at last. "But I was fond of the master, and I didn't want him to suffer. In a year of service I heard nothing but scenes against him. It wasn't fair, and if nothing else I wanted *her* to know there were witnesses."

"So," Guidi intervened, "according to you, what were the wrongful accusations that *Signora* Lisi made against her husband?"

"You think of it, she said it." As she grew animated, Enrica's face turned proud and nearly contemptuous, quite a transformation. "She said the marriage had ruined her *prospects*, when five years before she lived down from my house and bought her potatoes and cabbage in the market square."

"You knew *Signora* Lisi beforehand?"

"Not personally. But when the master hired me you could tell from the way she looked at me that the *signora* recognized me from the days we bought greens from the same vendor. Her *prospects*! Her father drank himself to death, and as far as I know her mother mended clothes for a living."

Bora made a calm gesture with his right hand, like a teacher asking for silence. Enrica interrupted herself just when Guidi could hardly wait to hear the rest.

"Please conclude your account of the accident," Bora said.

Enrica's hooded eyes travelled to the German, and settled on him.

"On Fridays the master expected a thorough cleaning, and there was always a clutter of chairs and rolled-up carpets until I was done. Half-asleep as I was, I stumbled on I don't know how many things before I got to the front door. When I got there, all I could see was that the master had fallen out of his wheelchair. It'd never happened before, and it scared me so, I didn't pay attention to the fact that the car I'd heard was not around. I ran down the steps to help him, and of course I could tell he hadn't just fallen. He was white like a sheet of paper, and this little trickle of pinkish blood was running from his nose." A shiver went through Enrica like a tired whiplash, so that her shoulders slumped. "It's useless to ask me what happened next, because I don't remember anything else about it. That's why I can't cry now. Something broke inside me. I started shouting, and the next thing I knew I was standing by the state highway. I couldn't even tell you how I got there."

"Who called the police, then?"

"I don't know. I don't know. If you don't believe me, ask the physicians at the *Ospedale Civile*: they signed my certificate; they'll tell you that for three days afterwards I couldn't even remember my name."

On his corner of the desk, Bora was motionless again. Guidi noticed a vein pulsing on the side of his neck, where a ragged scar disappeared into his immaculate shirt collar.

"Did you sleep with your master?"

There. Guidi heard Bora callously ask the question, and when the woman did not reply, rephrase it in the same tone. "Did you have sexual intercourse with your master?"

Guidi watched Enrica grow flushed, yet return Bora's stare.

"Yes."

"For long?"

"Yes."

Bora was also blushing, a strange reaction that seemed to have nothing to do with embarrassment. Was it arousal? Guidi couldn't tell.

"Had you been hired for that purpose?"

"Not for that *purpose*." She looked away from the German, unhappily. "I'd been hired because the master hoped his wife would carry the baby to term, and wanted a live-in maid for her."

Guidi sat up in De Rosa's armchair.

"When was *Signora* Lisi pregnant?" Bora asked, the coldness of his tone betrayed by the rise of blood to his face.

"About two years ago. She lost the baby very soon, by the third month. The master was heartsick. Heartsick. He had already bought toys, baby clothes. He'd already chosen the crib and the stroller. After that there was no more mention of children, because she didn't want any.

I even heard her throw it in his face that the baby had died because it'd been made by a cripple."

Bora winced, and Guidi noticed it. But Enrica was a schoolgirl again, clutching her cheap bag. "Some weeks went by, and then I felt sorry for him. What do you expect? The master was not a man to do without. He wasn't a monk, was he?"

"Do you mean the Lisis no longer had relations?"

"I never saw them in the same bedroom. And I was the one who *offered* it to the master, one evening when his wife went to painting class. He didn't say no."

For the past two minutes, Guidi had been nervously shredding a folded piece of paper with his nails, without looking at what he was doing. Only after Enrica Salviati finished speaking did he realize that he'd torn to bits a message signed by Mussolini, which De Rosa had apparently received with the morning mail.

Afterward, Bora insisted that he and Guidi stop at the beer hall in King Victor Emmanuel Square before driving back. "Have a pilsner," he suggested.

"Do you know beers?"

"No. I never drink beer. But I trust the taste of millions of other Germans."

"What will you have, then?"

"Nothing. I'm not thirsty. *You* look like you need a drink." Bora chose the table, and sat down. A pillar offered protection from behind, but his chair was directly exposed to anyone coming from the outside. Whether it was a tactical lapse or not, he seemed absent-minded and on edge.

"Are you thinking about what the Salviati woman said, Major?"

"No."

When the beer came, Guidi wetted his lips with the cool, bitter foam. He said, "I appreciate your courtesy, but there was no need for you to tell De Rosa that *you* shredded the paper from Mussolini."

"On the contrary, there was."

"Why?"

"Because I'm a German officer, and I can do as I please."

Guidi drank deeply. There was no way to judge whether Bora was poking fun at him or was being friendly. As usual, the German had given him neither the time nor a chance to decline the invitation, and had insisted on riding in Guidi's battered little Fiat. Since at other times he was not shy about driving his repaired and recognizable *Wehrmacht* BMW, it might, after all, be his way of offering some protection to someone travelling with him. Guidi took a long sip. But then perhaps Bora was just an egotist. Or he was afraid for himself, and was trying to escape another partisan attack.

In any case, here he sat, green-eyed, with that skullcap of dark hair that lent him the mien of a crusader. Barely thirty, Guidi judged, well bred and self-confident. Women were attracted to Bora, Guidi was sure of it. And this afternoon, God knows why, he was more than a little jealous of him. *And yet this is the face*, he told himself, *of a man who has just shipped men and women to imprisonment or death.*

"Major, if what the maid says is true, and the Lisis hadn't slept together in two years, why would Vittorio wait until four months ago to ask for a separation?"

Bora ordered another beer for Guidi. "I don't know."

"Even the Catholic Church grants an annulment if marital rights are denied."

"Perhaps Lisi loved her."

After the first beer, Guidi, who was a teetotaler, began to feel unusually merry. The second one worked wonders. He found himself happy that Claretta had kept away from her husband for two years, happy that Bora had brought him here. "*Love?* Come, Major. A man like Lisi, running after every skirt! Surely he wasn't the type to fall in love."

Bora removed an infinitesimal grain of dust from his left sleeve. "Are you engaged to marry?"

"No."

"Do you have a woman?"

"Why, no."

"Then what do you know about it? You must live with a woman to know what it means to fear that you might have to live without her."

Pluckily, Guidi guzzled the second beer. "I don't think you're the same type of man Lisi was."

"The comparison is irrelevant. I wasn't speaking about myself at all." With a glance at his new wristwatch, Bora said, "Time to go. Are you up to driving?"

Guidi smiled. "I never felt better." But for some reason the chair would not budge from under him.

"Fantastic," Bora grumbled. "Just what we needed. Give me the key to the car."

"Why?"

Impatiently, Bora stretched his right hand across the table. "Come on, come on, Guidi, hand it over. Now we'll have to make you down Heaven knows how much coffee! Why didn't you tell me you're not used to drinking?"

Guidi searched his pockets, giggling as he did. "Why should I have?"

"Because you're stone drunk."

Guidi found Bora's sternness irresistible. "Me? Drunk? I've never got drunk a day in my life!"

5

Less than an hour later, Guidi was taking a frustrated look under the hood. He said something to the effect of an apology, angry for apologizing when it certainly wasn't his fault if the old Fiat had broken down, especially when Bora had insisted on driving it.

"There's no chance it'll start again," he concluded. "It's happened before, and we had to haul it."

Bora stood a few paces away with his back to the car, reading the road map. Whatever he answered, the wind caught his voice, and Guidi didn't understand what he said. Even so, both knew the closest village was nine and a half miles away, and except for the unlikely passage of a military vehicle, they had a long walk ahead of them.

Bora tossed the map back in the car. "We might as well get going."

Guidi, whose intoxication had cleared enough for him to question whether Bora could manage the march, volunteered to seek help alone.

"Why?" Bora slammed the hood down. "This is *nothing*. Near Kursk I spent a week on foot behind enemy lines, with a broken arm and no ammunition."

"I see," Guidi said. It was difficult to assess how much daylight remained in the muted dimness of the afternoon, because the sky had been overcast all day. Shredded, furious clouds rolled in from the northern horizon in an ever-renewing carpet, dark and less dark, but always compact. A few birds flew askew in the gale. Guidi lifted his collar against that gale. He recognized the weather pattern. The temperature would drop soon enough. By sunset it would either turn to soaking rain, or, if the wind changed, to clear and frigid. He glanced northward for a break in the clouds.

"The forecast indicates fair weather tonight," Bora informed him. "We ought to have a good frost, too."

For a few minutes they walked, Guidi with hands driven into the pockets of his coat, all too aware of the raw blasts that came from behind to chill his ears, Bora seemingly indifferent to them but for difficulty in lighting a cigarette. They stopped, and Guidi made a cradle of his fingers, so that Bora could keep the lighter's little flame from being extinguished. After a few attempts, Bora's cigarette grew incandescent at the tip, and he passed it to Guidi to start his own.

"There's nothing like a walk to mull over a problem, Guidi."

On Bora's lighter, Guidi noticed, was an embossed *Luftwaffe* eagle. "Not that we have any solid leads," he said, idly wondering whether Bora had relatives in the German Air Force.

Bora took a quick draught of smoke. "On the contrary, I believe we have too many, and we haven't yet looked into half of them. De Rosa can run at the mouth about Lisi's golden heart, but you and I know Lisi's wealth had aroused jealousies within and without the Party, not to speak of slighted husbands, former and present wives and pregnant girlfriends."

"Well," Guidi spoke in the wind. "Could Lisi have been a gambler?"

"You've seen how padded his bank accounts were. If he gambled, they surely didn't bump him off because he couldn't afford to pay his gambling debts. Of course it could have been an assassination à la Matteotti. A political adversary is done in without witnesses, and even History is left wondering."

"Major Bora!"

"What? Isn't that what happened to Matteotti twenty years ago, and only because he was a famous socialist? I'm not stupid."

"You ought not to speak so lightly."

"Ha!" Despite the stiffness of his gait, Bora forced Guidi to keep up with him. "In our case, it's more likely the widow did it."

"Likely, but unproven. And between you and me, Major, if that were a fact – mind you, if it *were* a fact, could you honestly blame her?"

So that it wouldn't be snuffed out by the wind, Bora spoke with the cigarette in his mouth. "I told you once that I haven't been asked to handle this case in order to pass moral judgement. You're much more concerned about matters of ethics than I am." Bora pressed his lips and smoke escaped from his nostrils in a faint quick cloud, soon snatched by the wind. They had walked more than a mile when clear patches of grey evening sky began to float above the convulsed race of late-autumn clouds. "There's our fair weather," Bora observed.

Guidi, whose bladder was starting to resent the amounts of beer and coffee stored in it, had stayed behind for a respite. From the wayside where he stood, careful the wind would not spray urine against his trousers, he could see Bora waiting a few feet away. His back was turned, and he stood ramrod-straight as if the march were not affecting the pain in his wounded leg.

A minuscule star pricked the east like a pin. Another followed, and another, and soon the darkening sky was full of them, little lights now bold, now dim, as if panting with fears of their own. Already a frail, opaque moon sailed like a glass boat up high. Bora raised his eyes to the crescent. As wraiths of tardy clouds overtook it, it more and more resembled a delicate wind-filled sail overhead; rushing, finely wrought, the moon would not be so graceful again until after it went entirely dark, tomorrow or the day after. For reasons of his own, Bora showed no ill humour this evening, something that Guidi was ashamed to resent more than an argument.

"*Luna mendax.*" Quoting the Latin saying, Bora smirked, and kept his eyes on the moon.

"'The moon is a liar'?"

"Yes. You never heard the proverb? I'll tell you about it some time. You know, Guidi, we ought to check De Rosa's alibi."

The words came as an attempt at conciliation. Guidi, who tonight treasured the notion that Claretta had been long refusing her bed to Lisi, fell for it.

But Bora's indulgence sealed over like ice. "On the other hand, it is impossible not to see her as an ungrateful mate after what Enrica Salviati had to say."

Dusk gathered around them, and soon they were silent.

They had resigned themselves to wandering in the dark when the round hum of an engine rose from the distance behind them. Guidi glanced back in alarm. He couldn't help thinking that a partisan band was about to find him in the company of a German officer. Alongside him, Bora's only reaction was to unlatch the holster on his left side. Guidi, too, reached inside his coat.

A large car was approaching, the slits of its blackened headlights projecting feeble cones of glare ahead. Bora and Guidi couldn't make out how many people were inside, and kept on the defensive. The car scaled down its gears, creeping to a halt on the shoulder by them. From the semi-darkness of the lowered window, "*Wollen Sie mitfahren?*" The question floated to them over the idling of the Mercedes-Benz engine.

Bora and Guidi were both surprised, but while Bora's hand left the holster, Guidi's did not. The bald head of a stout old man emerged like a strange birth from the window. He smiled. After speaking a few sentences in German to Bora, who readily answered, he spoke to Guidi in Italian. "I saw a Fiat stopped a while back, and was wondering who might have left it there, with the curfew and the danger of night air raids. Now," he said, clearly pleased at the sight of Bora's uniform, "I understand. My house is less than four miles off that way." He pointed to the twilit flat countryside broken by hills like islands. "You are welcome to spend the night, and I can take you to town in the morning."

Bora did not trouble himself with consulting Guidi on the matter. "Yes, please."

They were soon travelling along in the ageing German car, toward sites unknown. Guidi marvelled at Bora's imprudence in accepting a ride just because the driver spoke German.

"By the way," the old man was saying now, "I know I shouldn't be out in a private car, but there's never any checking on this road. My name is Moser. 'Nando' Ferdinand Augustus Moser." He turned to the men seated in the back seat. "Austro-Hungarian subject by birth in Trieste, when His Imperial Royal Apostolic Highness still ruled this land. Good music and good cheer, and all that! My father, God bless his memory, was a physician in Franz Josef's court, but it was his elders who built the house some three hundred years back. There were scores of Mosers, when this was Austrian land."

Guidi tried to dredge from his Catholic school education that bit of Italian history. The Peace of Vienna came to his mind, though he wasn't sure of the date – 1866?

Bora said something in German.

"*Ja, ja,*" the old man agreed. "*Ganz genau, ja.*"

As they went along, only remnants of light, or perhaps it was the starlight, allowed the travellers to intuit shapes and distances. Guidi looked through his dusty window. The hills had grown closer to one another, revealing archipelagos of sparsely wooded terrain. Like a new continent of purple darkness, they set limits to the starpricked sky.

Bora didn't seem to pay attention to where they were being taken, so Guidi kept alert. Eventually he made out a long façade, and two colonnaded wings spreading out as if to embrace the cultivated grounds.

"It's not going to be any warmer inside, I'm afraid," Moser said in Italian. "No hot water. There never was. And no telephone. Tradition. But I'll show you the fortepiano young Mozart played when he passed by on his way to Verona in 1770 with Papa Leopold. It's a Silbermann, you know."

The qualification meant nothing to Guidi, but Bora seemed enthralled. "Really?" He sat up. "Built by Gottfried or the heirs?"

"By Gottfried himself."

"*Ach, so?* I played on a Hildebrandt piano in Dresden."

It was the first time Guidi had heard of Bora's interest in music.

The car had turned onto a brick or cobblestone path that led them bumpily to the main door. Moser asked Bora, "Saxon, are you?"

"Leipzig."

"Leipzig – not related to Friedrich von Bora!"

Bora did not elaborate. "He was my father."

"Well!" Moser kept smiling. "How fortunate for the Silbermann if you'll play tonight."

Bora answered nothing at all.

Once the great leaf of the main door was pushed back, a gaping, vast darkness received the men, compared to which the night seemed luminous. Moser groped alongside the wall, awakening faint light bulbs from the sconces to reveal a stage-like, seemingly endless hall. Echoes travelled unknown vaulted spaces above, the ceiling being all but invisible. Each step and each word sounded two, three times, as if ghostly feet and mouths populated the dark to imitate the living. Behind the sleek shape of the fortepiano, the powerful sweep of a staircase sought the dimness of other floors. It seemed to Guidi a frozen waterfall of alabaster, gleaming now opalescent yellow, now thickly white. The stairs lost themselves in the gloom, behind a baluster. Church-like, from unfathomed corners and recesses, stucco reliefs extended white and gilded limbs to the stolen pool of glare. Beyond these, lost to the light bulbs, the domed darkness hinted at a glory of windows and painted images, though nothing but a borderless mist showed at this hour.

Moser's hunched figure seemed out of place in the shadowy beauty. But there he was, rubbing his hands, with a nod inviting the guests to follow him through a low doorway.

If the partisans pop up and kill us now, it's all Bora's fault. Guidi thought the words, and still followed.

The door led to a cavernous kitchen, at the centre of which a wood stove seemed to be the only working thing. Moser went to toss a piece of cut lumber into it. He said, "When you're alone, there isn't much point in keeping up the entire house. The rest of the family is long gone, what in 1918 with the Spanish flu, and then with wars and age. The rooms upstairs are in good shape, but there's no electricity." Bora had remained on the threshold of the kitchen, half-turned to the hall. "Yes, that is the Silbermann." Moser acknowledged his interest. "Let me show you."

Guidi was not musically inclined, so he sat to warm his hands by the stove. The thought was taking shape in him that all this had happened for a reason after all. In any case tonight he'd find out more about Bora. He was thinking that finding out about Bora, at least tonight, was part of his lot in life. He overheard the men speaking German in the hall, Moser's lilting old voice, Bora with his calm tone like running water. The metallic sound of a few notes followed, and Bora's suddenly eager comments.

What a fuss over an old piano. But at least, Guidi thought with some guilty gladness, he was not wandering the Sagràte fields, hunting down a madman. Well, well. Corporal Turco was surely in a panic. Not to speak of his mother, whom he'd left fussing over home-made pasta.

"Cristofori wrest-plank as in the one made for Frederick the Great," Moser was telling Bora. "See? And yet little Mozart didn't like it as well as he would Stein's."

"With Stein's wrest-plank there was no more blocking of the hammer."

"Precisely."

Around Guidi, kitchen and house seemed to breathe as if by an inner weather system, winds and currents and rainless storms. The draught from the unused chimney must have once been formidable, a throat of brick and stone mighty enough to gulp rivers of air. How different it all was from Claretta's enclosed pink world, new and shiny like the inside of a shell. Tonight Guidi could not help comparing Bora's talkative, animated friendliness to the hard side he showed the girl, and everyone else.

He was presently returning to the kitchen with Moser, speaking Italian. "I spent my summers in Rome between the ages of five and sixteen, at my stepfather's ex-wife's. I know all the Roman church organs and historic pianos worth knowing."

Moser smiled. "And you still don't want to play mine?"

At once Guidi noticed Bora had not removed the glove from his right hand, so that the gloved mutilation of the left was not obvious. That he did so now, in a calm fashion, was not lost on Moser. There was an embarrassed rounding of shoulders, a turning away to handle an aluminium pot set on the stove. With his back to the kitchen, Moser said, "I hope you gentlemen won't mind a simple dinner."

"You shouldn't trouble yourself, *Herr* Moser."

"And why not, Major? How often do you think I have guests any more?"

Dinner was more than simple, even by war standards. In bizarre contrast with the fine plates on which it was served, a fare of soup and bread was all there was to it.

"The house eats more than I do," Moser forgivingly said afterwards, as if to condone the reality of it. "I don't know who'll feed her when I'm gone. Some things you can dispose of, but the house, the house – you're part of it. It's like disposing of yourself."

"Do you still own the land around it?" Bora asked.

Moser shook his hairless round head. "Gone years ago, along with the good times and all that. Only Mozart's little ghost stays, and I live here like Jonah in the whale."

German and Italian alternated, or mixed within the same sentence. His mind caught in the other events of the day, Guidi paid little attention, though at one point it seemed to him Moser addressed Bora as *Freiherr von Bora*. As far as he could tell, Bora had not shared the reason for their being on the road. And although his shoulders were at ease, aloofness was again a part of him, as when he had sat across from poor daunted Claretta. For an inexplicable moment it seemed to Guidi it might even be shyness, but it was absurd that one like Bora could be shy.

Could it really be *Baron* von Bora?

"It's best that the family's gone before it came to this," Moser chattered on. "My ancestors fought the Turks at Vienna and Zenta and Belgrade. They fought the Turks and won, and those who survived came here to treasure the conquered Ottoman flags. They built the house in this charming countryside and were ready to enjoy life, music, the good things. Soldiers and colonists and farmers these two hundred years."

Guidi repressed a yawn, his mind on Claretta's pouting lips drawn around the slender cylinder of her *Tre Stelle* cigarette. Here was talk of the dead, but Claretta was alive. Lovely, alone. Would *she* be able to keep her house and livelihood in the future?

"My elders brought back eastern superstitions," Moser went on, "such as never looking at the waxing moon through a glass pane. That's bad luck, you know. You didn't know it, Major? Well, it is, or that's what the Ottoman Turks said. It wasn't until my father, bless his soul, that we replaced the windows on the front with clear glass. And it may have been a foolish dare after all. But here, you let me do all the talking. *Signor* Guidi, what do *you* say?"

Guidi did not know what to say. He muttered some generic agreement, while Bora spoke to Moser with great composure. "I am like your ancestors. I have my own Turks to defeat."

They were the most suggestive words Guidi had heard Bora utter to date.

There was more talk of history and music before Bora and Guidi were shown to the Mozart rooms up the opalescent stairway. Hallways escaped candlelight to become lost in the dark, with fugues of unused spaces, panelled entryways. Guidi gave up counting rooms when Moser opened in front of him what seemed the void itself. From it came an overpowering smell of dank and long-accumulated dust, and a gust of icy air that swayed the tips of the candles.

Moser smiled at him. "I think you'll like Papa Leopold's room, *Signor* Guidi. This is the south side, so you'll be quite cosy. Good night." And, turning to Bora next, he added, "We go the other way for you, Major. If you don't mind the chill, you're welcome to Wolfgang's room."

"I don't mind the chill."

Guidi wore his clothes to bed that night.

After the clearing at sundown, the wind had taken over the dark, and now scurried all around the great house looking for chinks to blow into. If this was cosy, he hated to think of the temperature in Bora's room, which was on the north side. The strangeness of the evening deepened now that the candle was out. Insects ticked away in the wood, burrowing their minute channels along spindles and boards. Entering the bleakness of damp sheets was like slipping into an unknown pool of water. This is what he got for listening to Bora. Guidi lay as still as one resigned to drowning, until his body became accustomed to the cold.

Somewhere, this same night, the lonely convict also lay or sat up, with a deadly weapon and God knows how many rounds of ammunition. Perhaps through the brushwood he sensed the distant villages, dark with the curfew. Perhaps he heard the deep sounds of animals in stables and folds, and listened to the wind rustling branches and the spoils of corn in the fields. And if there was a scent of snow in the air, the convict would smell that, too. Perhaps he would move on. Perhaps he would shoot to kill tomorrow.

In his sink-hole of cold and dust Guidi sneezed, cursing Bora for landing him here. What irked him most was that Bora never showed himself vulnerable. He confronted men and women in his aloof, superior way, and never revealed himself. Tonight was the closest he'd got to it (but what did he mean by *his* Turks?), and had he cared for it, Guidi could have capitalized on the hints. *But no, look out, he's the same son of a whore who sent the Jews to their deaths.* Guidi sneezed. Searching his pockets for a handkerchief, he suddenly remembered that Claretta had handed him her card the other night. It was still in his coat pocket, where he groped through sandwich crumbs until he found it.

Holding the card to his nostrils, Guidi knew that Bora was dead wrong about her. Her perfume was not cheap, not irritating. And what if her face was patterned after movie stars in the magazines? There was no guilt in that. True, though, he hadn't said a word about Claretta to his mother. God forbid. Agitated by the discovery of lipstick smears, as late as this morning she'd asked if he'd finally decided to use some sense and get married. Married. *Sandro, darling, don't let me die without grandchildren.* Guidi slipped the scented card under the clamminess of his pillow, regretting that he hadn't kissed Claretta's hand as he took leave of her.

Is this what a strong mother and Catholic schooling do to a man? With all that *Jesus dear, Who the cross bore, may I love Him more and more*, one ends up awkward, inhibited with women, there's no denying that. Uselessly fascinated by symbols, tokens, fetishes. Even by odours, colours. It isn't as if he didn't, of course... But whores, afterward (and sometimes before as well) disgusted him. Being a policeman made no difference to that sensitivity. Damn it, he was Bora's age, and the thought of a woman he hadn't even kissed kept him awake, while Bora had a wife and one could only guess what variety of sexual experience behind him.

In his rancour, Guidi thought of Bora as strongly sexed, although he had nothing to go by but Bora's tenseness during Enrica's testimony. And perhaps his hostility toward Claretta. *Damn him, maybe he secretly hankers for Claretta, and she for him.* As if, more worldly, jaded in some ways, certainly more cynical than Guidi could ever be, Bora were responding in a resentful manner to women in general.

At the very least, Bora must long for his wife and for their lovemaking, with the potent yearning of marriage. In which case his contempt for women might be no more than loneliness and the forced continence of war.

Across the sealed darkness of the room, as Guidi lay shivering, music travelled up from the deep great body of the house. Faintly at first, coins of sound rolled lightly. Then, the notes became a tender and haunting and clear ripple across the Silbermann. The melody was known to Guidi. He couldn't attach a title to it, but it was a voice saying things he had somehow heard or intuited before and only half-understood, a voice young and vulnerable and wise. Questions and answers creating a sequence without echoes but unmistakably Mozart, and unmistakably, by the repentant interruption of it, played by Martin Bora.

At daybreak the next morning Bora left with Moser, and however he managed to direct his business, he was back by half-past eight with an army car and driver.

Guidi had meanwhile awakened in his heavily draped room, where worn velvet here and there showed the morning sun through webbed patches. His rising from bed caused a storm of dust motes. He went to the window and peered out, fearing that if he touched the drapes they'd crumble in his hands. Through the chink he could see little: only a segment of the portico below, bearing a worn crown of limestone statues white as bones.

When he walked downstairs, the house's decay was more evident in daylight. Thin cracks in the walls ran ominously close to the stucco decorations and up the painted cupola, celebrating overhead the apotheosis of some military ancestor. In gruesome old cabinets built into the corners, blood-red Ottoman flags stood fading and cracking at the creases. Guidi glanced at them and then neared the long body of the fortepiano. He plucked at the keyboard, and tinny notes were all that came out of it. What a waste of time, this entire interval. It made no difference that they'd likely have had to spend the night out of doors otherwise. And now there was the car to repair, as if he needed further trouble.

He wondered what Claretta was doing at this hour. Bathing? Sipping coffee? Lounging in bed with the little dog at her feet? In the name of justice, if nothing else, he had to persuade Bora to let go of his hostility toward her. It wasn't Claretta's fault if Bora carried his own luggage of Puritanism or misogyny, different from a bachelor's but no less there, and more bigoted. *What if he isn't Catholic at all, and only went to church to entrap*

Monsignor Lai? Bora liked reading features, and what he unfairly detected in her pink looks was not the fragility Guidi perceived. Unfair, unfair. This morning Guidi was determined to find another motive for the murder, and another murderer. What about money, power and lust? They were strong motives, perhaps in excess of jealousy. But then Bora would likely say that at one time or another each of the four motives had entered Claretta's curly head.

When the German army vehicle entered the curved space of the portico, followed at a close distance by Moser's dusty car, Guidi was anxious to leave. On the doorstep, compared to Moser's worn shabbiness, Bora looked every inch the soldier. Guidi was not about to even enter his slept-in clothes in the competition.

"I called Verona from the closest public phone I could find," Bora took him aside to inform him. "There is news. Clara Lisi has been arrested for her husband's murder."

"What? How is it possible, Major? Why? What has changed from yesterday?"

Bora said he did not know. "I haven't the time to look into it now. I have urgent business to attend to at my post, and so should you."

It was true enough, but Bora's arrogance was out of place. By the time Guidi entered the army vehicle, he was in a quiet rage, which Bora's coolness only made worse. Soon they were leaving the overgrown garden in a cloud of ice crystals and vapour, spewed by the exhaust across the chill morning air.

Back in Sagràte, Guidi did not hear from Bora for the rest of the day.

What he did hear was the rattle of machine guns and automatic rifles in the foothills, and now and then the dull explosion of a mortar shell. The head of the local *carabinieri* – that overzealous, royalist army branch of the police – stopped by Guidi's office just before noon. He reported how his patrol had encountered a group of partisans at the edge of Sagràte's territory.

"We didn't exchange one word," he shared in a noncommittal way. "We ignored one another. And I'm not telling the Germans about it, either."

"You could have at least asked them if they saw anyone fitting the convict's description, or if one of them was killed near the ditch at Fosso Bandito."

The *carabiniere* shook a plump finger. "I don't talk to partisans. Besides, judging by the looks of them, they're having a tough time these days. The German major at Lago doesn't give them a breather. If he doesn't go after them in person, he sends his men. Do you hear them? They've been at it since before dawn. Thank God once in a while a German gets it, too, and just the way he had it coming."

Guidi had no reason to feel alarmed at the words, but he did. "What do you mean?"

The *carabiniere* pointed to Guidi's wall map. "You mentioned Fosso Bandito. Are you familiar with the thicket of holm oaks beyond it, near the old watering hole? One of my men went searching there yesterday afternoon, and found a dead German in the brush. We knew soldiers and partisans had been in the neighbourhood because of the shooting."

From the next room one of the policemen, deep in paperwork, began whistling a song under his breath.

Guidi found it out of place, but not enough to silence him. "Well?" he urged the *carabiniere*.

"Well, the dead soldier was there, dead as they come, so there was nothing to do. We resumed our work. If they care to, the Germans can go look for him on their own."

"Had he been killed by rifle shots, or what?"

"He had a hole this big on his right side. A chunk of meat was missing from him. I thought maybe a mortar shell had grazed him, and he'd dragged himself off to die in the woods."

"Was he wearing his boots?"

"He was."

"But I bet it wasn't the partisans that killed him."

Here the paper-shuffling policeman started singing out the words of the song, so that Guidi wheeled toward the door to shut him up. "Cavuto, what *is* it with you? Go sing *La Strada nel Bosco* somewhere else!" But it might not be an accident that Cavuto – who played dumb but wasn't – should sing about hidden trails in the woods when they were talking of partisans.

Whether the *carabiniere* agreed with Guidi, he did not say. "At any rate," he added, "whoever killed him, I stand by my decision to leave the soldier where he was. It's too complicated to explain to the Germans where and how it might have happened. And you know about this morning, eh?"

"No, I was away. What about this morning?"

"News came that the truck that left Lago yesterday – the one with the Jews in it – got in trouble somewhere along the way. The Germans must be mad as hornets."

"Is a search party what they're up to now?"

"Don't know, but their commander has joined them in the hills."

Less than half an hour later, in the holm-oak woods, Lieutenant Wenzel lost his temper with the corporal, who'd doubled over to vomit at the sight of the dead soldier.

"Wenzel," Bora said sharply, "get back here."

Wenzel obeyed. He was somewhat myopic and, though he did not wear glasses, he had an expectant way of staring at those who addressed him.

"Don't look at me." Bora pointed at the body. "Look at *him.*"

"Yes, *Herr Major.*"

Bora took the deference as a given. He'd known Wenzel since their private-school days in Leipzig, where Wenzel was a first-year student and he an upperclassman. Wenzel maintained the younger student's admiring respect, reinforced now by the difference in rank.

"When did you notice that Gerhard was missing?"

As ordered, Wenzel stared at the dead soldier. "As I wrote in my report, *Herr Major,* we had suspended fire no more than five minutes earlier. The men were spread out in a fan, three or four hundred yards across. Some had advanced more than others, and Gerhard had been keeping to the left. According to plan I did not suspend the operation at sundown. However, now that the bandits had disengaged, I decided to gather the men and return to the post. We'd had two serious casualties, plus one fracture, and I was now informed that Gerhard was missing. We didn't know if he'd been wounded, or had got lost. I ordered a search until it became impossible to see our way around, and then re-entered."

"Why didn't you resume the search first thing this morning?"

"Because with *Oberfeldwebel* Nagel escorting the Jews and you gone, I decided to wait for you to come back to Lago, *Herr Major.*"

From where he stood, Bora could fully see the massacred side of the dead soldier. A file of ants scaled his thigh, seeking the edge of the wound. Gerhard was not even twenty, and had the stunned, wide-eyed, beardless face of an ignorant child. Bora thought, *Now he's learned at least one thing, poor Gerhard. But what good is it to him?* "Have Nagel gather Gerhard's belongings," he said out loud to Wenzel, "and draft a letter of condolence for me to sign."

Just then in Sagràte, Guidi's mother was listening to a woman's voice on the telephone. Bewildered as she was, she fought off the temptation to ask why the message for her son was being conveyed to his home rather than at the office.

"When is the inspector due back?" the woman enquired.

"He's a busy man," *Signora* Guidi said stiffly. "I usually expect him back for lunch at about one."

"I see. Then do me a favour. I'm calling from a public telephone, and don't have much change with me. Please tell the inspector that Enrica Salviati needs to see him again, and ask him if we can meet Saturday afternoon in Piazza Victor Emmanuel here in Verona, near the park fountain."

"Near the park fountain," *Signora* Guidi repeated. She was trying to estimate the woman's social standing from her tone and inflection, and how old she might be. Her accent – Venetian, maybe. "Any other messages?"

"Only that the appointment is at two. Thank you ever so much."

"My pleasure, I'm sure," *Signora* Guidi spoke back in a falsetto more honeyed than required, and hung up the phone. Pleasure? She was thinking of Sandro's handkerchief. Too bad she couldn't see the woman, or smell her perfume. The voice was neither here nor there. Polite, that was all, but try as she might, she sounded accustomed to speaking dialect. And she had little money with her, called from a pay telephone. Guidi's mother fretted. What if Sandro spoke the truth about the street-walker?

Bundled up in his chilly office, Guidi had his own phone troubles. He could hardly make out the far-away voice of the Verona prison warden floating to him through the earpiece, seemingly saying that no prisoner had ever been allowed to converse by telephone.

"I am very sorry, Inspector. Regulations are regulations, you know better than I. We're in Verona, not in America."

What did America have to do with this?

"At least let me know how she is," Guidi said irritably. "The investigation has been assigned to a German officer, and it is of the utmost importance that *Signora* Lisi be treated well. We have not yet concluded the interrogation."

The warden's quivery voice came and went through the wires. "...has had breakfast... feeling well. Don't worry, Inspector, we'll do our best. You may come and see the prisoner at any time during office hours, and in the case of a resumed interrogation, we can supply office space."

Noisily, Turco trundled into the office with an armful of green wood.

Guidi looked up from the phone, covering the mouthpiece. "Why are you bringing in that garbage? You know it only gives out smoke, and the air gets unbreathable."

"We're out of dry wood, Inspector."

"Wrong! There's some under the stairs, go and look."

Turco backed up. A moment later there followed the crash of wood on the floor. Judging by the blast of cold air and the curt German comment that came at the same time, Guidi knew that Bora had entered the building in haste and slammed the door against the exiting Sicilian.

Within moments, Guidi found himself standing behind his desk, noticing that when Bora was angry the afflux of blood under the skin darkened his eyes, and the scar on his neck looked livid. He was saying, "I just brought back one of my men to the post, dead. I have good reason to believe he was killed by your escaped convict."

"*My* convict, Major? He doesn't belong to me any more than to you. I'm sorry about your soldier. Where did it happen?"

"In a holm-oak grove north of Fosso Bandito. The blast tore a fistful of flesh and bone from his left side. I have not come to tell you this, Guidi. I am perfectly aware that I risk my men's lives each time I send them out on patrol. It's seeing them killed for no motive that enrages me."

No motive. And what about the Jews you carted off? Guidi was within a hair's-breadth of saying it, but he knew it wouldn't help matters. "Excuse me." He reached for the ringing phone. "Mother? What are you... Yes. Really? Who was she, did she say?" He called Bora's attention with a meaningful nod, and jotted down for him "Enrica

134

Salviati wants to add to her statement" in his notebook. "Listen, Ma," he said, "if she calls again, tell her it's all right, I'll see her on Saturday at two. No, I won't need the good shirt. Just tell her I'll be there."

Bora read the words, and walked back to the door. Grumpily he crushed an empty cigarette packet in his right hand and tossed it across the room into Guidi's waste basket. "Don't expect me to come with you to Verona. For the rest of the week I go after the coward who assassinates my men."

Yes, and the prisoners who got away from you. Guidi said, "As you prefer. Any questions you want me to ask Enrica Salviati?"

"Yes. Ask her if Clara Lisi has a lover."

"I wonder how much you can trust the testimony of a rival."

"Don't worry about that. Simply ask Salviati the question. I'll take care of asking Clara Lisi directly."

Bora's intentions were not destined to be carried out. Having failed to find him in Lago, the SS had come looking for him at the Sagràte post. There was no wriggling away from confrontation, and Bora only thanked his stars that Wenzel was still in the woods. This afternoon the anonymous *Standartenführer* wouldn't trouble himself with leaving the car.

"Things don't look good, Major," he rolled down the window to say.

Bora ordered the soldier guarding the doorway to go inside. "*Things* is a vague term. I take it you refer to specifics."

"Please. Let us not play games. I have difficulty reconciling your present clumsiness with the high degree of achievement you displayed in Russia. If you could break out of Stalingrad with your entire unit, you could surely get fifteen Jews to Gries."

"Mechanical failure happens to the best of us. The Republican Guard delivered the prisoners in a disgraceful lorry. The front tyre rod gave in, and the Jews went off the road in the mountains. It's a miracle I didn't lose my men in the accident. It was night-time, and the Italians were too drunk to be of any help. I will have to report, of course, the fact that two of my soldiers were pulled out of an anti-partisan operation because of your request. In view of the impeccable record I seem to hold here as a rebel-hunter, doing without any of my highly trained men places my continuing success in jeopardy. As for the prisoners, we will leave no stone unturned in hunting them down. The rugged terrain hampers us considerably, but I am hopeful."

"The hell you are. Negligence is the least you'll have to answer for."

Bora was careful to show no alarm. "You're making a lot of fuss over fifteen Jews. I must say I am astonished by your lack of interest in my pursuit of bandits. They're much more dangerous than Jews."

"Nothing is more dangerous than Jews."

"I stand corrected."

"Corrected? That, I'm going to make certain you are."

On Friday, Bora was grateful for the call ordering his immediate presence in Verona, where the drafting of a plan for a joint military action on Lake Garda was under way. The combined German–Italian operation was expected to begin on 15 December. He even looked forward to a night in some lonely hotel room, unless Colonel Habermehl offered him hospitality in his bachelor flat behind Palazzo Maffei. By evening, it was raining in Verona, but it turned cold enough for ice to form on the streets in the morning.

"Thank God you've come to visit. I die of boredom at night if I have no one to talk to." In shirt-sleeves and grey braces, Colonel Habermehl poured a Scotch into his glass, and after a moment of hesitation added no ice to it. "You're sure you don't want one, Martin?"

"No, thank you."

"Too bad." Habermehl gulped the liquor with a toss of his head. "What generation is this of yours, that would rather get killed than make love?"

"I wouldn't go as far as that, *Herr Oberst*. If I had a choice in the matter—"

"As if I don't know you. When I heard about your accident in September I told myself, 'Here goes my best friend's stepson, without even enjoying his wife for a straight month.' You should have insisted on evacuation to Germany, and at least a couple of weeks' furlough. Even without your left paw, I bet you could have figured out how to entertain her."

"Times are hard."

"Times are always hard for somebody. You must learn to extract as much as you can." Habermehl returned to the bottle. "Just a drop, what do you say? Let's drink to our little Paul Joseph Goebbels' intimation that 'Our will to win is unshakeable'. Or, no, better yet: let's drink to his 'Hit a rogue more than once!'"

"No, thank you."

"Have it your way. Speaking of little men, this morning I met De Rosa. Puffed-up as always, like a bantam rooster. He told me he'd tried to telephone you without success."

Bora sat upright in the armchair, where he'd slumped until now. "Was it in reference to the Lisi affair?"

"Yes. I even wrote it down somewhere. You know I have no memory. Now, where did I?… Oh, I know. I'll check the interior pocket of my tunic." Quickly for a man of his size, Habermehl walked out into the hallway. He returned holding an envelope, on which he had scribbled with a fountain pen. "It washed out, sorry. It was raining when I took it down. See if you can make it out, Martin. Or else call De Rosa from here."

Bora recognized a few important words. *Girl's father – first abortion – money – argument.*

"May I use the telephone, Colonel?"

"Go ahead," Habermehl answered from the liquor cabinet. "It's in the hallway."

Soon after, at his address on Via Galileo, Centurion De Rosa cut a less than martial image in his pyjamas, even though he was clutching a handgun. That he was hardly expecting Bora to show up on his doorstep and at this late hour was obvious by the embarrassed way he put the weapon away.

"One must always be ready, Major." He stammered an excuse. "Traitors, political enemies, partisans – one must be ready for unforeseen events."

Bora overheard a rustle in the bedroom, and assumed that *events* might include jealous husbands. Without waiting to be invited, he stepped in.

"You didn't answer the phone when I called you twenty minutes ago."

"I was busy."

"Well, I must talk to you. Colonel Habermehl gave me your message."

"My message? Ah, yes. Yes. The story of the abortion and the girl's father." Sweeping a furtive glance toward the bedroom door, De Rosa stretched on his bare feet to whisper in Bora's ear. "Give me five minutes. It's a delicate question, a married lady."

"You have five minutes exactly. Be quick about it."

De Rosa kept his word. Bora heard him speaking *sotto voce*, and a somehow familiar woman's voice answering in a distinct vibrato, "Thank God. I was really scared for a minute."

When he came out in his stockinged feet, pulling up his army breeches, De Rosa found Bora standing in the living room with a disapproving look, as if not wearing one's boots were for a German more inexcusable than having a married lover.

Bora said, "You told Colonel Habermehl how the father of a girl who died during an abortion had a row with Lisi over money. When did the incident take place?"

"After 8 September, I don't recall exactly when. The only reason why I even thought about it, Major, is that you insisted on hearing if Lisi had enemies. The way I see it, there's no way to prove that any of the girls had even *been* with Lisi, if you catch my meaning. I told you they swarmed around him like flies."

"Does the man in question have a first and last name?"

"He has both. Neither one begins with a 'C', though."

Bora sat down in an unpadded armchair, without taking off his cap. "This is very interesting, and I wish to hear every detail of the argument. Tell the lady in the other room to make herself comfortable for an hour at least. There are other things I wish to ask you."

"Now?" De Rosa gave him a hateful look. "Major Bora, I understand you're a man of action, but we can meet tomorrow and nothing will change. It is absolutely necessary that I take the lady home before one."

Bora checked his watch. "Go ahead. I'll wait here."

"But—"

"It's already half-past midnight. Obviously the lady doesn't live far from here. Do your bidding and return. I'll wait here."

Rapid-fire whispering ensued from the bedroom, then a completely dressed De Rosa walked angrily toward the living-room door. Bora heard the clicking of a woman's heels following him out of the flat to the landing, and then the metallic clang of the elevator cage closing shut.

Alone in the house, Bora looked around. It was an unremarkable place, devoid of books, with a diminutive kitchen off the living room, a single bedroom and a bath. On the writing desk, inside an ashtray encrusted with sea shells, sat two tickets for the past opera season, and some receipts. Flyers from expensive hotels – the Grand Hotel in Gardone, the Metropole Suisse in Como – were stuffed in a manila envelope. Political junkets, Bora thought.

The kitchen was impractically narrow, but outside it a trellised balcony with lawn chairs extended to the bedroom. There, hooded lights floated the dark-sheeted bed in an underwater azure glare. The scent of woman was deep in the room, and Bora withdrew from it.

Ten minutes later, the front door was slammed open.

Surprised at not having heard the sound of the elevator cage beforehand, Bora glanced up from the newspaper he'd been browsing.

"Swine!" From the hallway a voice came to him strangled by rage and the exertion of climbing several floors. "I caught you without the bolts on the door, swine!"

Bora put away the newspaper.

A distracted middle-aged man flew into the living room and, having done so, he remained agape long enough for Bora to light himself an American cigarette.

"Are you looking for Centurion De Rosa?" he asked.

The man took a step backward. "I thought…"

Bora looked away from the man's humiliation, from the absurdity of the situation. Half-heartedly, without lying, he said, "Centurion De Rosa isn't here."

At three in the morning, Colonel Habermehl found the De Rosa episode much more amusing than it had seemed to Bora. Laughing until he had tears in his eyes, he asked for more details.

"There isn't much else to say, *Herr Oberst.* I was bracing myself for a tasteless scene, Italian-style, but Bruni's husband was so disappointed to find me alone instead of De Rosa in good company, he couldn't even keep up his fury. He started bawling in front of me, and gave me an earful about faithless women."

"And you? What did you tell him?"

"Nothing. What could I tell him? My only reason for being there was to find out the address of the man who fought with Lisi. I needed to keep De Rosa in one piece for the time necessary to hear the information. Fortunately Bruni left without seeking redress. A few minutes later De Rosa showed up, out of breath. It seems he hid himself in the porter's booth on the ground floor, and had been praying to all the saints while Bruni climbed the stairs to catch them by surprise."

Habermehl poured himself an abundant nightcap. "Good thing you chanced upon the love scene! Tomorrow we're stuck with the joint operation plan, but you will follow up on the new lead the day after tomorrow?"

If he shut his eyes, Bora could see the ants labouring up Gerhard's bloody side. "No, sir. The day after tomorrow I'm on patrol."

6

The new hospital complex lay north-west of Verona, between the Adige's riverside and the foothills of Quartiere Pindemonte, where houses gave way to fields and the Industrial Canal could be seen steaming in its banks. Before joining Habermehl and the others at German headquarters, Bora had an early morning appointment with the head surgeon, who'd treated him on the day of his wounding.

"Sunday is a good day." A smiling nun preceded Bora down the perfectly scrubbed, phenol-scented corridor. "Doctor Volpi is less busy than usual. How is your left leg?"

Bora was not surprised to be addressed with *lei* here. He knew the Vatican had instructed its religious to "abstain with garb and prudence" from adopting the Fascist mode of address. The abstention clearly included addressing Italian-speaking *Wehrmacht* officers.

"Better, thank you. Do you remember me, Sister?"

Her hands in the folds of her sleeves, the nun halted in front of a glass door, which she opened for him. "Yes, indeed. Your other leg sent some good kicks my way."

Bora entered.

"Good morning, good morning." Unceremoniously the surgeon had Bora undress and sit on the examination table, and started to cut the bandages around his knee. "Just as I thought, it's become infected again. How many times must I tell you, Major? All this activity, with badly healed wounds – you had better watch out."

"I'm busy, I can't."

"Do less, or do otherwise. The human body deserves respect, and you're paying none to yours at the moment." After disinfecting the wounds, the surgeon probed for the metal fragments still embedded around Bora's knee. "At least a couple must come out today, more if we can. You'll have to lie down for it, it serves no purpose for you to watch what I'm doing. Mark my word, without sulpha drugs, without antibiotics, one of these days we won't be able to prevent a serious infection. What then? Do we amputate the leg we fought to save, or do we let you go to your Maker with septicaemia?"

While the surgeon dug into the taut flesh, Bora stared at the sterile blankness of the ceiling. It cost him a muscle-breaking effort not to let fear overtake him, as he again lay on the table, smelling disinfectant, smelling blood.

"Did you know you're running a fever?"

"I don't feel feverish."

"Put this under your arm." A thermometer came his way. "Ah, here is one of the fragments," he said, as if Bora didn't know from the burst of pain travelling up his thigh. "Just a little more patience, it's coming."

Bora held his breath until he heard the clink of metal being dropped into a basin. A warm stickiness ran down his knee, sponged off at once.

"Does it hurt?"

"A little."

The carving into his flesh resumed.

144

"You should thank God that you were holding a brief-case on your lap that day, or else you'd have got a burst of shrapnel into your belly. You'd have lost more than one hand, and we wouldn't be here talking about it. Wait, the other piece is coming out. Frankly, I can tell you now, when they brought you here I knew you wouldn't die only because you struggled like an animal."

Bora glanced at the surgeon's white crew cut, low over his bloody knee. "Sister, out there, told me I kicked her."

"You also nearly crushed the bones in her hand, as for that. Give me back the thermometer."

Disinfection, bandaging. It was then the arm's turn. The amputation seemed to be healing. Bora said nothing about it, but the surgeon fingered the stump with a frown.

"Don't tell me it doesn't hurt. I cut my share of arms and legs and hands during the Great War. In my opinion, there are neuromas forming at the nerve tips. Not the sort of pain you chase with aspirins. If you have someone at the post who can give you shots, I'll give you morphine to take along."

Bora was in pain even now, and the words gave him a sinking feeling, as though the room were trying to slip from under him and he'd have nothing to hold. "No."

"Well, think about it."

"It's out of the question. I can't possibly make use of such strong medication."

The surgeon went to wash his hands in the sink. "It's your call. You've got a high fever. I advise lukewarm compresses on your arm, rest in bed and antipyretics." Standing by his desk, he dried his hands with a spongy cloth, then scribbled something in his prescription book. "Meanwhile here's a prescription for plain old Veramon.

Take it. Providing of course that a bland painkiller does not contrast with a soldier's stiff upper lip. You'll find a pharmacy at the end of the street."

On the same day, Guidi arrived in Verona for his appointment with Enrica Salviati. Although it was already one in the afternoon and milder, with rain beginning again, a lacy, white trim of frost still edged the tramway tracks.

The girl waited by the park fountain, a sombre, sleek-lined silhouette turned away from him. Guidi approached her, and she returned his greeting.

"I'm sorry I made you come all the way here, Inspector, but the other day I couldn't tell you the whole story. That's why I had to see you alone."

Guidi nodded. "If it's because of the German officer, haven't they explained to you that we're working together on this case?"

"No, it isn't because of the German. It's the other one."

"De Rosa?"

"Yes, him. I didn't want to say anything about him that he could hear from outside the door."

Guidi was suddenly hopeful and curious. Fascist plots and revelations that could alter the game tumbled like playfully tossed cards in his head. "Tell me," he encouraged her. "Tell me everything."

On Enrica's bare head, little drops of rain sparkled like broken glass in the blackness of her hair. She said, her doleful face upturned, "I had seen De Rosa before. He came a couple of times to visit the master. They would lock themselves inside his office. And you could tell from the way he showed up that he was coming to ask for favours. He crept against the walls and asked 'May

146

I?' every five minutes. If the *signora* was in, he'd bring flowers or chocolates. When he talked to the master he even called him 'Your Excellency'."

Guidi was impatient. "Fine, fine. And then?"

"You could just feel the master didn't want to talk to him." Enrica chewed on her clumsy Italian. "You know? You can tell. For two days in a row he told me to say he was not at home, and De Rosa took it badly. He bullied me to find out when he'd be back. One afternoon, about six weeks ago or so, he came on Sunday, and you could hear them argue in the office. The master didn't want anyone on the ground floor when he discussed business, so I couldn't make out what it was all about."

"What did *Signora* Lisi do, during these visits?"

A grimace discomposed Enrica's dark beauty. "*When* she happened to be at home, you mean. She'd have to stay upstairs, like me. She'd listen to Rabagliati records or paint her nails. She couldn't care less about the master's business, as long as she had *schei* – I mean money – to spend. I think the master didn't want to meet De Rosa in his house, because once I heard him call back to him from the door, 'The next time we meet in Verona, or we don't meet at all.' But, as I told you, six weeks ago De Rosa was back, hat in hand as every other time."

Guidi noticed that Enrica was shivering. Although they had stopped under one of the trees in the park, they were getting thoroughly wet.

"Let's go to the café across the street," he suggested. "We'll catch pneumonia out here."

Reluctantly Enrica followed him, arms folded, head low in the rain. "I can't stay long, Inspector. I have an appointment."

147

"Yes, but I want to hear whatever else there is. It can't be all you had to tell me."

Guidi was disappointed, and he knew it showed. He'd hoped for a more sensational revelation. Of course Lisi apportioned favours and exacted obeisance; it didn't take Enrica Salviati to figure that out.

They entered the café. The place was crammed full with people who had come in from the weather. Squeezing among shoulders and backsides, Guidi remembered what Bora had told him to ask, and was suddenly resentful of the charge.

At first Enrica pretended she did not hear, or else the hubbub of the crowded room truly kept her from hearing. Guidi repeated the question, and she turned slowly to him.

"If she had a lover? It isn't you who wants to know."

"Never mind who wants to know. What do you know about it?"

"Nothing, that's what. If I knew I'd tell you, you can be sure, but the *signora* was not stupid. If she played around, she did it away from home. Since they were practically separated, it wouldn't be that difficult now, would it? She came to visit only when she needed money."

Even in the crush of trench coats and folded umbrellas, Guidi felt a liberating sense of relief at the words, as if Bora's spite and Enrica's jealousy had been smashed against the impeccable wall of Claretta's conduct.

"So, what you had to tell me is that De Rosa frequented Vittorio Lisi. You never saw *Signora* Lisi with other men, either. Anything else?"

"Yes, something else. Just before the separation – it must have been around the end of May – there was a telephone call at the villa. I was in the kitchen, and the *signora* answered herself. I don't know who it was, but she closed the parlour door and whispered for a good half-hour, and her eyes were red when she came out. The master had told me to report any telephone calls that came while he was outside gardening. He loved roses, he was very good at growing them and he'd won prizes for it. When he came back in, I informed him someone had called, and his wife had answered. I don't know what tales she told him afterward, but for sure she didn't tell him she'd been crying over it."

By the force of his skinny elbows, Guidi had cut through the crowd to reach the counter, followed by Enrica. "How did Lisi travel from the country to Verona? How did he travel by car? I heard nothing about a chauffeur."

"He'd ordered a one-of-a-kind car from Fiat in Turin. It cost him a fortune, but it was designed so that he wouldn't have to use the pedals. He always drove it himself."

"There were no cars in the garage."

"Well, Inspector, ask De Rosa. The Fascists came to pick it up the day after the incident. I heard it was given to an army general who lost his legs in the war."

"Very well. Let me know if you remember anything else, but make sure you call me at this number."

Without comment Enrica took the slip of paper with Guidi's office number. She then told him she was looking for employment, and was due at Via Mazzini for an interview at three-thirty. Guidi bought her a cup of coffee, and let her go.

Only after he left German headquarters did Bora recall he was supposed to stop by the pharmacy. He instructed the driver to stop by the first one on the way, and began rereading the report on anti-partisan warfare the Italian officers had given him. The rambling document went into great detail about the organization of partisan bands in the valleys of north-eastern Italy. Bora, who was familiar with the manual published on the subject in '42, was not surprised by the bad news. With resignation, he read carefully and did not grow angry.

Brusquely the BMW came to a halt. "Are we at the pharmacy?" Bora asked without lifting his eyes from the paper.

"No, *Herr Major.* There's a traffic jam ahead."

Bora looked. Given the scarcity of wartime traffic, he could hardly believe the confusion. Immediately ahead of the BMW was a delivery van, and in front of it two German army trucks, part of a convoy that had somehow become separated. A tram idled across the street beyond, and passengers clustered at its doors to get off.

The driver lowered the window to hear if the anti-aircraft alarm was sounding somewhere. Only a freezing, needling rain, on this side of becoming snow, ticked on the car and pavement.

Bora left the car. Even if it was a partisan manoeuvre to isolate and assault German vehicles, he'd rather face the danger out in the open.

As things went, the driver of one of the army trucks had already walked ahead to see, and was now coming back with a swinging step.

"What happened?" Bora asked.

The soldier saluted. "Just an accident, *Herr Major.* The tram ran over somebody; it will be some time before they clear the tracks. We're taking the parallel street. If you wish, you can follow with your car."

Bora looked at his watch. He had a headache, and even the dim light of day bothered his eyes. Damn, he thought, the surgeon should never have told him he was running a fever. Re-entering the BMW, he told his driver, "Forget the pharmacy. Follow the trucks and let's get out of town."

Early on Sunday, Bora buttoned his tunic in front of his window at Lago, with deft small movements. He had slept poorly, but coffee kept up his alertness for the time being. Nagel and the other soldier who'd accompanied the guardsmen had returned the night before. Debriefing had lasted two full hours. Bora had kept Nagel in his office longer than that, and shaken his hand after the interview. Guidi's pre-dawn phone call had jogged him out of sleep, but did not vex him. He'd agreed to go out with the Italian party because snipers, crazy or not, were his business too.

And here it was, a dull-edged glassy day that promised more snow. Minute crystals came down in serpentine spirals even now, from a mackerel sky that seemed not to have enough in it to produce snow. Bora looked up at the speckled clouds creating an illusion of tiered space loosely drawn between horizons. The sun was trying to peek out from one of the layers, prying through with long shafts of light. Bora found himself humming along with the piano music from his radio, though it was not a merry piece. But not a sad one either. Like Guidi's pale long face, it shared information without revealing immediacy of moods. God forbid, Bora thought, perhaps Guidi had no sense of humour.

Thumb and index clasped the hook of his collar, and he was ready. With the palm of his hand Bora cleaned the window pane that began to grow cloudy under his breath, staring beyond it at the smoke from distant chimneys so as not to look at his hand, whose perfection as a physical tool abashed him now. Smoke drifted white from the chimneys only to turn a cheerless blue higher up, against the tangled brown of trees. It was the sterile blue of Russian skies, a colour Bora had hoped never to see again. Against that sterility, where the low sun took hold of it, the curl of smoke grew orange.

Guidi's car was stopping in front of the command post. Guidi came out, wrapped in overcoat, scarf and hat. Around him, bits of snow continued to fall askew and in spirals, as if the invisible moon overhead were shedding its skin to nothing.

Stepping back from the window, Bora glanced at his hand, closed into a moderate, controlled fist. Forgiveness came hard to his body. But for all the nights he still felt scooped out and empty, he was hyperactive with energy most of his days.

Guidi was incredulous at the first words Bora told him.

"The father of the dead girl is around? Why didn't De Rosa tell us about it earlier?"

"It's a moot question, Guidi. Be thankful he chose to tell."

"And how long has this person been around?"

"Zanella is the name. He was in Verona at the time Lisi was killed. Since neither his name nor his daughter's name begins with a 'C', De Rosa said he felt the suspicion didn't apply. But the man did punch his way into Fascist headquarters about two weeks before the murder. According to De Rosa, he was asking for money, since it was far too late to discuss the dead girl's honour. De Rosa says Lisi refused to pay."

Unconvinced, Guidi watched Bora check and replace the magazine in his P38 pistol. Somehow he wanted to believe, but he had to say, "These late developments are suspicious, especially coming from De Rosa. What else is there, Major? Please don't tell me Zanella has conveniently disappeared so that we can't interrogate him."

"Not exactly. His name is among those drafted last Tuesday by the Organization Todt for labour in Germany. Drafted as an ambulance *driver*, you'll be interested to know. But you can't blame his removal on De Rosa. He only told me about the man because I grilled him at two o'clock in the morning about the matter of Clara Lisi's car."

Despite Guidi's efforts, the rise in his interest had to be obvious, because Bora made a rather long, somewhat amused pause.

"It seems that I was right in suspecting that De Rosa had Marla Bruni in his sights. The soprano got the car and De Rosa got the soprano. Will I ever learn about the rottenness of the Italians?"

Although Bora smiled saying the words, Guidi was offended. He was about to refuse the offer of a cup of coffee, but remembered Bora always had the real thing at his disposal, and let the major pour him a hefty cupful. Briefly he reported on his meeting with Enrica Salviati.

"We're practically back where we started from, Major."

Across his gleaming desktop Bora pushed a sugar bowl toward Guidi. "Why? You can talk to Zanella's wife. I have her address."

Guidi promptly unfolded the piece of paper Bora gave him. "Thank God it isn't far from Verona."

Bora seemed pleased. Too pleased, in fact, for someone who'd lost the prisoners entrusted to him. Guidi assumed they'd been recaptured, or shot. "Now that I've lifted your spirits, let's go hunting. We can talk on our way down to the cars."

When they drove through the fields, cackling flights of crows drew ever-changing, incomprehensible scribbles against the white foothills. The snow on the highest saddlebacks was already tongued yellow by sunlight rifting the clouds.

Bora paid attention to colours and textures, noting how the same light appeared tender on one surface and crude, cruel on another. Indifferent on farm walls or where it lit up the frozen squares of sheets hung to dry, it turned into a fat, happy light on round objects, meagre and dour on angular ones. Light knotted narrow bands in between trees, but lay lavish and exacting like enamel on their branches facing east.

Russian colours, Russian season. Bora remembered writing to his wife about the light in Russia, sending her sketches that according to his mother she had not yet had time to unwrap. In the yawning blue beyond the fleece of clouds, the dark of the moon stood out like a ghostly circle, barely bluer than the sky. No liar moon, this one. It resembled a communion wafer to be held on one's tongue until it melts.

The cars stopped in a windless lot by the road, and Bora got out to meet Guidi. Patting the woolly heads of his German shepherds, Bora gave clipped instructions to their handler. Then he said, "Tell me all you know about the convict, Guidi."

"Other than that he was being transferred from one jail to another when he escaped? Well, he was an infantryman, and on furlough from Albania for shell shock at the time he knifed his mother to death over an unshined pair of boots. There's no telling where he got the gun and ammunition, but from what I showed you, he did."

Bora nodded. Quickly he pulled a leather glove onto his right hand with the help of his teeth before saying, "I will be honest with you, Guidi. If my men and I happen to surprise him, we'll deliver him to you gladly. If he fires at us, we'll gun him down."

"I expected you to say that."

"Only so that you know."

Like fleece growing tighter, the sparse clouds overhead were closing in to create a compact layer, soon to seal over the rising sun. A dry sprinkle of snow came down to powder the dogs' backs. Wherever sunlight still peered through, the flakes glittered like bits of foil. Bora, who was still running a fever, appreciated the cold air. He started across the field ahead of Guidi, and though his knee ached sharply, he kept pace.

When Guidi caught up, Bora said, "There was a prisoner of war while I was in Russia – I never knew his name or patronymic, but we called him 'Valenki' because of the winter boots he wore. He wasn't what you call a 'well man'. And, like your convict, he had a fascination with footwear. Instead of moping around and begging like his companions – you haven't seen begging until you've seen Russian prisoners of war do it, Guidi, it makes you sick instead of angry – he'd squat by the fence of the compound and look at the soldiers go by. Soldiers and refugees, because at that time we were still advancing rapidly. Well, Valenki stared at everyone's feet, and in all seriousness predicted who would die before long. The other prisoners laughed at him, and so did those among us who spoke Russian."

Flanked by Turco, Guidi watched his step on the stony, snow-covered terrain.

"Do you speak Russian too, Major?" Turco asked admiringly.

"Yes. But I never laughed at Valenki."

It galled Guidi that Turco was warming to Bora. "Well, there's no need for foreign explanation here. The fugitive needs a pair of shoes, kills for them, and discards them if they don't fit."

"My soldier was still wearing his boots."

Guidi didn't want to say the *carabinieri* had happened on the body immediately after the killing, and kept mum.

"Shoes or no shoes," Corporal Turco intervened from behind the foul little cloud of his cigarette smoke, "this girl" (he used the Sicilian word *picciotta*, nodding toward Lola-Lola) "will take us straight to that *lazzu di furca*."

Bora turned to him. "Fine weather for tracking, eh, Turco?"

The Sicilian seemed flattered by the familiar address. Despite his protestations to Guidi against the Germans, he now looked at Bora with respect, vigorously assenting. "Why, sir, that's a fact. Does *vossia*… Does the major hunt?"

"Not animals."

Talking, they had reached the place where they would part ways, on the side of a narrow irrigation ditch stopped by ice. Through Bora's binoculars it appeared like a scar in the snowy earth, rimmed here and there by dry stalks of furze tall as a man and ruddy like rusted metal.

Bora passed the binoculars to Guidi. "*Pyrej*, the Russians call that plant. If you're really hungry you can make bread out of its flour." He glanced around at the cheerless countryside. "I see plenty of things one could live on, if one had to."

Guidi scanned the edge of the field and the hills beyond it. He found Bora's superficiality unbearable in light of his *other* involvements, his *other* duties. A cold-blooded killer seeking justice against a cold-blooded killer. How did he justify deportations to his arrogant self-righteousness as faithful husband and honourable soldier? Even Russia was a pretext to show his ability to handle things. Claretta's survival must not register on the scale of what mattered to Martin Bora.

Soon they had come to the irrigation ditch, where Guidi and Bora synchronized their watches. "You keep to the flat land," Bora said, "and we'll edge the hills. We will spread out in a semicircle and join again with you here at eleven hundred hours. If you hear firing, don't come. You needn't trouble yourself with what else we may be doing in these parts."

An hour later Bora and his men reached a clearing at the foot of the northern hills, where a ledge overgrown with brushwood formed a small recess that offered a shelter from the wind. Snow had been falling steadily for the past thirty minutes, and the northerly scattered it in gusts of powdery consistency. The white sprinkle adhered to dead leaves and trunks and the men's winter uniforms.

Against the rock wall of the recess, traces of a fire built from twigs and small branches were rapidly being covered by snow. Nagel took a stick, poked the fire with it and felt the stick with his bare hand.

"Still warm, *Herr Major.*"

Bora could see how young trees at the top of the ledge had been snapped to provide fuel.

"And the fire's so small, sir, it doesn't look like there was more than one man. Slept or sat here overnight."

"Yes. Whoever it was, he moved out all right, but he could still be near by."

Cautiously the soldiers started up the incline. Looking back at the fields, past an undulating curtain of thin snow, the houses of Sagràte were haphazardly sprinkled like pebbles along the road. Bora could no longer see Guidi and his men, because a sparse growth of trees intervened. No doubt the dogs had started after a trail, and if they hadn't come here directly, it meant the fugitive was elsewhere.

Bora climbed ahead of the patrol. His boots found firm footing at times, at times they slipped, and he had to resist the urge to hold out his left hand for support. But being outdoors was invigorating to him. The cold earth smelled clean and good under his steps.

What did Guidi understand? The Russian winter had nearly killed him, but it was summertime Russia that frightened his soul. If he just closed his eyes, the sinister triangle of the airplane rudder rose like a dead fin out of the sea of sunflowers in bloom. The snow was gone, the task at hand, gone. Those immensely tall and unbending stalks rose up, thick as a man's arm and hairy with a razor-sharp bristle, through which he struggled in his nightmares. He fought and wrestled against them, his strength against theirs, squeezing among them until he could not breathe. Tirelessly he drove himself through until he made it to the airplane.

"More tracks, *Herr Major*."

Nagel's words startled him, so that Bora stumbled and had to reach for the closest branch in order to keep standing in the snowdrift. *It's the fever*, he thought, and, *Thank God it is wintertime.*

Perhaps because of his flimsier clothing, Guidi had less appreciation for the cutting wind riding the flat land. The snowfall was thickening, and soon they might have to interrupt the search. Even Lola-Lola ran about distracted by the weather, not to speak of Blitz's wanderings. Guidi's shoes had grown uncomfortable, and his feet stiff and numb in them. Bora and his soldiers had disappeared in the distance. Another hour and fifteen minutes had to pass before the rendezvous at the ditch; the ditch itself was invisible as the plain grew white and uniform before and behind Guidi's men.

Ahead of his group marched Turco, shoulders rounded, rifle slung muzzle down the way his Mafia cousins carried them. Calling out to the dogs, the snub-nosed German soldier followed his own trail; three other men advanced in a broken line. Snow stuck to the front of their clothes as they went.

Despite the weather, the policeman in front of Guidi hummed in his low, off-key voice. Cavuto, of course, judging by the fragments of words floating from him.

"Come, there's a trail in the forest / I'm the only one who knows of it / D'you want to know it too…"

Then Turco called out. "*Accura!* Inspector, somebody's been through here!" He had reached the edge of a wooded patch, and pointed to footprints that the canopy of trees, bare though they were, kept from being filled quickly.

"They're not German boots, are they?"

"No, there are no hobnails."

When Guidi joined him, Turco had stepped further into the woods. Guidi followed him, after ordering Cavuto to stand ready to cover them. Cavuto nodded, oddly singing down to a hum. "Down there among the trees / Woven with blooming boughs / There's a sweet simple nest / Just as your heart desires…"

He's scared, and sings to calm his nerves, Guidi thought. *Or else he thinks that singing of hidden trails will reassure the partisans if they're on the lookout.*

"It's one man's footprints, Inspector."

"Stop moving around, Turco, you're confusing things. Where do they go, can you tell?"

The Sicilian kept an intent, puzzled face to the ground. "Here and there, looks like. Like he was pacing back and forth or something. He stopped here, and then took a few more steps. I can't tell, Inspector, but he had shoes on."

"It's only been snowing hard for the past hour, so we're pretty close to him. Keep your eyes open, men. God willing, we're wrapping this up today."

The dogs had suddenly become single-minded again. Lola-Lola pawed at the trace, and Blitz squirmed with enthusiasm. Following them, Guidi and his group walked the depth of the wooded patch and then began edging

160

it again, eventually coming into the open, where snow circled hard against them.

The song had got into Guidi's head, reeling like a noxious fly.

"It seems like a wonder / The woods and the moon / Passionate tales they tell…"

Right. Enchanted forests, my foot. Now it's all partisans and Germans. And madmen on the loose.

Here footprints were being obliterated rapidly, though the dogs were not mistaken now and strained to reach the rise in the land that heralded the hills.

"Come, there's a trail in the forest / I'm the only one who knows of it / D'you want to…"

A rifle shot cracked among them, whipping down from the incline. The bullet went past Turco and grazed the arm of one of his companions. Echoes rolled after it from the piedmont.

"Get down!" Guidi shouted.

Another shot came, and then in quick succession three more, from a different angle. Guidi recognized these as from the Germans' semi-automatic weapons. More echoes slapped the hills, growing fainter. Nothing followed this time.

"*Marasantissima*, they must have got him!" Turco rose from the snow, clumsy like a calf when he's first born. "Either that, or he's run off."

The two groups met on the wooded hillside, which Guidi's men reached by climbing, and the Germans by following the length of the ridge.

"We found blood," Guidi informed Bora. "There's a good amount of it some fifty yards on that side, and the snow is very disturbed. You can see there are drops and trickles here, and here. The dogs are going crazy." As he spoke, Guidi realized that Bora was ordering to call the dogs back. "Why did you do that, Major?"

"We put at least two bullets in him, possibly three. I guarantee you, he's not going far." With his boot Bora smoothed the bloodstains on the snow into a pink mash. "He won't live until morning."

"Until morning? Do you mean you're not continuing the search now?"

"Don't speak nonsense, Guidi. This is no terrain to go rummaging through unless there's a damn good reason. I'm not risking my men's lives to run after a murderer. We gave you a hand, and now we're going back to Lago. If you want my advice, you'll get out of the hills before the shots bring the partisans out. They know German rifles when they hear them." And because Guidi was visibly frustrated by the proposal, Bora added, "I wouldn't have given the order to shoot had he not opened fire. We had caught sight of him and were following at a distance, when apparently he saw your group and opened fire. I told you we'd shoot."

"I'm staying until we find him, Major."

"I'm not."

Within minutes the Germans had left the hills and were walking back to the road. The snow, which for a time had subsided, was starting again to blow white and blinding and nearly horizontal as the wind carried it. It would, before long, cover the blood.

On Wednesday, 8 December, an air raid struck Verona.

Each in his office, Guidi and Bora witnessed the eastward passage of impossibly high formations of Allied bombers plough the sky in long furrows of vapour. Before long the rumble of anti-aircraft guns reverberated, a deep and dark hammering of the air that shook the window panes at Lago and Sagràte. Frightened birds scattered from the riverside. Bora's Iron Cross tinkled against the mirror where it hung by its black-red-white ribbon. And during the return flight there was a dogfight between American planes escorting the B-17s and German or Italian fighters, high above the ridge of the northern hills. Guidi could not tell them apart, but Bora recognized the Mustangs' rat-like profiles, and the Messerschmitts' squared, slim cockpits.

Half an hour later, although Guidi had an appointment to see Bora that day, Bora acted as though he didn't expect him. "In case you wish to call Verona from here, my telephone line is down as well," he began. "And I have no time to speak to you. One of the fighters went down south of the state route: I'm going out to the crash site."

Guidi was sick with worry about Claretta, it was true. He just didn't think it was so apparent.

"I'm not here to telephone," he said. "You promised to share the work you did on Lisi's accounts, Major."

"Later, later!" By quick fingering of his right hand Bora was securing the pistol belt around his waist. "Wait here if you want to."

"May I come along?"

"Absolutely not." Bora pushed him out of the room ahead of himself. "Move, Christ!"

In front of the post a handful of soldiers were boarding a half-track. Guidi had walked downstairs with him. "So," Bora said, impatiently waiting for the BMW to be

163

brought around to the kerb. "Did you find the convict, yes or no?"

"Not yet."

"I could have told you that. If it's not too cold, the dogs will smell him in a couple of days."

The half-track had barely left the sidewalk when Bora's car braked sharply in its place, door swinging open to receive him.

"May I at least wait here, Major Bora?"

"Do that." Bora went in, and at once the small convoy was speeding out of Lago on a narrow country lane.

Now and then the tyres slid on glassy ice patches, but Bora would not let the driver adjust the speed to the conditions of the road. He kept watchful fixed eyes on the horizon, where a stalk of black smudge fingered up to the sky in the stillness after the snowstorm. Within minutes the car had left the lane and negotiated a snow-quilted trail in the fields. A dip in the terrain concealed the horizon for a time, then untrimmed poplars created a haze of branches that hid the smoke and crash site. Bora sat tightly to ward off his tension. Arm, leg, head. All hurt again, and anxiety made things worse, though he had no hope of finding the pilot alive. Heartbeat clogging his chest, he was the first to get out, the first to find his way through the blackened brushwood to the breach in the martyred earth.

It was well past noon when the patrol returned to Lago. From the doorway of the command post, Guidi watched the vehicles park head-to-tail. Soon Bora approached with his hasty, limping step. Oil and bloodstains visibly smeared the cuffs of his coat when he walked in. He gestured to Guidi to follow him upstairs. In his office, without a word he reached his desk, where he placed a canvas bag. He went to sit behind it, still silent and hard-faced.

Guidi walked to the window. He made no attempt to speak first, turning his back to the room, to create an illusion of privacy between them. His concern about Claretta trapped in Verona was turning to fear; he sensed anxiety in others well enough.

Before long, small sounds indicated that Bora had emptied the canvas bag on the desk.

"Was it a German airplane, Major?"

"No. It was an American machine."

When Guidi looked, Bora was examining the few objects from the crash site, and it seemed to him that he was very grieved. A log with snapshots in it, keys, a lighter and identification tags seemed to be all there was. One by one, Bora stared at the photographs before laying them aside, and then tilted his chair until the back of it touched the wall.

"Did you retrieve the body?"

Bora nodded with his lips tight. He stretched to take out of a drawer a notepad thick with numbers and handed it to Guidi. "My *work* on Lisi's bank accounts."

During the time it took Guidi to read through the pencilled amounts, Bora simply sat balancing his chair with his eyes turned to the window.

"I knew there was something to it," Guidi said in the end. "Lisi was lending money, and not only to De Rosa. There seem to be accounts that were not settled."

"There always are when you die suddenly."

"And the interest he charged! My God, it was thirty-eight per cent, calculated bi-weekly. I wouldn't be surprised if one of his debtors did him in. Thirty-eight per cent. You wonder who'd ask for money under such conditions."

Bora did not comment. He took out of his pocket one of the receipts found in De Rosa's flat, and gave it to Guidi.

"De Rosa is a gambler?"

"So it seems." Having returned the chair to its front legs, Bora reached for the telephone. He appeared to be thinking of something else entirely. "Here," he said after listening to the receiver. "The line's back on. Why don't you call Verona?"

Guidi didn't have to be asked twice. Only with difficulty, however, was he able to secure communication with the city jail. He listened with relief to the warden at first, then his optimism fell. "She has been formally charged with Lisi's murder, Major."

"Count your blessings that she's survived the air raid. When you're done, I'll call De Rosa at militia headquarters, if they haven't blown it sky-high."

Guidi perceived much tolerance in Bora now, contrary to the inconsiderate haste of his departure. Yet tolerance, like self-control and physical energy, seemed painstakingly sewn over him, until it fitted too tightly for him to escape or reveal anything else about himself. Whatever De Rosa was telling him now by phone, Bora answered in German, coldly and without pause in what Guidi took to be a reprimand with no chance for rebuttal.

"He had the gall to tell me they started the paperwork to deprive Clara Lisi of any inheritance," Bora volunteered after slamming the receiver down. "Things are moving too fast. Raid or no raid, we had better get to Verona as long as there's daylight left." He walked out of the office to snap instructions at someone, and returned to gather the airman's belongings into his drawer.

"The last time I did this it was near Kursk," he mentioned in a quick careless way, as if the issue didn't matter really. But the shattered canopy shone and loomed in his mind, a million pieces of blood-lined thickness like the explosion of a glass world, the breaking of an immense vitreous eye that tumbled into the summer sky noiselessly. Not even his own blood had cried out in outrage to him as his brother's blood on his hands.

In Verona, smoke mixed with cement dust rose from the periphery struck by bombs, and an odour of wet plaster filled the air.

Bora could still smell it when he entered De Rosa's office, bypassing the obsequious Italian guards. He said at once, "Why didn't you tell me Lisi lent money at usury?"

De Rosa had been reading a newspaper, which he now quickly stuffed into a drawer. He stood, flushed with embarrassment and spite, and went to close the door before answering. "I don't know what you're talking about, Major."

"It would have made the investigation much easier and saved us time!"

De Rosa swallowed hard. "Well, why did you get that provincial cop mixed up in this? We came to you for the job, and you got that limp noodle Guidi involved in it. The whole idea, I thought we had agreed, was secrecy."

"Secrecy? Secrecy about what? As if Vittorio Lisi were worth it! Come out with it, did he lend money to you and to others in the Party, yes or no?"

"Major, I resent your barging in here just after a raid blew our railroads into disarray."

Bora could have smacked him. The urge was irresistible for no more than a moment; still he had to stiffen to repress it. "I couldn't give a damn about your railroads. Did he lend you money or not?"

"He *gave* money to the Party, for God's sake! He contributed generously, that's all. To me, he extended some financial courtesy, I don't deny it, but I always paid back every cent." As he spoke the words, it seemed to dawn on De Rosa what else Bora had in mind, because his whole expression changed in an instant. "Major Bora, I am appalled, *appalled* by your insinuations! Do you really believe the Verona Fascists would stoop to kill for money? You insult us all by even thinking of it. Besides, Vittorio Lisi was a consistent and willing source of revenue. Why should we kill the goose that laid the golden egg?"

"It seems to me the Party acted with admirable haste in manoeuvring to delete Clara Lisi from the will. What are you planning to do about the other wife: bump her off, maybe?"

"Major, Major, Major! You're being unfair. Had we something to hide, why would we come to a German brother officer for a solution to the crime?"

Bora had no ready answer, which was enough for De Rosa to try to seize the moment.

"Believe me, Lisi was very secretive about his business. Wherever his money came from, it was hardly our concern. All we want to know is who killed this prominent man. We can't feed a scandal to the people of Verona. I gave you a clue about the dead girl's father, Zanella. See what you can do with that. But keep in mind it's money he came to ask for, not moral satisfaction. And there's no signature on pregnant bellies, is there?" When Bora gave him a disgusted look, De Rosa changed his tune. "You must concede that an upstart, spendthrift wife with a dented car and no alibi is highly suspicious."

"So is someone who fixes the dented car for his lover. As far as I can tell, you have no alibi for the afternoon of Lisi's death."

De Rosa opened his mouth. No immediate sound came out of it, but the caterpillar moustache cambered as if it'd been stung. "I refuse to submit to—"

"Spare yourself, it's my profession to find out things. No one in your office seems to know where you were. You left at ten and didn't come back until the following morning."

"You should have no problem divining were I was," De Rosa said acidly.

"Marla Bruni, you mean? I'm sure she'd cover for you. But who covers for her?"

"I… we… man to man, Major Bora, I was with her in my flat, and we made love during that time."

"For twenty-four hours straight? God in heaven, I'm a damn good lover, and I couldn't pull off that kind of marathon!" De Rosa's provoked face was laughable, but Bora could not bring himself even close to laughter. His headache was turning into a nauseous need to vomit. All morning his left arm had ached, and from the maimed wrist agonizing stabs travelled to his shoulder and up the nape of his neck. Just above his riding boot, the mortified flesh of his knee throbbed like a second, painful heart. Bora steadied himself enough to put a cigarette in his mouth, but did not light it. "I want to know what else there is, who else there is. It comes down to money, so I want to know who might have killed the man for money."

De Rosa frowned until his eyebrows drew a furry right angle on his forehead. "What about Clara Lisi, who wanted more money than he was willing to give?"

"Never mind about Clara Lisi. I'm going to see *her* next."

Bora did. His headache made the prison's bright lights a sea of malicious sparks, through which he waded, growing angrier by the moment.

In the beginning, Claretta withstood his uncompassionate questioning. Then she burst out crying and asked for Inspector Guidi. In the end, because Bora was not about to relent, she let herself go into a half-swoon in her chair.

"She hasn't eaten all day," the guard who came to assist her told Bora. "With the fear of the air raid besides, she's taken ill."

Bora was sceptical, but the faint showed no sign of turning into consciousness again as long as he stayed around. Finally he left, with little more than exasperation to his credit. Not looking where he was going, at the front door he whacked the incoming Guidi out of his way.

"Where the devil are you headed, Major?"

Bora said nothing.

The darkening street was alive with a furious wind. From the street, in the moaning dusk Guidi watched Bora hastily limp to his car and sit behind the wheel without starting the engine. It was exceedingly cold. Too cold to snow, even. Still Bora sat in the car, and all that was visible of him was the firefly glow of his lighter when he lit a cigarette.

Guidi crossed the threshold to enter the prison.

7

Nando Moser shuffled to open the great door of his house. "*Na, Herr Major!*" he greeted the visitor. "Come in."

Bora acknowledged the invitation, but did not move from the threshold.

"I realize it's late in the day," he said, by way of apology. The truth was that he was almost too weary to take another step.

"Only six o'clock. Not late at all." After letting him in, Moser latched the door again, and followed Bora to the poorly lit centre of the hall. "It's good to see you again. What brings you here?"

Bora was staring at the Silbermann piano. "I don't know, I just drove by." He was grateful that Moser faced him from a distance, without forcing him to talk. The very act of standing here, of speaking his native language, affected him tonight. Bora felt as if an immense burden were trying to roll off his shoulders, a burden he wondered at having carried as long as he had. He was tired, inside and out. "I only need a moment," he said, shamed by the awkwardness of his words.

Were the burden physical, no less pain would weigh on him than did now. Bora looked at the piano and nearly let go enough to shiver, but would not allow himself that weakness.

Moser, too, turned to the Silbermann.

"This house was built as a haven, Major. Army men need a place to go. I'm glad you came, and I'm glad you played, the other night. You're very good."

Bora shrank back at the compliment, feeling repugnance for the word "good", when he knew what "good" had been.

But Moser smiled. "Music is something we were taught to judge, in this house. I heard your late father conduct *The Flying Dutchman* at Bayreuth, in 1913. It was Friedrich von Bora's last and grandest performance. Walter Soomer sang lead, if I'm not mistaken."

"Yes. My mother owns a recording of it."

"What excerpt?"

"*From the distance of times long gone before.*"

"It fits us well."

"It fits us well," Bora repeated. He glanced away from the piano, and at the old man. "I really don't know why I came. I needed a respite, I think."

"To get away from your Turks?"

"Inner and outer, yes. The inner ones are the worst."

"All the same, I shouldn't let you stand here. Would you care to sit down? We could go by the stove."

Bora was already walking toward the staircase. He sat there, his back against the wall. He removed his cap and laid it on the next step.

Unobtrusively Moser came to sit on the piano stool.

Bora couldn't look at him just now, nor speak. Vulnerable like glass, like thin glass, he avoided looks and

172

words as unsafe, when he had a craven urge to weep for his dead brother. Far from any concerns about career or safety, his brother's death was tonight's great burden. Also his loveless wife, his loneliness. The burden weighed with all the unwept deaths in his life, the unwept losses suffered and yet to come. Ever since driving to the crash site today he'd carried the urge inside, like a wound more cruel than those healing on his body, a sore that was intimate and endless and could no longer be sewn shut like the rest.

So Bora chose not to resist physical pain. It was perhaps the first time since September that he did not oppose some resistance to it. Tonight he'd rather mind the flesh than his grief. In the end, in the end he cared nothing about himself, which was why his body would not forgive him. He was grateful that Moser sat quietly in the semi-darkness, hands on his knees. Silence and shadow were all Bora could endure now that the burden was about to fall.

Pain racked him then. Still, grief was absolute and full of guilt and useless anger. Such frustrated grief, such long-frustrated grief. Pain was less frightening. Bora looked at it, and did not dare pick up the burden again. So he sat and gave himself up to pain. There were other weights, other responsibilities. Tonight he refused them all. He did not want to seek out those who had killed Lisi. He resented Lisi, Lisi's wife, Lisi's money. The very task disgusted him tonight. It unnerved him, God knows why. Perhaps because others had something to gain from solving the crime, and he did not. Nothing would come to him from a solution. No relief, no peace.

"It's difficult to find peace." Moser spoke calmly. "One never finds it outside. Conquering the enemies outside only gives you spoils to build a house with."

Bora faced the wall. He said, "It's worse than that, when one can't give up."

"Sometimes one must, Major, and it's more heroic to do so."

"I can never give up."

"Then I am sorry for you."

Bora shut his eyes, resting his forehead against the cold wall. "Why? We make our choices and fashion our enemies; unless we kill them, they kill us. And when they're dead, we despise their corpses. We let someone else find them."

"Sometimes."

"No, always. Always. Unless we turn scavenger, we must let the dead be. I *know* that."

And because he'd chosen pain, Bora's pain grew and strained him. Leg, arm, shoulders, neck: he laboured to control his voice, but could do little more than breathe with inert animal patience, slow and hard.

"You seem extremely tired, Major. Are you unwell?"

Unwell? Bora was losing the battle. He could no longer keep from trembling, nor could he care that it showed. His teeth chattered in his mouth. "I am ill, *Herr* Moser. And I am in terrible pain."

Bora said it with shame, as if exposing a tainted part of himself, from which filth would smear the room. Fearing it would do so. But the room stayed clean and unpolluted beneath the great painted vault as under a merciful indoor sky.

174

"What can I do to help you, poor man?"

Bora turned his face away until the tendons in his neck ached with the rest. Nothing would help, nothing.

Not unless you can give me back my dead brother, or give me back my hand, my wholeness, my wife's love.

Bora was trembling not to cry out. In the dark behind him, the dark of shut eyes and an empty house, mornings flashed like lightning, quick visions sank into nothingness as soon as they rose to memory. His brother at the station, smiling their mother's smile. The exquisite line of Dikta's hands, cupped to hold his face when she kissed him. Russia. Russia. Russia. The car's windshield bursting in. Groping in the blood for his wedding ring, and the shred of his hand still bound by it.

Can you give anything back? Oh, Christ. Oh, Christ.

It was the voice of the Silbermann, dangerously close, that answered him. Sharp, each sound a keen edge. Melancholy, unforgiving, cruel and innocent, unwilling or unable to lie.

If Valenki had at least told me when. *If I knew* when.

Anguish sliced through him, as if dammed blood from the inner wound were being lanced free to cleanse it, to wash over him and drain him of grief. Nothing would be given back to him. But the ancient music opened each vein of bitterness to bleed into streams, dark pools, so that Bora did not weep with tears. Because men do not outwardly weep.

The music said no.

It was a long time before Bora could move or speak again. The music had ended, and the house was deadly quiet. Pain was strong enough to stun him.

175

"*Herr* Moser, I am looking for someone I don't want to find," he said.

"But you will."

"We found him," Guidi informed Bora in the morning, calling from his house. "Not far from where we first saw the blood trail. If you have time in the noon hour, come and see."

Bora only said, "I'll come."

Guidi put the receiver down. An insistent clatter of cups signalled that breakfast was ready in the kitchen. Pulling up his socks by the window, he saw a day clear like a washed mirror; all things stood minutely etched in it and even grains of dust cast shadows on a day like this. This was the morning he knew he would capitulate and tell his mother how the lipstick had come to be on his handkerchief. And *why*, which was in the end less wearisome than arguing with her or exchanging monosyllables across the table three times a day.

So he told her.

On her feet by the sink his mother accepted the truce, hands tight in a knot under her apron, not so gracious in victory as she was appeased in her righteousness. Guidi took a hefty bite of bread to keep from embellishing the confession. She poured him chicory coffee. Funnily enough, this morning his mother's eyes appeared fixed and curiously round, like the eyes of a chicken that has watched the worm emerge from out of the soft earth, and by a steady glare hopes to further its inching out.

"So you were joking that she's a street-walker."

Guidi sent down a swig of coffee after the bread. "What would I give my handkerchief to a street-walker for, Ma?

Let's leave it as it is. She's someone the authorities are working on."

"Of course. I'm not curious about your job. I never ask." But there she stood, counting every bite he took.

"Her name would mean nothing to you, Ma. You don't know her. You never even spoke to her. Besides, she's in jail."

"In jail? What for?"

"Murder."

The worm had unfurled out of its burrow entirely, but the chicken was not sure it wanted it now. Complacently Guidi found himself reminding his mother this was the kind of profession he was in. "Your husband was in the same line of work all his life and paid the bills with it. You never seemed to mind that."

"Sandro, *do not!...* I'd be grateful if you didn't drag your father's memory into this."

"God forbid." Guidi gathered the last of the bread in his mouth, drank the rest of his coffee and decided to leave her with something to pick on for the day. Hands spread on the table as he stood from his chair, "You know, Ma," he said, "I do go to bed with women."

At half-past noon, the temporary morgue in Sagràte was open, and reeked of phenol-disguised decay.

Bora stopped by the entrance to hand his greatcoat to Turco, who carefully draped it over his arm. "Is the inspector already in, Turco?"

Guidi heard the words from beyond the glass panel of the next door, and walked out to meet him. Bora said, "I told you my dogs would find him."

They walked in, and faced the body on the table. At once Guidi caught Bora's intent observation. "But your dogs were not the first," he remarked. "Look at his feet. Some creature has been gnawing at them."

Bora spoke, with his eyes on the body. "Where was he, exactly?"

"Not far from where we met on the hillside. Minus the dogs and with snow coming hard, we didn't realize he had fallen behind a tangle of roots and branches. You were right in that he didn't live long. He bled to death, and he's starting to lose rigidity already."

"How many bullets in him?"

"Three. See, two in his chest."

"And no shoes on, obviously."

"That's the strangest thing. He had been wearing them when we tracked him."

"So, he did not kill to secure footwear for himself. I thought so."

Guidi shrugged. "It seems he removed his shoes before dying. A few feet away we found another pair, presumably those of the man who was shot in the ditch. He set his own like a cross beside himself, we'll never know why."

"Set in a cross, eh?" Bora drew closer to the table, so that his uniform touched the impure edge of it. "Had you shown an interest, I'd have told you the rest of Valenki's story."

"Does it matter?"

"It does." Leaning forward, Bora examined the dead man. His head was shaven, a reddish stubble barely shadowing the pallor of skull and cheeks. His neck had arched back in the throes of agony but was losing rigidity, as Guidi said. Eyes and mouth gaped open. Much blood had flowed from his lungs up his throat and nose. Bora looked closely, and the survey struck Guidi as an excess of morbidity.

"What do you hope to read in his face, Major? He just looks dead."

"Indeed." Bora took a careless step back. "He does remind me of poor Valenki. Did I tell you how one day I asked Valenki how he could be sure about his predictions?"

"No."

"Well, he answered that God had appeared to him in a blaze of clouds and granted him the gift of reading people's destiny. 'How?' I asked. By seeing those about to die barefoot even though they might be wearing shoes. He said, 'The dead don't wear shoes, *uvazhaemiy* Major, and so I see them wearing no shoes, as they will be soon.' I can't vouch for the civilians, Guidi, but those of my men whom he pointed out did die shortly afterward. Even though it didn't take a prophet to anticipate disasters on that front. It's neither here nor there, Guidi, but the example goes to prove that shoes may have meant something very peculiar to this poor man. And it isn't out of the blue that I told you Valenki's story: it suggests a possibility we ought to consider." Bora took out a cigarette and put it between his lips. "Just as it isn't clear to us what the madman meant by stealing his victims' shoes, we don't quite know what Lisi meant by scrawling a 'C' in the gravel. Perhaps, Guidi, we ought to learn a lesson from our defunct madman: whether we flatter ourselves that we understand them, whether they escape us altogether, things seldom are as they appear."

"Yes, well. Whatever, Major. So, what happened to Valenki?" Guidi asked.

Bora lit the cigarette. "Poor Valenki. This story of the shoes and the dead went on for a while, until one day I saw him crouching away from the fence, with his face in his hands. It was not like him to cry, so I called out to him. I asked what was wrong, which made him even more miserable. He said, 'Ah, esteemed Major, I've seen my own two feet bare, and I know too well what it means. May the Mother of God have mercy on me.' I felt sorry for him. I handed him a cigarette through the fence – he loved to smoke – and scolded him, 'Come, Valenki, these are all tales. Put them out of your head.' But he wouldn't take the cigarette. He looked at me with eyes starting out of his head. 'I see your mother and my mother weeping, esteemed Major, but my mother is not weeping as hard as yours.' Cigarette?"

"No, thanks, Major." But when Bora showed the pack of Chesterfields, Guidi took one, and gently placed it in his chest pocket to keep it from breaking.

Bora took a draught, and slowly let the smoke out of his mouth. "I tried to take it in good part, you know. 'Don't be silly, Valenki, you don't even know my mother,' but I must confess that his words hit home. My younger brother had just volunteered for the Eastern Front, and I worried about him enough, even without predictions. As for Valenki, he just shook his big shaven head. '*Gospodi pomilui, Gospodi pomilui,*' he wept, crossing himself as he asked God and the Virgin Mary for mercy." Bora looked straight ahead, but Guidi saw him blink. "All the same, he tried to escape that night, and the guards shot him dead."

"Were your men responsible for it?"

Bora seemed genuinely surprised. "*My men?* Do I seem to you the kind of officer who would be assigned to a prison camp? My regiment was stationed near by, that's all. But God knows I've been thinking more than once of poor Valenki and his shoes. We chatted almost every morning. He'd look over as we prepared to move out and call, 'It's no good today, esteemed Major. Watch out this morning.' And without telling my men, if Valenki said to watch out, I would surely watch out."

Guidi smiled just enough not to offend the German. "But you did not believe him."

"Why not? Why shouldn't I believe him? Couldn't the Lord God have spoken to Valenki? He was as good as any of us, except that he was Russian. He was crazy, too, which likely made him better than most of us. You see, Guidi, 'The dead don't wear shoes.' Being barefoot equals being dead. Half a world away, poor Valenki would agree. Anyway, good for you. You must be pleased you solved this case at least. By the way, could you tell whether anyone else had come across the body before you?"

"You mean partisans."

"It's exactly what I mean."

"We saw no other footprints."

Cigarette in his mouth, Bora placed his fingers on the dead man's lids, and held them closed. "That's a good piece of information. Now I would like to collect this fellow's carbine and the ammunition."

"They are at the police station."

"Kindly send your corporal to retrieve them. You know, this poor fellow does look like Valenki. All the same, you're rid of him."

"Yes, while Lisi's killer is still at large."

Bora spoke back with sudden irritation. "It amazes me that you're so sure, because I'm not. The difference of course is that whoever killed Lisi is not a random murderer."

Guidi's own hostility had been stored overnight, and the words fuelled it beyond their import. He tasted anger, and for once liked the taste. "And you, what did you *do* to Clara Lisi last night? She was in hysterics by the time I saw her."

"How gullible you are. I did nothing to her."

"But you saw fit to inform her about the abortion of the Zanella girl."

"I also asked her if she has a lover. You wouldn't ask such a question, and I think it's relevant."

Guidi felt blood go to his head. "Why don't you just lynch her while you're at it?"

"On the contrary, I plan to stay clear-minded about her. And about everybody else. The flaw of you Latins is that you confuse firmness with cruelty."

"Sure, the same firmness that made you cart off a load of innocent people!"

Bora reacted as though he'd been struck. "Don't you *dare*, Guidi. Don't you *ever* discuss military operations with me."

It was all he replied, but Guidi saw a change go through Bora so complete as to make him wonder. He started to add something, and angrily Bora kept him from it. "No. No." The silence between them was flimsy and unstable, threatening on Bora's part as it was insecure on Guidi's, a moment when things could go either way.

Just as quickly, though, Bora regained his aplomb. "Let's hold to the business at hand. You asked me to come here. I came. Is it Clara Lisi you wanted to discuss – what I *did* to her? Or you wanted to show me what remarkable shots my men are? I will be visiting the Zanella woman tonight. You can come if you want to, or I'll wrap this thing up on my own and give my recommendations to the Fascists in Verona."

"What recommendations? You haven't figured this out any more than I have!"

"No, but I have no bias, and that's why I will. Did our precious Clara Lisi tell you what I managed to get out of her?"

Guidi spoke through gritted teeth. "I can't wait to hear it."

"She was engaged to be married when she met Lisi."

"So?"

"So I looked into this suitor of hers, and I've already found out his first name is Carlo."

Guidi clammed up. They left the death room together, and because it was sunny, Bora chose not to wear his greatcoat again.

"What about you, Inspector?" Turco enquired.

"I'm not German. Give me my damn coat."

Outside the small building, the crust of intact snow alongside the cemetery path allowed the slender, graceful shadows of the cypress trees to draw a phantom fence on the white ground.

Bora went to walk in the snow. "I love this," he said, crushing the bright crust under his boots.

As if there had been no tension between them a moment ago, he was trying to abstract himself, to pretend the investigation and the people in it were nothing to him. Guidi knew, and would not let Bora get away with it. Keeping to the sunny side of the path, he smugly said, "Well, what have you discovered, other than that the name of Claretta's ex-boyfriend starts with a 'C'?"

Bora looked over. "I thought you'd never ask. The fellow was from Vicenza, and as of last report he served on a submarine. The Ministry of the Navy informs me he began his career aboard the mine layer *Pietro Micca*. Presumably he did his duty then. I have already phoned the police in Vicenza to find out more, and was promised an answer by this afternoon. Clara Lisi swooned when I asked her, so I'm still curious to know how this boyfriend took it when Lisi wheeled onto the scene, and whether or not he kept in touch with her." It seemed the right time to remind Guidi of what Enrica Salviati had told him at the café – the call Claretta received and cried over – but Bora did not. Unaffectedly he walked among the graves, ankle-deep in the snow.

"Aren't we grasping at straws?" Guidi chose to say. "You assume the boyfriend was jilted, but we don't know that."

Bora's answer was casual, almost easy-going. "We'll see." Stopping in front of this or that headstone, like a curious museum-goer, he looked at and read the inscriptions. Leisurely, for Bora's impatient nature, he observed the wilted flowers in gilded tin vases, the snowy wreaths resembling sugar-dusted buns. "We'll see."

"In any case, five years seem like an awfully long time to keep up with a woman who's no longer interested."

Bora halted. "On the contrary. It is not a long time."

At the far end of the cemetery, in a shady remote corner, were the pauper graves. Seeing that Bora was headed in that direction, Guidi made a point of remaining in the sun.

"What are you looking for, Major?"

"Nothing."

The Vicenza police called at three in the afternoon, while Bora sat in his office, reading a letter newly arrived from his mother.

According to the police, Carlo Gardini's family had not objected to the breaking of the engagement, all the more since Claretta had no money. "All the same, Major, Gardini didn't take it well. He went to her house a couple of times and, according to the neighbours, in both instances he made a scene. We also have a 1937 report about a public altercation between the parties. Some slaps flew back and forth, it says here, 'on account of her incipient use of peroxide for cosmetic purposes'."

Bora found it difficult to pay attention while his eyes were still on the letter from home, so he laid it face down on his desk.

"Any recent reports of Gardini's activities?"

"We enquired of his father. The family received occasional news through the military post, but after the navy disaster at Cape Matapan there were no letters, and no official communiqués. He is not listed as a prisoner of war, nor as missing, nor as killed in action. After the confusion of 8 September, who knows. Two months ago an acquaintance told the family she was sure she had seen him in Vicenza, but more likely than not it's a case of mistaken identity."

Bora wrote on a blank sheet: "Remember to go higher in the Ministry of the Navy".

"Very well," he said. "Thank you. Let me know if there are developments."

He'd barely put the receiver down when De Rosa called. Without wasting time, "Major," he asked, "did you happen to read yesterday's news in the *Arena*?"

"No, I don't get the paper here at Lago. Why, what should I have read?"

"Vittorio Lisi's housemaid, the Salviati girl..."

"Well?"

"A tram ran her over the day before yesterday near the station."

Bora remembered the traffic jam in Verona, the passengers crowding to get off the public car. "Is she dead or alive?"

"Dead. Eyewitnesses reported she slipped while crossing the tracks, either because of the ice or because she took sick. They transported her at once to the hospital, but she was dead on arrival." De Rosa paused for effect. "Now don't tell me I don't keep you posted."

"Is it possible someone pushed her?"

By De Rosa's hesitation, Bora wondered if he'd said more than he intended. "I'm reporting all I know, Major. Meanwhile that self-styled first wife, Masi, says she wants to go back home. She says that if you or Guidi have other questions to ask, that you go about it soon. I don't mind putting my office at your disposal, but need to know when you might be using it."

Bora folded his mother's letter, and placed it in his breast pocket.

"I prefer that you bring Olga Masi here," he said. "Tonight, preferably. Nineteen hundred hours sharp. I'll make sure the inspector is in attendance."

His planned trip to see the Zanella woman was out of the question.

At seven o'clock, De Rosa punctually delivered Olga Masi, who was still wearing the clothes she had donned at the funeral. She showed no timidity in the German's presence, other than that she clutched her knitted gloves and handbag to her chest.

All she knew, she told Guidi and Bora, was that Vittorio was dead and she wanted to go home. No one had ever bothered to keep her informed of Vittorio's doings before, so there was no point now. She had put her mind at rest long ago. "Vittorio was what he was. Handsome, manly, he liked women. There was no changing that. Better to pretend nothing was happening. When he married me" – here Olga Masi turned to Guidi in a fluster – "*g'avevo solo la dota del Friul: tete e cul...*"

Guidi glanced at Bora, whose lack of reaction might mean he had not understood that a poor girl's dowry is "ass and tits", or else pretended not to understand.

"My Vittorio..." Olga Masi sighed. "Whenever he took off, I'd wait for him to come back. I knew he went after somebody else as soon as I turned my head. He was like a blast of wind at the street corner: here, then gone. This *Signora* Clara you speak of was really stupid if she didn't understand how it was with Vittorio. I want nothing from the will. I have said it already to the lawyer the major sent to me." Here Guidi looked at Bora, who leaned against the window sill and did not acknowledge the glance. "I never asked Vittorio for money when I needed it. Now that my folks are dead and I have a small piece of land, I don't need anything else. I have no children, no grandchildren. What do I need money in the bank for?"

Guidi's attention shifted to De Rosa, whose martial face and occasional crimping of the moustache betrayed an effort to keep from smiling at the good news.

"The only thing I want," Olga added, "is to take back Vittorio to Roveredo, where I married him. And maybe the money to get him a cemetery plot big enough for the two of us and our little girl. I have already spoken with the priest, who said it's all right even if Vittorio had been a socialist and we never did get married in church. As long as we tell the bishop, he said."

"I don't know about that," De Rosa interjected. "After all, Vittorio Lisi belongs to the Party, and the Party should decide. There's already a granite monument in the works."

"*Idiotisch.*" The German word came contemptuously from Bora, and both Guidi and De Rosa looked his way. "Keep the money, but at least let her have the body. Haven't you already got all you could from Lisi?"

De Rosa grumbled. At the edge of her chair, Olga Masi adjusted the drooping black velvet toque that kept slipping over her eyes. "For once in my life I get to keep Vittorio all to myself. There's satisfaction in it, gentlemen."

After the meeting, Bora and Guidi remained alone in the office. Bora walked to his desk, and sat down. He'd grown stiffer of gait, and Guidi had noticed how his handshake tonight had been overly warm and dry. But Bora revealed nothing about himself. He flipped on a desk lamp, asking, "Did you bring the book I requested?"

"I'll fetch it from the car."

When Guidi returned with the legal tome, Bora had brought a chair to the side of the desk, and was resting his booted left leg on it. Spread on the desk were a few black-and-white snapshots he'd got De Rosa to take for him of property Lisi had acquired in Verona. "He had good taste," Bora said without sharing the pictures with Guidi. "A flat near Porta Borsari, a pied-à-terre facing Palazzo Bevilacqua, a fancy flat on Corso Porta Nuova. If only his taste in women had run so high."

Guidi dropped the book on the desk. "I suppose you have a good reason for wanting this."

"Yes." Bora looked up. "In five minutes or less, explain to me the legislative aspects of bigamy in Italy."

Guidi did not answer at once, though the question had come with characteristic hurry, a sign Bora was up to something. He opened the book under the desk lamp, searched for the right page and read out loud from it.

"The act of bigamy is regulated by Article 359 of the Zanardelli Code, and is now considered a crime against the institution of matrimony. Earlier they considered it adultery," he explained. "Since 1929 a religious marriage is legally binding in the eyes of the civil authority, as by Article 34 of the Concordat between Church and State. A church marriage is recognized as binding by the civil authority, as long as it is transcribed in the State register in observance to the letter and spirit of the law."

"What about a marriage that was not celebrated in church?"

Guidi turned the page, peering through the crowded script. "Among the causes for annulment in case of a previous marriage contract they list 'lack of free consent' on the part of the unaware spouse."

Bora nodded. "That is, if the spouse does *not* know about the pre-existent contract. What if she knows?"

"If she knows, Major, the annulment is possible only if said spouse denounces it within one month from the beginning of cohabitation, or from the moment he or she discovers the existence of the previous tie. As far as the agent of deception – Vittorio Lisi, in this case – his action is considered as aggravating, according to Paragraph One, Chapter 555, of the Rocco Penal Code."

"Yes, but since Lisi is dead, the aggravating nature of the crime is nothing to him. Who decides about the validity of the first marriage?"

"Usually a penal judge. But the penal judge can defer resolution of the issue to a civil judge, as by Optional Preposition, Article 3 of the Rocco Penal Code."

Bora lowered his leg from the chair with difficulty. "So, any way you look at it, Clara Lisi's marriage is invalid."

"I'm afraid so. And matters are complicated by the legal separation proceedings."

"Hm. If bringing up the first wife was a ploy to threaten Clara's eligibility to inherit, they went through a lot of trouble for nothing. I seem to understand the second spouse has no rights whatever, especially if she knew of the existence of the first marriage."

"This is your assumption."

"I am free to assume a great deal, Guidi, I'm not a policeman. What I'm wondering is, did Clara Lisi know about a first wife – and if she knew, did she pretend ignorance for motives of her own? Finally, I'm dying to know if she was the one who anonymously summoned Olga Masi to the funeral."

Guidi forcibly laughed at the words. "What would she gain from that?"

"The complete invalidation of her marriage to Lisi. Even the Catholic Church would agree to annul such a contract, incidentally clearing the way for remarriage."

"And what makes you think Claretta wanted to marry again?"

"The ex-boyfriend and the tearful phone call are suggestive."

"You don't know who made that call, nor if it really took place."

"That's fair." Slowly, Bora rubbed his left knee. "But someone must be telling the truth in this mess. After all, the victim did as he pleased from the beginning of his married life. Why would Clara Lisi wait five years to ask for a separation, if she hated her lot? Now, if a former lover had recently appeared, or *reappeared* on the scene, separation might become attractive."

"Well and good, Major. But with a legal separation Claretta would automatically cut herself off from any hope to inherit."

"What does it matter? If she is not the murderess, there was no way for her to know Lisi would die so soon after they parted ways. His doctor says he'd have lasted a good long time, and she might have wanted to be free to remarry."

It was the first sign of Bora's willingness to doubt Claretta's guilt. Guidi found that he accepted the hypothesis with admirable composure.

"And if Clara Lisi knew Vittorio had already been married," Bora continued, "it made sense for her to wait until his death to expose the first marriage. Had she dared do it while he lived, he'd have likely crushed her. All the same" – and here Bora changed tone, as if unwilling to let Guidi feel somehow vindicated – "she is the superficial, acquisitive type. She could have decided to get rid of him because he pulled the purse strings or suspected her of having a lover. Here." Bora pushed the photographs toward Guidi. "Do you want to take a look at Lisi's houses?"

"No. But before I go, Major, can you tell me who it was that bought a fine burial plot for the fugitive?"

Bora looked him straight in the face.

"I have no idea."

It was nine o'clock when they parted ways. Bora had received intelligence of partisan activity north-east of the state route, and would lead a patrol before dawn. He did not speak a word about it, of course, but Guidi noticed the cases of ammunition piled in the hallway below.

At his return home Guidi found no supper – the second time it had happened in two days. He made himself an omelette sandwich and ate in the kitchen. The radio was on in the parlour, a religious programme. An exaggerated, crisp flipping of magazine pages also came through the open door. In order to avoid his mother, Guidi also avoided going to the bathroom to brush his teeth. He went directly to bed, and dreamed he was Claretta's ex-boyfriend, back from the sea.

In the post at Lago, when it became obvious that he couldn't relax enough to sleep, Bora sat in his office to reread his mother's letter, studying every sentence written in her quick, minute hand. The letter was in English, as was all the correspondence they had ever exchanged.

Yes, Martin, she has received your mail. She will answer soon, give her time to adjust... and: *My poor darling, how difficult it must be to become reconciled to such permanent injury* and also: *Try to understand.*

He understood, oh yes. He read through the pain of his mother's mourning for Peter and for him, and through the diplomatic, self-conscious brevity of her words.

My dear Nina was the only answer he wrote on the blank page, *ask Dikta if she still loves me.*

8

At eight in the morning, shafts of chaste light fingered through the windows. Framed by the kitchen door, Guidi saw his mother puttering around the wood stove in that oblique glare.

"Morning."

He crossed the floor to make himself a cup of coffee, and during the operation she neither turned nor looked over, as she slowly stirred the soup. Guidi went as far as placing two teaspoons of ersatz mocha in the aluminium coffee-maker, and this on the stove. He even had time to put cup and saucer on the table. He knew perfectly well how sitting down to coffee in the kitchen was tantamount to surrendering, but he was sick of the tension.

His mother waited until he took the first sip before saying, "I know what it's all about, Sandro, don't you think otherwise. These silent bouts don't work with me. Mysterious phone calls, trips at night, every other moment off to Verona when until now I had to drag you in chains to accompany me to a cinema or a department store. She's a married woman, isn't she? With children, maybe. One of those city women, those Verona tarts who have always had the reputation they have had."

Guidi drank his coffee. Instead of anger, he felt an amused curiosity to hear what his mother had concocted in three days of silence. Just to provoke her, he answered, "She's married, as a matter of fact. How did you know?"

His mother dropped the wooden spoon into the soup. "I knew it. I knew it. It's all because of Verona and that cat-eyed German who has got on his conscience God only knows how many crimes." She picked up the spoon, sending a tomato-red squirt across the air. "And to think you could have married the daughter of a Court of Appeal judge!"

Guidi managed to laugh. "Right. If only she'd wanted *me*."

"She'd have accepted, had you been more insistent. Didn't she end up marrying a schoolteacher? A pencil-neck with less career opportunities than yourself, who did go to university!"

"That's the way it went. I guess I let the chance of a lifetime escape me. As far as my trips to Verona with Bora—"

The spoon dived into the soup again, and for good. "Your blessed father would turn in his grave if he knew you're working with the Germans. He, who fought them in the Great War and was decorated with a silver medal."

"Well, blame it on Mussolini and the King, who got in cahoots with the Germans."

"Don't you dare touch His Majesty."

"Who'd want to touch him?" Guidi walked to put cup and saucer in the sink. "As if your own father wasn't a Republican, Ma."

"Leave my father alone, too. *He* was not about to rub elbows with a killer of poor innocent folks."

"The King did the same thing in Libya thirty-some years ago."

"Not the same thing, Sandro. Those were Africans. You can't compare."

"Why, it makes it all right if you do it to Africans?"

"Say what you want, I would not be seen with him. I wouldn't want people to think I agree with him. This is all going to come back to haunt him—"

"Him, him, him. Ma, he's got a name. His name is Bora. And nothing's going to 'come back to haunt him'. You're just doing what you always do, projecting your sense of punishment on God, or whatever it is you believe in. Get it straight once and for all. Nothing happened to those who killed your husband, nothing's going to happen to Bora *just because*. If he gets it, he gets it. But not because you or God said so."

"Go ahead, blaspheme in my face. I want to know about this woman of yours."

"And I'm not telling you." Guidi put his coat on, and his greatcoat over it. "Just hear this. When I fall in love, that's when I'll get married. And the sooner you let me off the leash, the sooner it's going to be." He opened the front door to a gust of wind that ruffled the wall calendar in the hallway. "If you keep badgering, I'll ask for a transfer to Sardinia, where at least I'm rid of you." Guidi slammed the door behind him, taking an unusually deep breath of winter air. From the doorstep he heard his mother recriminating alone in the kitchen.

"Married, and a murderess! Why didn't I die when the blessed soul did, before all these tribulations?"

*

197

In Verona, only a dense echo of daylight filled the prison courtyard, and little of it entered the room.

Claretta had hoped the visitor would be Guidi. Bora knew it from her countenance when he stepped in and greeted her with a nod. He'd driven here directly from night patrol, nauseous and feverish, taking only the time to shave in the warden's lavatory.

"I have come back for a few more questions," he said. "It is of the utmost importance that you answer with perfect candour, since your innocence can only be proven by honesty and the facts."

It was, admittedly, the opening expected of a German officer. Claretta's sickened glance told him as much. She sat down, folding her arms. Her breasts rose with the motion, a quick heave under the cloth. Still, in her grey frock she looked dejected and common, displeasing to him in ways Bora could hardly justify.

"What do you want to hear this time, Major?"

"Only two things. Did you know, yes or no, that your husband had already entered into a marriage contract in Friuli, and, if so, was anyone blackmailing you or your husband?"

As Bora spoke, Claretta's face went suddenly white. Her unretouched cheeks took on the appearance of fresh cheese. Far from feeling sorry for her, Bora wouldn't forgive her even the folding of arms, seeing malice in it.

"What?" she stammered.

Her response was genuine, but could have many motives. Bora said, "I have reason to suspect that when we first met, you told an untruth concerning your marriage to Vittorio Lisi."

"I don't know what you mean. What other wife are you speaking of? Vittorio never told me he had another wife!"

"He may never have told you, but I'm not sure you knew nothing of it. Does the name Olga Masi sound familiar?"

"Never heard of her."

"Do you know she is still in Verona as of this morning?"

Claretta wetted her lips. She said, looking elsewhere in the bare room. "How should I know, if I never heard of her?"

"Well, someone in Verona knew of Olga Masi's existence. Not only that, someone informed her of the death of Vittorio Lisi, who had married her twenty-nine years ago in Friuli. Someone told her you were currently married to him. Someone directed her to the place where his funeral was held."

"I don't believe you."

"You don't believe I'm telling the truth, or that she is in Verona?"

"There is no other wife. You're making it up to make me admit to something I have not committed, I know your type."

"I doubt very much you know my type." Bora showed her a piece of paper. "A civil marriage certificate. It just came in. See for yourself."

Claretta clutched her elbows, as if she were cold. She made no effort to reach for the paper, or to look at it. "Put it away," she said. "I don't want to read anything. Put it away."

Bora did. "Now tell me the truth, because I'll find out on my own sooner or later."

"I'd rather speak to Inspector Guidi. Why isn't he here?"

"Because he has other things to attend to. Tell me if your husband was being blackmailed about his first marriage, and I promise I'll send Guidi tomorrow."

Claretta lowered her head. The rows of blond curls cascaded on her forehead with a girlish, perhaps studied effect, but she was really pale. "I've told you a hundred times, Major. I know nothing of my husband's business. You're wasting your time."

"Wasting time is something I never do. If you don't collaborate with me regarding Olga Masi, I assure you I will endeavour to prove your guilt, and at this point it wouldn't take much."

"Please leave me alone. I'm not feeling well."

Bora stepped to the door, and opened it. "Tell me the truth, and I'll leave."

"You don't understand!" Claretta bent over, locking her arms together. "I'm sick," she moaned. "My head is spinning."

"I'll call you a physician."

"Just leave me alone!"

Bora started out of the door, asking for the warden.

"Wait, wait." She spoke with her head in her hands, swaying slightly from side to side. "I don't want to see anyone else. Ask me again."

Bora closed the door, and stood with his back to it. "I have two questions. Did you know about Olga Masi, and did anyone blackmail *you?*"

For a good minute there was no answer, then Claretta dug her hands into her hair, lifting the curls from her temples, a world-weary gesture Bora had seen actresses make in bad movies.

"Here's all I know, Major. On the night of the day when Vittorio died, I found a typewritten note under the door of my flat. Four lines telling me Vittorio had another wife up north. If I wished to avoid a scandal, I'd have to deposit five thousand lire in a waste basket by the train station. At first I thought it was a very bad and cruel joke, because people knew Vittorio had money. I didn't take the note seriously. When I found a second one in the mailbox the following day, I burned it in the fireplace as I'd done with the first. The third day I didn't even bother to open the envelope."

"Did you burn this one as well?"

"Yes."

"You should have shown it to the police."

"Why? If it was a bad practical joke, they'd do nothing about it. If it was true, why should I tell the police there was another wife somewhere? Anyway, by the third day after Vittorio's death they started watching my flat, so they wouldn't believe anything I had to say."

"It may be because you lie so often."

Claretta turned her childish white face to him. "And what's wrong with it? Everyone lies, and if you tell the truth, no one believes you anyway. I'm alone now, and I must take care of myself. What do I care what others think? Whether my marriage is valid or not, I get to keep the jewels and furs Vittorio gave me. They're plenty, you know. And if I ever get out of here, Verona has seen the last of me." She leaned forward in the chair, and the flimsy frock showed to advantage the wealth of her breast.

Clumsily Bora rummaged in his tunic for cigarettes.

"Besides, Major, they tell me I'm an attractive woman. If that's true, I should not waste the only gift I have.

When Vittorio and I went to Venice in 1940 I was introduced to Blasetti, the film director. He told me I have magic eyes and look like Clara Calamai. He told me he knows Calamai personally, and that if you put us side by side you'd think we're sisters. Therefore, I have some confidence I might succeed in motion pictures if I put my mind to it." Because Bora had just succeeded in finding the pack, Claretta said, "May I have a cigarette, too?"

Bora obliged her, and left the room.

In the hallway, the warden told him Inspector Guidi was on the phone.

"You may use my office, Major."

Guidi reported that De Rosa had just called. "He said he'd tried to get hold of you and couldn't. He made it very clear that's the only reason why he would even speak to me. He's in a tizzy, and claims there's no time to lose."

"Why?" Bora squashed the cigarette in the warden's ashtray. "What happened?"

"Apparently one of the plain-clothes men De Rosa assigned to watch Claretta's flat noticed a suspicious character in the neighbourhood two nights ago."

"Man or woman?"

"Man. The subject rang her doorbell twice, and when no answer came, he paused to observe her balcony and windows from the other side of the street, and then left quickly. The plain-clothes man was not allowed to leave his post, but worked it out so that he'd be back and free for action last night. He waited in a distant doorway, and the same scene played itself out. Ringing, no response, looking up at the windows. By the time the plain-clothes man approached, the other had already turned tail and was gone."

"Did De Rosa give you a physical description of the suspect?"

"Between the late hour and the blackout, all we know is that he seemed young and of medium build. Hardly enough to do anything with, but De Rosa made me swear I'd inform you."

Bora knew by the pain awakening in his body that he'd let his guard down for the first time since going on patrol. Fever added malaise to pain. He said, "Just in case, I'm staying in Verona. Join me as soon as you can. You'll find me at Colonel Habermehl's. Here's the address."

That evening, Colonel Habermehl faced the oak liquor cabinet with a fond expression. Drink gave him a perennial rubicund cheer, and for all that he'd managed to keep his career in harness thus far, he was no good whatsoever after three in the afternoon. The blood stagnating in the minute vessels all over his face would trick him one of these days, by his own admission.

"Hell, a stroke is the way *I'm* going," he said tonight. "There are worse ways. 'Hit a rogue more than once' says Paul Joseph – so, here's a third shot of poison!" And then, "Something's up, Martin, you're not fooling me. Have a cognac and tell me what it's about. I opened a *Napoleon* I brought from France, and I'll be insulted if you refuse."

Bora had no intention of refusing. He let Habermehl pour him a double shot in the paunchy glass, and emptied it at once. "It's nothing, *Herr Oberst*. I'm not sleeping well. The usual worries at work."

"I think you're catching a seasonal disease, whatcha-macall it…"

"Influenza, in German and Italian alike."

"There, influenza. Well, cheers anyhow. 'Believe in the future. Only then can you be a victor', blah blah… What news from home?"

"They're all well."

"Your wife?"

"She's well."

"When did you see her last?"

"Last autumn." Bora helped himself to another cognac, which he partly drank.

"Last autumn, on furlough from Russia? And that's all? I was right. You should have got yourself airlifted to Germany after the accident. It's better when they see you right away, when there's a serious accident. Women get all mushy then."

Bora put down the cognac. He had nothing to answer Habermehl, and it was fortunate that Guidi's arrival was announced next. "Tonight we might be able to secure Clara Lisi's blackmailer," he said quickly. "And he in turn might lead us to the assassin."

Habermehl downed a fresh drink. "Well, good luck. Too bad your wife didn't see you when you were laid low. Now it'll take some convincing to make her see she's lucky you're alive."

As if he needed the reminder. Bora walked out of the parlour, into an elegant waiting room where Guidi introduced the plain-clothes man to him.

"I had a public notice posted on Claretta's door, Major. I will explain while we drive there."

"Are you armed?"

"Yes. But please, we have no proof this man has anything to do with the matter, and in any case we don't want to kill a potential witness."

Bora showed the latched holster. "You must think I have nothing to do other than going around shooting. I do not intend to open fire, but you'll never find me unarmed." With an unexpected grin, he added, "Wouldn't Yanez behave the same way?"

"Yanez?" Guidi thought he had not heard right.

"Of course." Bora preceded Guidi in the street. "Just because I'm from Saxony, it doesn't mean I only read Karl May as a boy. Once I went through the Old Shatterhand and Winnetou tales, I fairly devoured the adventure novels of your great Salgari, during my summers in Rome. I can't tell you how many times I smoked my *nth cigarette, à la* Yanez, while I was in Poland. Of course, this was before many other things happened."

If Guidi expected to hear more, he was disappointed. Bora only said, "Make sure your safety catch is off, Guidi."

The plain-clothes man was a blond, heavy-set man with a boxer's mug and the unlikely name of Stella. Asked by Guidi to report, he flipped through his notebook with a saliva-sleek thumb.

"It went like this. Both nights the suspect showed up between six and seven. The first night it was twenty past six, and last night twenty to seven. He walked from the cross-street on the right, rang the bell, looked up at the house front, and left the same way. I could have stopped him last night, except that a German truck was coming down the Corso." He glanced at Bora, who kept his peace. "That must have startled him. He'd cleared out by the time I made it across the street."

Bora asked Stella to draw an approximate map of the city block, and to mark on it the movements of the unknown man. "Did you notice any accomplices? Vehicles?"

"I heard no sound of engines. But he could have been dropped from a car at a distance, or else used a bicycle."

Bora studied the map. "Where's the best place to wait unseen?"

"There's an alley down from the front door, on the left. You can't see much after curfew. If the moon doesn't come out tonight, it'll be tough. If you want, I'll come along."

"No," Bora said.

"Yes," Guidi said, preventing with a gesture further objection from Bora. "We need a third party, Major."

"I meant to use German soldiers."

Stella ripped the map from his notebook and gave it to Guidi. "Better not. The movements of German troops are closely watched. If they're noticed anywhere in the neighbourhood, it's likely that no one will show up."

From his seat near the liquor cabinet, Habermehl overheard the Italian conversation without understanding a word. But in the fifteen years he'd known him, he had learned that Bora acted most sure of himself whenever he had the least reason for it.

"Martin made an enormous mistake when he got married," Bora's stepfather had told Habermehl at Christmas-time last year. "This marriage of his won't survive the War."

The street by Claretta's house stretched dark, and whatever moon there was, the passing clouds hid completely.

Bora had parked the BMW in the alley, lights off. Without smoking, hardly speaking at all, he and Guidi waited in the front seat. It was freezing cold outside and inside, but they kept the windows rolled down to avoid fogging up the glass. Guidi had the impression that Bora was trembling, which was unlike him to say the least.

"What is it, Guidi? What are you looking at?"

"I'm looking at nothing. I'm waiting, as you are."

Bora apologized. A moment later he took off his cap. Although he turned his face to the side window, Guidi could see – no, he could not quite see, only make out by the broken light through the clouds – that he was wiping his face and neck.

"Guidi, I haven't told you the incidental details I learned from the midwife. But if we're to visit Zanella's wife before long, you might as well hear them."

"Do they add anything to the investigation?"

"They don't. But aside from insisting that Lisi ordered her to go on with the abortion – I did tell you that – she said the girl was frightened. That they were both scared, in fact. It was a full moon, and according to the midwife, every abortion she performed with a full moon came to some kind of grief."

"Poppycock."

Bora lay back against the seat. "I am merely supplying you with the incidentals. She said the foetus moved for some time, but was dead by the time the placenta came out."

Guidi, whose notions of obstetrics were those of any bachelor, limited himself to a nod. On the other side of the street, against the darkened façade of Claretta's house, the piece of paper posted on the door was the only thing visible. Stella was lost to view in a recess, but undoubtedly waiting. "Anything else, Major?"

"She declared she never did know the name of the girl. It's safe to assume it was the Zanella girl. All the midwife claims to know is that the girl's father was in the army."

"Not a particularly helpful hint these days."

"No, and the midwife admitted it wasn't the first time Lisi had brought her girls in trouble. He'd wait down in the car every time, and usually drove them off himself. But usually the girls were in the first trimester, and things went well with them. If you can say that under the circumstances."

Guidi's feet were stiff with cold. He wiggled them in his shoes, and blew on his thin-gloved hands. "What about the other midwife?"

"Thankfully she left town at the end of August. I've heard more about abortions than I care to know."

Suddenly alert, Guidi hunched forward. "Look." The notice Guidi had posted on Claretta's door was nothing but an announcement of changes to the tramway schedule, but the intent was to attract attention. So far the dimly white stain of the leaflet had stood out in the dark, but now it was blotted out as if something, or someone, had come in front of it.

"He's here, Guidi."

"Maybe."

A pale triangle of asphalt came into view where a gap between roof edges allowed an incipient skinny moon to cast light on it. The human figure had emerged from the dark of the houses into the pale triangle, and was now facing the posted notice. It was far too dark to read, and Guidi had purposely chosen a faded, badly printed specimen. The wavering, quickly extinguished flicker of a match came and went in the breeze, followed by another, and a third one.

"He's trying to figure out if it says anything about Claretta. Let's go."

Bora and Guidi silently left the car, and slipped out of the alley. Guidi followed the wall to reach a wholly dark spot from which he could cross the pavement and reach the opposite street corner. From where he stood, the stranger's hand gathered to protect the tremulous glare of the match was red and translucent like raw flesh.

As for Bora, by habit he unlatched the holster as he approached Claretta's door nearly in a straight line. The wind was against him, and covered his booted footfalls. He understood from the wind-borne faint tinkle that the stranger, disappointed in the notice, was ringing the doorbell. Three short rings, like a signal. From the corner of his eye Bora realized Guidi had turned the street corner. The night swallowed him up. Nothing was visible on the left side. The electric doorbell rang three more times, deep in the body of the dark building.

Guidi was already too far to hear the bell. Noiselessly he walked to the end of the narrow street, where he set himself to wait again. The moon blinked and was sealed over by clouds. *Liar moon*, Bora thought, taking another step forward. He was conscious of the pain in his left leg, as one participates in someone else's suffering, intellectually. Tension offered him a temporary stay from physical distress, and within it he moved carefully, secure. It was just a matter of moments before Stella approached the stranger. The rest would follow quickly and to a good end, with Guidi barring the way out.

Holding his breath, Guidi was counting the passage of seconds.

Bora perceived motion to his left.

And at that instant, without warning, the air-raid siren let out a loud, tearing wail. It spiralled to a deafening pitch from a nearby building. Bora cursed in the uproar.

Whether he was on to the ambush or not, the stranger dodged at the same time that Stella lunged for him. There was a brief scuffle, a close-range shot impossible to hear in the noise, like a fiery silent burst.

Bora stopped thinking. He pursued and tackled the running shadow from behind, and the weight of his tall body knocked the stranger over. Stella groaned on the pavement as the men stumbled over him. "He's got a gun, Major!" And Stella's moving about made Bora lose hold of the adversary. Blindly he struggled against an arching, kicking body full of elbows and bony angles. Impeded by the greatcoat, Bora used his size to gain an advantage, but it wasn't enough. He struck with his right fist in frustration, and still the stranger slipped from under him with the benefit of two sound legs. Bora wouldn't let him go. He kept after him, as if the godawful noise didn't mean bombs might be falling at any minute. Pain and the dizziness of fever had disappeared as if a sponge had wiped them off. Chasing the stranger down the street where Guidi had gone before, Bora no longer felt his body. "He's armed, Guidi!" But not even Bora could hear what he was shouting. From a few feet away, a bright-tongued shot blasted out of the dark, missing him. Bora returned fire this time, aiming low.

Pausing to take some kind of aim was enough to break the spell. Agony sliced through him with the terrifying ease of a razor. Bora, who'd just thrown his dead weight forward not to lose his prey, blacked out for a moment, even as he collided full force against him. In falling, he brought him down, and lost him again.

Guidi was ready. At the end of the street, where the dark was belted by a waving dance of spotlights and gunnery beacons, he made out the stranger coming straight at him, saw him at the last moment try to swerve. Guidi could have fired, but didn't. They scuffled, and then Guidi managed to throw the man over, shoving him flat on his back. He made out the clump of the handgun and stepped on the squirming wrist, kicking the weapon out of the way. He had no way of knowing if the others had been wounded, or worse. But at least the wail of the siren finally cranked down, winding into an immense, stunning silence.

Guidi called out in the dark, "Major Bora! Stella, how is it going?"

Stella answered from afar in a strangled baritone. "Son of a bitch, he got me in the blooming shoulder!"

Bora came to his knees. He didn't know where the voice came from to answer that he was fine.

The air raid never materialized. It was likely another false alarm, caused by a play of night clouds in the spotlight. No engine sounds, no distant explosions. The criss-cross of anti-aircraft beacons ceased over the rooftops. In the newly made darkness, Bora sped toward the hospital, carrying Stella, who staunched his wound with a rag and blasphemed in his teeth, and the prisoner under Guidi's armed guard.

Picking up speed, braking, gears changed every moment, Verona was coming to after the alarm. Thrown out of bed by the air-raid alarm, drowsy tenants climbed back from basements and shelters, ghosts stumbling in their night clothes, here and there crossing at their own risk in front of the BMW's spanking clip. Stella was let off before the hospital. By the time they reached the central police station in Piazza dei Signori, Guidi found that consignment of the prisoner and all the explaining fell on him. Bora had disappeared with the excuse of washing his face.

"There's a German officer with me," Guidi told the policeman on duty. "I'm sure he wants to have his say, too."

"Well, where is he?"

"He's coming."

"Have a seat, Inspector."

Guidi did not sit down. Only after handing over the prisoner did he take a good look at him. "Sooner or later you'll have to open your mouth," he said blandly, and watched while the policeman frisked him. Something about the pinched young face was familiar. Half-lit by the crescent of electric light from the floor lamp, the features seemed not exactly known, but familiar. He was undergoing the search in a straddling stance, grim-eyed, hostile and familiar. Guidi stared. "You'll have to talk." *Where the hell is Bora?* he was thinking meanwhile.

Steps approached in the hallway, but it wasn't Bora. Two brunettes in short, huge-shouldered furs shuffled by, hoarsely complaining to a fresh-faced patrolman about being brought in. An exchange of looks passed between them and Guidi as they went by, a wary, cynical glance, and no interruption in their groaning. The young patrolman prodded them forward. "Shut up, whores."

Guidi couldn't imagine what had happened to Bora. He stepped to the door and looked out into the hallway. There, slumped at an impossible angle on a chair, a drunkard snored, hands palms-up on his knees like a beggar. Next to him a diminutive man with a black eye stood in his pyjamas, and at the other end of the hallway sat a boy with a vice-ridden grin, scratching with a nail the wooden surface between his open thighs.

Guidi turned back to the room, where the prisoner now sat in handcuffs.

"Of course, these documents are false," the policeman was saying with contempt. "Typical fake *Papier* they use to take in the Germans. He's a 'technical assistant' same as I am, this one." He showed Guidi a personal pass that read on one side, *German Command of Engineering Liaison*, and on the opposite side, *Feldnachrichten Kommandantur*. It authorized the carrier to circulate freely "at every hour of the day or night, even during air raids", and informed those whom it may concern that the carrier's bicycle could under no circumstance be seized or requisitioned. "It's a good thing he didn't have the two-wheels with him, or you'd never have nabbed him. Doesn't want to talk, but before tomorrow morning I promise you I'll have him cough up his name. Look here." The policeman pointed out to Guidi the date on the papers. "They haven't even bothered to write 'Year XXI of the Fascist Era' after 1943. Eh, you! Who was the baboon that made you this lousy *Papier*?"

Guidi's knuckles were beginning to ache from the blows he'd landed on the man's face. He glanced away from the papers, and at the prisoner's face again. "I think I know who he is," he said, surprised that it had taken him this long to remember. Out of the room, down the hallway and down the steps, he walked into the street, where the BMW was parked. Surprisingly the major had forgotten to lock it. Guidi took from the front seat the folder Bora had obtained from the navy and, leafing through it, climbed back into the police station.

The photos were what he wanted. He unclipped a group photograph of sailors from the rest, looking for the circled figure. Sure, the beard had been shaven clean. A wintry pastiness had replaced the tan. Some weight had been shed. But the face, especially the grim deep-set eyes, and the straddling stance were the same.

"And a civilian gun licence? How did you get it?" the policeman was braying at the prisoner when Guidi re-entered the room. "This is an English gun, you son of a whore, where did you get *this*?"

A few steps away, with his back to the door, Bora stood listening.

"Finally, there you are," Guidi said. "Major, you don't know who we've got!"

Bora looked over. He had his usual countenance, cool and undemonstrative. Aside from a pronounced pallor and the fact that he seemed to have held his head under the faucet, nothing looked amiss. "Who did we get?"

"This is Claretta's ex-boyfriend!"

"I see." Bora turned his attention to the prisoner, without any anger whatever. "He's tall for a submarine sailor."

214

They remained at the central police station until about ten.

Once the prisoner had been removed to a cell, Bora spent some time convincing the policeman on duty to refrain from interrogation until he received "further instructions". He'd minutely examined handgun and false papers, photos and navy documents. "This is very interesting, Guidi," he said. Soon he dialled a number on the policeman's telephone. The paleness on his face had extended to his lips, a paper-white, dead man's paleness. It stood out as a silver stain above the field-grey collar, even in the half-light of the floor lamp. When the call went through Bora spoke in German, perhaps to his headquarters, perhaps elsewhere.

Guidi understood he was asking for a captain in the SS.

"*Ja. Ja. Ich glaube, dass er ein Bandit ist,*" Bora said in a low voice. And he betrayed himself by briefly closing his eyes, as if the revelation or the simple effort of speaking exhausted him.

Guidi tried to understand whatever else he could from the whispered German conversation. So, Claretta's ex-boyfriend was a partisan. It wasn't the first partisan he'd seen, but this one seemed bellicose and intractable like a wild bird. Contrary to expectation, it wouldn't be easy getting anything out of him. Hence Bora's phone call. Guidi left the room.

In his cell, deprived of ammunition and what little else he had, the young man sat in his shirt-sleeves and barefoot, without even his socks on. Guidi thought of the Russian prisoner Bora had spoken of. "Poor Valenki", as Bora called him. And he thought of the madman the Germans had brought down with three shots in the body.

With a battered, dark air of challenge, Carlo Gardini, Class of 1915, avoided Guidi's stare.

"It is all arranged," Bora informed the policeman as he and Guidi prepared to leave. "At seven hundred hours tomorrow, a representative of the Security Service will come to interrogate him."

A delicate layer of sleet had fallen on the city in the meantime. When Guidi and Bora walked out of the police station, the few cars parked near by had shiny, granulated white roofs. It was bitter cold, an aching cold. Guidi tied the scarf around his neck. Too bad he hadn't worn his hat. This was one of the times he regretted not listening to his mother's advice, waiting for Bora to precede him inside the BMW. But Bora handed him the keys.

"You may drive."

It wasn't like Bora to entrust himself to others, especially when it came to speed and timeliness. Without comment, Guidi took the keys and sat behind the wheel. Bora leaned against the other door before letting himself in. Once inside, Guidi heard him breathe laboriously, and try to control his breathing. "Here we go," Guidi said, and turned the key in the ignition.

The car had a powerful engine. Guidi was not used to anything of the sort. It zoomed on the icy surface from its parking place, grazing the opposite sidewalk before regaining an even keel. Guidi did his best. Even on the city streets he had to take care at each corner to keep from skidding. Soon enough he was gaining speed and stepping on it, across train and tramway tracks. Bora did not criticize him, and by the time they left downtown,

Guidi had gone from prudence to a measure of pleasurable foolhardiness.

They roared through the suburbs. Guidi even regretted having to stop by the German roadblock in the open countryside, where all documents were duly asked for and read. Bora presented his papers first, and when the soldier peered in to see who was at the wheel, he briefly added, *"Polizeikommissar Guidi, mein Freund."*

Then they were in the lonely countryside again. Dark houses, abandoned factories and farmsteads rolled by, eaten by the night behind them. No perspective, no horizon was visible for a long time, then the sealed obscurity began to break into luminous stripes, fleeting and colourless, as the rising moon filtered among the clouds. A river came up, like a strip of foil.

"Be careful, there's already ice on the bridge." Despite his efforts at self-control, Bora was trembling, and his voice gave him away.

Guidi glanced at him. "I will." He slowed down, approached the bridge at a moderate speed and crossed it without incident. "What will happen now to Carlo Gardini?"

Bora did not answer at once. "The Security Service will take over the interrogation," he said after some time. "Gardini carried an Enfield with plenty of ammunition. It isn't a revolver easily found in Italy. It's a good war weapon, I had one in Spain back in '37."

"If the SS take him into custody, the Italian authorities can forget about a chance to interrogate him."

Guidi's words fell into several minutes of silence this time. From what he could make out in the darkness,

Bora was sitting back, breathing hard. Whether he was fighting not to tremble, or trying to stretch his left leg, he didn't seem to consider there wasn't nearly enough room, and his knee struck the edge of the dashboard. Guidi sensed a whiplash jerk going through him, and was aware of how precariously Bora hung on to self-control.

"Are you all right?"

Bora mumbled a strained sentence in German. Correcting himself, he added in Italian, "I'll speak to *Hauptsturmführer* Lasser. He knows why I have to do it."

"Who's Lasser? And why you have to do *what*?"

Bora didn't say.

Half an hour later, Guidi was wondering what in God's name he should do. He kept talking to Bora and Bora answered less and less lucidly.

"Should we stop a moment, Major?"

"No. Keep going, keep going. I'm fine. Just a little tired."

"It may be better if I take you directly to Lago and then have Turco come and get me."

"I told you, no. Mind the road."

Silence followed again. Bora leaned away from him, and all Guidi could hear was his quick, laboured breathing. When the first sparse houses of Sagràte grew out of the darkness alongside the road, followed by church and town office and finally police station, Guidi drew a sigh of relief.

Bora's strained voice said, "Do not stop here. Drive straight to your house."

"I can walk from here, Major."

"To your house."

Guidi drove to his house, which was at the opposite end of town. His mother's window was dark, but he wagered she was sitting there, waiting.

Bora asked to have the keys back.

"Should I call Lieutenant Wenzel, Major?"

"No need."

But Bora knew he couldn't possibly manage the few miles to Lago. He drove back toward the police station, and past it, stopping as he'd done many times in front of the army post near by. He could see that Wenzel was still up by the barely visible line of light that marked his blackened window on the upper floor.

It seemed suddenly absurd that he should find himself here. Bora wondered how he had arrived here, and why. He wondered where *here* was, certain for a moment that this was Russia and that never in his lifetime would he leave Russia again.

His hands trembled too much for him to pull the key out of the ignition. He struggled with it, grasping at it until he succeeded. Next, he opened the car door to get out, or perhaps it was the soldier on guard who did it for him.

Bora answered the salute. This he knew. He took the few steps that separated him from the entrance to the post, and said something. He had no idea what he said. The door was tall and black, astonishingly narrow, menacing, dangerous somehow. When Bora tried to enter, it slipped away from his field of vision, sinking deep under him.

Early in the morning Turco stuffed rolled-up newspapers into the wood stove, careful not to stain the cuffs of his shirt. He had found some dry wood too, and crisp chestnut peels to start the fire.

Guidi found him crouching there.

"Good morning, Inspector. *Ossequi.*"

"Hello, Turco."

"Have you by chance spoken to the major this morning?"

"Bora? No." Guidi took off his greatcoat. "Why, has he called?"

Satisfied with the way the fire was going, Turco closed the stove door and regulated the valve. "*Nossignuri.* I thought that maybe he told you what happened next door."

"At the army post? I didn't notice anything as I drove by." Guidi unrolled the scarf from around his neck, without removing it altogether. "Why, what do you think happened?"

"*Vah,* you know last night I was on duty. Since I know you don't like it if I smoke inside, at two o'clock I stepped out for a moment to roll myself a cigarette. The door of the Germans' place was wide open, and there was an ambulance parked near by."

9

Bora woke up in a hospital room, with a nun praying at the foot of his bed.

"I must be worse off than I feel," he told her.

"Oh, don't worry about this." The nun put away her rosary. "I do this every chance I have."

Bora heard himself trying to laugh, though there was hardly a motive.

"Don't move," the nun added. "You just came out of surgery. Doctor Volpi took advantage of the fact that you couldn't keep him from it, and cleaned up your knee once and for all. He worked on your arm, too."

"How did I get here?"

"I don't know exactly; I was in the chapel. It seems you were running a terrible fever. Your men urgently called the local physician, who gave you a shot of ephedrine and, fearing septicaemia had set in, sent you our way at once. You were unconscious when I first saw you, and the doctor says your blood pressure was down to nothing. You've been here two days already. I'll shave you, if you wish."

As his whole body began to wake, Bora was starting to feel pain, and it was rather more than he wished for just now. Nausea was setting in also.

"I can shave myself, Sister."

The nun made a self-conscious, shunning little gesture, and walked to a metal table to fetch a basin with soap and water. "Stay down, be good. Give me a chance to earn Paradise."

With deft, experienced gestures, she began to lather his face. Her hands were bony, lukewarm. Safe hands. Bora recalled the grasp they had offered him to escape the bite of death, and it seemed impossible they would have the strength. "I'm sorry I kicked you in September," he said.

"Never mind September, Major. You should have seen how furious Doctor Volpi was this time. He started calling here and there like a madman until he found some military hospital where they had some penicillin. Taken from the Americans in Sicily, they say: the Lord knows how they got it all the way here."

Bora had no desire to find out more about his health. He knew he should be asking if there were messages for him, but didn't want to. He felt worse by the minute, and resigned himself to let the nun work on him. "What day is it, Sister?"

"Tuesday, 14 December."

"Tuesday. And I'm here wasting time!"

The nun put the shaving kit away. She walked to adjust the wooden blinds of the drapeless window, dimming the harsh flow of daylight. She told him, as she prepared to leave the room, "You should try to love yourself a little, Major Bora."

Unlike her, Doctor Volpi had no sympathy in voice or manner. He stepped in as soon as the nun left, with the untactful crankiness that revealed more than worry. "You don't even deserve to feel as good as you feel. I only had colloidal silver on hand, and that brings about fever in itself. If it wasn't for the penicillin I scrounged... You owe your skin to a non-commissioned officer at the Padua military hospital, a Sicilian by birth. Thank goodness he kept in touch with those of his brothers who managed to avoid confinement – and not confinement for political reasons."

Bora understood. The Mafia gave information to the Americans in exchange for precious medicines, and sold them for high prices elsewhere. He'd have protested were he not facing Volpi, who said, "The non-com owed me a favour, and as a *man of honour*, he would not default. Have I injected penicillin into you these past forty-eight hours! You'll have a hard time sitting for a while, but it's nothing compared to what could have happened."

Bora was beginning to recognize the room. Off-white nuances, details. Blinds, the veined marble window sill, small cracks in the plaster of the wall beneath it, like a horse's head. Nausea. The smell of disinfectant. Even the mutilation of his left wrist was bandaged as on that day in September. He said, as an apology, "I can't imagine what happened."

"You *can't imagine?* A streptococcal infection strong enough to catapult you to your Maker, with a collapsed pulse we failed to detect three times in a row. My father was right when he said that you Germans are like animals: you're hard to kill. I told Sister Elisabetta you're not to leave the bed for any reason. And as for you, remember I'm laying the responsibility on her. It falls on you not to make her transgress my orders."

Frustrated that lying motionless did not lessen the pain, Bora turned on his side. "You will at least let me go to the lavatory."

"Absolutely not. Sister Elisabetta, come back with a bedpan. Well, I'm off to my other patients, Major. By the way, a police inspector has already called twice, and a German colonel came to enquire about you. I sent both of them to hell."

The nun came as requested. Bora knew she was there only by the rustle of her skirt, because he would not look at her. Weakness and pain made everything insufferable, even the little things. He said, with his eyes to the window, "Sister, I am ashamed. Can you accompany me to the lavatory?"

"I can't. If you prefer, I'll wait outside."

"I'd rather not do it here."

The nun laughed a little. "Why? You're a married man!"

"But I certainly don't empty my bladder in front of my wife, or in bed."

"The doctor said you're not to get up. Be patient. These too are trials."

Her words made him wretched. Bora fought not to give in, not so well. "If you knew, dear Sister. I have done nothing but face trials for the past year."

"That means God loves you."

In Sagràte, Guidi read the mail Turco had brought him.

"No, Turco, I don't think he's dead, because Wenzel would be more frantic than he is. But there's no telling what happened to Bora. Since they won't tell me a thing about him by phone, I'm going to Verona, and that's that. Just what we needed, Bora walking off the scene the

224

moment we nabbed the witness. Now God knows what the SS are doing to *him*." Guidi set aside the important letters, tossing the rest in the waste basket. "Use them to light the stove tomorrow. If De Rosa calls back, tell him I don't know where Bora ended up. And since he speaks fluent German, he can find out for himself. I don't feel like talking to him."

Because Turco did not move from the side of his desk, Guidi looked up. "Well, what else is there?"

"A farmer found a pair of shoes laid in a cross behind his barn by the river. They were buried in snow, so they must have been there a few days. *Diu nni scanza e liberi*, Inspector: maybe the convict managed to kill other victims we never did find." Turco went to stoke the fire. "But it does seem like a thousand years since we were running after him, doesn't it?"

Guidi gathered coat, gloves, scarf and hat. "I'm on my way. Oh, and listen closely. If my mother insists on knowing where I went, you're to say you don't know. If she keeps on pestering, tell her I asked for transfer to Sardinia."

The truth was, Guidi did not like hospitals. He avoided them whenever he could, and this trip was a chore made worse by icy pavement, roadblocks and his resentment for Bora, whose fault it all was.

Sister Elisabetta was the one who greeted him, leading him down an impeccably tiled hallway with high vaults. Guidi held his breath against the medicinal stench wafting from the half-open doors left and right.

Bora's room was at the end of the hallway. The chatter of German voices could be heard from here. Colonel Habermehl was in fact leaving now, encumbering the threshold with his blue-grey mass. "*Sorge dich nicht*, Martin!" He was smiling.

As soon as Guidi walked in, Bora said, "I must speak to you."

"How do you feel?"

"I've been better. It's the matter of Gardini. Colonel Habermehl tells me not to worry, but I have good reason to worry. Today is the third day since he was taken into custody by the Security Service. It is imperative that we gain access to him. I asked the colonel to pull strings on my behalf. De Rosa will keep you informed."

There was a chair at the side of the bed, but Guidi chose not to sit down. *The matter of Gardini.* It was Bora who'd turned him in to the SS. If there were strings that were being pulled right now, they were Gardini's. "Well, Major, I came to talk about that very thing. Since I'm here, I also plan to go by the prison. What are we to tell Claretta?"

"You might as well tell her the truth. Try to find out if she and Gardini saw each other, if he went to see her at night. Tell her that, if the details are right, his alibi can support hers, and the crime of adultery is in her case preferable to that of premeditated murder."

Guidi did not react to the words, though they galled him. He shifted his weight from one foot to the other, looking straight at Bora. Freshly shaven, Bora had his usual sternness. He was wearing no prosthesis, and from his left sleeve only a heavily bandaged wrist was visible. *Wenzel must have packed his pyjamas*, Guidi thought, *because these aren't hospital issue. I bet his wife gave them to him, or his mother. And I bet Claretta thinks he's good-looking. He* is *good-looking, after all.* "So," he said, "you don't suspect Gardini of killing her husband."

Bora adjusted the pillow under his head. "I never know anything until I have the facts. I merely suppose a great deal. We still have to wrap up all interrogation, including that of the Zanella woman. I intend to leave here the day after tomorrow, if I have to step over the dead body of my physician to do so. You'll go see Clara Lisi, of course." Bora reached for a book on his bedside table, where bandages and medicines waited for use. He opened the book – it was in German, a biography of Mozart judging by the title on its spine – and pulled out a folded piece of paper. "When you return to Sagràte, do me the courtesy of giving this note to Lieutenant Wenzel. Poor Wenzel, I have given him a good scare."

Guidi left. The day had turned clear, with a blinding winter sun that made the interior of the Verona prison seem cavernous and dingy.

Minutes later Claretta was sobbing in front of him, her face in her hands.

"I'm sorry for the bad news," Guidi said. But he was jealous of her reaction, and helpless before her unrestrained show of grief. "Come, come. Don't be so upset, he's only been arrested." He watched her round shoulders shake with weeping. How fragile and pink she was, even in this grey room. It'd be easy to give in, and embrace her so that she would no longer cry. He limited himself to touching her elbow. "Come now, they haven't done anything to him."

What a lie. Claretta was not taken in. "It's all my fault, because I gave you his name!"

"No, no. We'd have found out anyway. You needn't cry."

She let Guidi lift her head, dab her face with his handkerchief. "Why didn't *you* come the other day? I don't want to see the major any more."

"You won't. You won't, Clara. He's in the hospital."

"Good!" Angry-eyed, she grabbed his hand in a wet grasp. "I hope he dies, I hope he dies this very minute!"

The moist warmth of her clasp travelled through him with blissful pain. Guidi was aroused and moved by the touch, anxious not to let go. "Tell *me* at least, Claretta. Were you meeting Carlo Gardini at night?"

She stood from the chair, and impulsively hung from his neck.

As the surgeon entered Bora's room, Sister Elisabetta was saying, "What a beautiful girl. Write to her, write to her. The poor thing, do not let her be in anguish for you." Bora was showing her a photograph of his wife, which he now removed from his wallet and placed as a marker in the biography of Mozart.

"Time for another penicillin, Sister," the surgeon interrupted. "Inject it higher up, we've punctured the muscle enough."

The shot burned like hell. Bora held on to the book, trying to give himself a countenance by keeping his eyes on *Travels Through Italy*, but he couldn't even see the words. Fire seemed to grow out of the small of his back, and for a minute or so afterward the pain down his leg was crippling. After dismissing the nun, the surgeon sat at the bedside and handed him a thermometer.

"Turn over. Put this under your arm, and we'll see how you're doing. I'm against smoking, but if it lifts your spirits, you may ask Sister Elisabetta to light you a cigarette."

Bora had to wait until the pain subsided before speaking. "I don't need to smoke, but I have a favour to ask."

"Only if it has nothing to do with getting up."

"I'm looking for a piece of information."

Having heard what Bora was asking, the physician scowled. "What kind of request is it, just after showing the family pictures? What have you done, knocked a girl up?"

"No. I'm just curious."

"Give the thermometer back." The surgeon read the temperature with visible relief, which he did not share with Bora. "Well, we have several specialists in Verona. Practically any physician can handle the matter, but if it is the specialists you're looking for, I know two that I would recommend."

"I'm interested in those who have private practices, not those associated with hospitals or clinics."

"And what do you want with their names?"

"I'd like to contact them by phone."

"Forget it. You're not getting up."

"Will you at least ask Sister to call for me?"

"Ask her directly. If Sister feels like being your secretary in addition to turning you in bed, it's her business."

Minutes later, the nun's little hands, cracked by soap and alcohol, vanished inside the depths of her cuffs. She repeated the question Bora had instructed her to ask. "Is that all, Major?"

"Yes, but I should warn you it is a lie."

"And you expect me to lie?"

"Only to good ends, Sister. According to the principle of double effect, a little transgression will be more than offset by its worthy result."

Sister Elisabetta smiled. "So now you're teaching me religion, Major Bora."

That evening, back home in Sagràte, Guidi crossed the kitchen floor without greeting his mother. Distractedly, with his greatcoat still on, he walked to the sink, lathered his hands, dried them without rinsing and sat down at the table. When his mother poured him soup, he stood up again and took to pacing back and forth. At one point he walked to the front door, opened it wide, slammed it shut and resumed his pacing.

Whatever amount of unchecked passion showed through, his mother was at once frightened. "Sandro, what happened?"

"Nothing."

"Are you sick?"

"No." Again Guidi sat at the table, staring at the soup. He unbuttoned his coat without taking it off. "Here." He stretched his arm out to give her his handkerchief, crumpled and stained with mascara. "I have this to wash, Ma."

Even early in the morning, one could smell liquor on Habermehl's breath, despite the Valda mints he constantly chewed. Too big for his uniform, the blue-grey Air Force breeches stretched every which way, and when he sat down at Bora's bedside, the fabric seemed about to burst on his knees.

"Martin, I spoke to the direct SS superior of *Hauptsturmführer* Lasser. He promised me he'll keep the prisoner in

Verona for another twenty-four hours. You have access to him, but he let me know that I was asking a great favour. Whatever your business with this Gardini fellow is, hurry up, because we don't know what they'll do to him next."

"If it were up to me I'd be out already, *Herr Oberst*. No matter what, I am leaving tomorrow." Although Sister Elisabetta spoke no German, Bora grew quiet when she looked in from the threshold.

"Major, there's a Republican Guard officer here by the name of De Rosa. He says it is urgent."

Habermehl recognized the name. He took his cap from the bedside table. "Do you want me to leave, Martin?"

"No, *Herr Oberst*, stay. Let's hear what's new. I might need your help again."

De Rosa swept in. He stiffened in a Fascist salute, and addressed Bora in German with all the exasperation he was obviously feeling.

"Major, it has come to my attention that a partisan leader has been arrested, and treacherously taken from the Italian authorities. I have come to ask, since it was you who handed him over to your compatriots, that you have him released to us at once."

Indifferent to Italian politics, Habermehl had left the chair and was leafing through Bora's book by the window. He found the photograph of Bora's wife, and lifted it to the light to study it. When he realized that Bora was about to flare up at De Rosa, he burst into an amused laugh to avoid the incident. He laughed to make De Rosa understand the absurdity of his request, and also because he knew fanaticism, and hated it.

*

At seven thirty on Tuesday morning, when Bora went to take his leave, the surgeon wouldn't even look him in the face. "I wash my hands of it. Do what you want, it's your skin."

By eight o'clock SS *Hauptsturmführer* Lasser, who looked very much like Alan Ladd and might or might not know it, spied Bora's ribbons before speaking.

"Haven't we met somewhere before, Major?"

The same question, from a different SS man. Bora said, "It's possible, Verona is a small place. Perhaps at the funeral of Vittorio Lisi, the other day."

"No, no. I'm speaking of military assignments. Weren't you in Poland back in '39? Yes. Now I remember. Cracow, Army Headquarters. You served under Blaskowitz."

"We all served under General Blaskowitz. He was head of the *Generalgouvernement.*"

Lasser's office, one of many in the requisitioned insurance building – the "INA Palace" – was cold enough for the men's breath to condense. Behind his puffing little cloud of irritation, Lasser was not falling for his calmness, Bora could tell. He'd brought up the issue because Army General Blaskowitz had the reputation of being hostile to the SS, and in Poland his young staff officers had dared to expose abuses against the civilian population. Bora, who had hand-delivered written reports on SS activity to Blaskowitz in his hunting lodge at Spala, knew where Lasser was headed. "Well, we left Poland behind a good long time ago. At least," he said, lowering his eyes to Lasser's ribbons, "you got France afterward. I did two years in Russia, Stalingrad included."

"You volunteered to go there, as you did in Poland. Now what do you want from us?"

"Only the opportunity to speak to your prisoner. After all, I turned him in to you. And I believe Colonel Habermehl explained that my presence here has nothing to do with politics."

Lasser's eyes narrowed. "This bandit, this Gardini, he is the worst of his kind, stubborn and impudent. He likes to push his luck, Major. If I'm not mistaken, for all your lying low in the Italian countryside, you're one to understand that feeling."

"I think you're mistaken."

"Weren't your men the cads who let a truckload of Jews escape just last week? I know all about it."

"Then you know that the vehicle broke down. It was night by then, the terrain was wooded and treacherous, and the guards were overpowered. That's all. It should have been apparent to your commander that my unit isn't trained for that sort of duty."

Lasser could not stare him down. But as he encumbered the doorway, Bora had to walk around him to get out. Carefully, because every brusque motion still caused pain and sparks of light to dance around him.

"You have five minutes," Lasser shouted after him. "So be quick about it."

After Russia, Bora had not believed he could suffer from claustrophobia.

Lack of horizons had haunted his late summer days there, and then the autumn and winter. Haze or rain or snow had in one way or another kept the end of that world from sight, so that he had led his men along as one lost, despite all maps and directions.

Today, the stinging rain and high-walled courtyard near the Palace closed in upon him like a lidless box, and made him unsympathetic and moody. That he'd been able to get these few moments was already miraculous, in the way that Habermehl could perform miracles with his influence. As things were, there was no time to get the information he wanted, but try he must.

Gardini was already seated inside the army truck, under armed guard. One prisoner, one soldier. Bora knew well enough what this "transfer" really meant, and he only wondered whether a sack for the body was being kept in the truck's cab, or if they wouldn't bother with that. Rain created chained links from the flap of the truck's cover, a sad necklace, and each scene like this, each death, was for the past two years like a rehearsal for his own, which added no egotistical pity, but only weariness at the long wait.

Gardini likely believed he was being brought to another jail. He said nothing about it, and neither did Bora. Bora would not climb into the truck, not only because his leg still hurt too much, but because that damp space would soon be polluted by death. So he stood in the rain by the tailgate, with Gardini looking down at him.

"We haven't much time," he said, aware of the irony of his words. "So it's best if you tell me quickly. Clara Lisi is in jail, accused of the murder of her husband. I imagine it matters more to you than to me." He ignored Gardini's scowl. "So, if you have anything to do with this case, spill it out. You cannot get in worse trouble than you are. And after all, you must have guts, or you wouldn't have sneaked into town three times, knowing you might be caught."

"Four times. I came four times."

"Well, good for you. I understand how important it is to see the woman one loves. Did you kill Vittorio Lisi?"

"I have nothing to say."

Bora declined with a gesture when the soldier offered to let him into the truck, and out of the rain. He didn't mind the rain. From his seat, Gardini only said, as if spitting the words, "You're a bunch of idiots, if you think Claretta did it."

"That's true, we're idiots at times. Enlighten me."

"I didn't even know Lisi had died, the scum. Much less that they had arrested Claretta. I came because I had to see her again."

"You *had to*, or you *wanted to*?"

Gardini stared at him with hostility. "What's it to you?"

"It makes a difference."

"I had to and I wanted to. How's that?"

"I expect you were the one who telephoned her in the country some time ago. Did you inform her you were planning a visit?"

And even as Bora was talking to the man, the odour of rain on the flagstones of the courtyard meant another time, and another place. Standing to kiss Dikta, before the War, unsure about her love even then but all taken up by their lust for each other, which did conceal love in him, enough to make him hope it did in her, too. His parents' country house in Gohlis, a venerable Bora doorway to a world of polite spaces, corners still friendly from his childhood, but now less innocent as he visited them again with her. Rain had for the longest time reminded him of that kiss.

That he should be standing here with a man who would be dead in an hour's time was like being dropped from a free space of possibilities into a trap. The courtyard, the task at hand, his career – traps one inside the other. And he was not the one to die today.

Gardini said nothing. Lasser's men had clearly worked on him. Bloodstains on his sleeves marked where he might have staunched a nosebleed. From the way he sat, Bora recognized the discomfort of a body that has been beaten.

"What I really want to know," he continued, "is whether you were with Clara Lisi on the afternoon of 19 November."

"I'm not telling."

"Were you in Verona that day, or anywhere around Verona?"

"I've told you all I'm going to say, Major."

Time was up. Bora walked away from the truck, and Gardini waited until he was nearly out of earshot before calling him back. He had a different anxiety in his voice. The grudge had diluted, or else it was not the most important feeling at this moment. "How is she?"

"She's fine."

The truck's engine started, and there was really nothing else to say.

On the second floor of the SS headquarters, Lasser's office no longer had Lasser in it. The nameless *Standartenführer* with the scarred lip stood there instead.

As Bora walked by, he called him in. Without closing the door, he announced, "I have your report here, Major," and when Bora said something, he rudely cut him off. "Save your breath. We know you're good with words. There's no way we're ever going to beat you at the game of words. But we're not in your philosophy class."

Bora heard himself losing prudence. "If that's your assessment, then I hope you'll let me go, since I have plenty to do, and being complimented on my writing is really a waste of your time and mine. Regarding the incident, you should be protesting with the Italian authorities. According to Article Seven, it was ultimately their transport, and their responsibility."

The eyes of the SS officer stayed on the folder he had in hand. "You *are* Martin-Heinz Bora, lately assigned to O.B. South, and before that, to O.B. East, Army Group III?"

"I am."

"Was not your assigned area within the 1941 operational range of *Einsatzgruppe* B?"

"I expect it was. If I recall, *Einsatzgruppe* B stretched from north of Tula to south of Kursk. It was difficult not to fall within its range."

"Does the name Rudnya mean anything to you?"

Bora regained enough prudence not to comment. "It's a place name," he said.

"Near Smolensk, is it not?"

"It's a place near Smolensk, yes. I hope you're not testing my proficiency in Soviet geography."

"Far from it. I have here a copy of Operational Situation Report USSR No. 148, dated 19 December 1941. There is a reference to the execution of fifty-two Jews in it."

"You must not refer to Rudnya, then. There were ten times as many executions there. The fifty-two were captured in Homyel and shot for passing themselves off as Russians."

"No thanks to you, Major."

It was uncanny how one could sweat in such a cold room. Bora said, "It was hardly my job to assist the

Einsatzgruppe. It seemed to be doing quite well by itself."

"Were you not called in to answer for your refusal to lend army support to the Rudnya and Homyel Special Units operations?"

"No. I was in the field when both requests came, and by the time I returned to base camp, the operations had been carried out."

"But you were not out in the field in Shumyachi."

"No. In Shumyachi I simply said no, as Paragraph 47, 1.b of the Military Penal Code directs. My reasons there were primarily related to my men's morale. Half of them had children of their own, and somehow a skin infection didn't seem to warrant shooting the whole paediatric ward."

"You're hardly qualified to judge medical conditions."

"But I'm highly qualified to judge troop morale."

It was clear that the folder held much more than his report about the 1 December incident. Bora could not distinguish the other documents from where he stood, but they resembled typewritten reports to the Army War Crimes Bureau, such as ones he'd authored and signed himself.

The act of tightening his mouth stretched the scar on the SS officer's lip. "Your report may say what you wish, Bora. I will tell you what *I* think. I think you have done nothing to prevent the escape of Jews, and nothing to secure their recapture. Thanks to the shabbiness of Italian equipment, I cannot prove you physically tampered with the truck, though a ball joint at the end of the front tie rod was loosened. You selected the worst route, and planned it so that the transport would be effected at night. Furthermore, I believe you got into bed with the local church, even to the point of staging the arrest of a priest who guided the rest to locations off-limits to us. This is consistent with reports we have of you from the East, where your army smarts suddenly got stupid when it came to Jews. There were nests of Jews hiding in the countryside up and down from your command at Lago, and now there are none. Somebody tipped them off, right in your backyard. Too much for a coincidence, I say. If you didn't have the friends you have, I'd call you a Jew-lover."

As on the emergency-room table, Bora was suddenly past anguish. He said, angrily, "I don't like the term."

"Fuck what you like or don't like, you big-mouthed aristocrat. If it weren't for your connections, we'd have taught you a lesson long ago. I want you to know I'm going to make it my personal business to pry your friends' hands off your shoulders. We'll see how long your luck holds up then."

Guidi waited for Bora in Piazza Cittadella, at the back of the INA Palace. "Major, did you have to have Gardini brought here, of all places? Do you know how many make it out of that door?"

Little did Guidi understand. Bora was catching his breath, and not only from having just come down two ramps of stairs from Lasser's office. "I don't wish to appear egotistical to you, Guidi, but to date I have lost several men and one hand to the partisans. If you add the ideological questions, which for me are more important than the personal ones, you'll see why I acted the way I did. Your Gardini killed at least three German soldiers

239

and managed to blow up a petrol depot. He knew what he was doing, and where he'd end up if caught."

"Did you at least tell him that Claretta is in jail?"

"Yes, but he likely thought I invented it to make him talk. He needed to believe I was lying, I think. One dies better if one leaves no worries behind. Don't make that face, Guidi. In Russia we strung partisans up by the wayside."

"What about Claretta?"

Bora knew he was being cruel, but he didn't feel charitable at this moment. "If she's guilty, she stays in jail. If not, since you're so concerned, why don't you go ahead and propose to her?"

They left Verona shortly thereafter, bound for the hamlet of San Pancrazio. Guidi sat silently next to the army driver, preparing the questions for *the Zanella woman*. In the back seat, Bora ostensibly read about Mozart's travels in Italy, keeping his left leg stretched out to rest.

Rain had washed out the snow. Fields ran in brown strips and squares, parted by willows and trash trees, grooved by ditches full of lead-coloured water. Farms went by, with their dishevelled haystacks and muddy yards. Guidi watched them file past. As he did, he caught through the corner of his eye how Bora was, in fact, contemplating his wife's photograph in the safety of the open book.

Mud had iced over and melted in front of the farmhouse. Guidi, who was the one who went to knock on the door, sank in the mire to the edge of his shoes. Wiping his soles on the doorstep, he said, "*Polizia.*"

A fair, wide woman answered the door. The sight of Bora's uniform visibly agitated her, and it took Guidi's mild approach to assure her that nothing had happened to her husband in Germany. Once inside, he did the asking, while Bora listened standing by the door.

"We don't want to hear that name mentioned in this house," she began. "Don't expect me to pronounce it. He was a filthy rotter, Inspector. God knows he's given us grief and tears, and may he roast in hell where he is. Whoever killed him, God bless him."

"Or *her*," Bora said from the door, eyes low.

Guidi ignored the comment. "You needn't go through the story of your daughter," he offered. "We know how it was."

"Do you?" She bared square, yellow teeth in a humourless grin. "*Do* you? And from whom do you know it? From the midwife that butchered her? From *his* friends? From the wife he bought himself, and who wasn't enough for him?"

Bora glanced up. But for the language, he could have been in the East right now. One after the other, the stoic faces of Slavic women came back to him, pleading without tears, or asking for justice. He'd killed their men, their farm animals, taken over their houses. He'd reopened their churches, given them food, sat with them for evenings. This was one more life-worn mother's face with a story to tell.

She said, "I went out as hired help when I was young; don't you think I know how rich men are with their servant girls? I told my daughter, too. God knows I told her. But who'd think an ugly cripple who could be her grandfather would do what he did. My daughter, she was young, and that's all I have to say for her. Children don't do wrong."

Guidi nodded. "Your husband came home after the army was disbanded, and from what we know he immediately went to Lisi."

"Sure he did. I only wish he'd kept his rifle so he could have done justice to him right then."

"What did he tell Lisi?"

"The things a father would throw at a swine like that. And he had the gall to offer us money, as if money would give us back our child. But that's just the way rich people are. They throw *schei* at you, and everything is supposed to be made all right. Well, it wasn't made all right for us. No, sir."

Guidi glanced at Bora, whose silence was as it had been when Enrica Salviati had been interrogated. He wondered, God knows why, if it wasn't after all an aristocratic shy reserve.

"Well," he continued, "they say it was your husband who asked for compensation."

Like bones set in a double line, her teeth showed again. "*Who* says? Whoever says that is a swine and a rotter! The swine's money wasn't good enough for us to wipe ourselves with."

"Did your husband have access to a car?" The question came from Bora, who'd walked to the kitchen's only window and looked out of it.

"Why do you ask, because he was an ambulance driver in the army?" sourly the woman spoke back. "That's why you took him to Germany."

Bora was suddenly impatient, though he wouldn't look at her. "I personally have no use for your husband. The war effort needs him. Just answer my question, please." He knew she was staring, but there would be no tears.

It was raining again, on a world flat as Russia but not so desolate and immense. Bora thought of his mother, of her lovely face and the tears Valenki had said she would cry for her sons. He couldn't remember his wife crying, ever. When he turned from the window, the woman was clasping her hands. This gesture, too, he knew so well. He stared at the knot of swollen fingers, bulging with blue veins.

"Is that what you want to know?" She familiarly motioned with her head for Bora to draw close, but Bora ignored the summons. "If that's what it's about, listen good, because I'll tell you how it went. Could my husband get his hands on a car? He could. He did. He had a car at his disposal on the day the cripple was killed. Got it from the army depot. Had a friend there, I don't know how he managed, but he drove back here in a car. Everybody knew the cripple had separated from his wife and lived alone with a servant woman in the country. My man told me, right here, at this table, that he'd made up his mind to go and get it over with. Yes, to *kill* him, what else? If that's what you wanted to hear, you heard it. Except that God didn't grant him the grace of doing it."

Guidi didn't know how Bora could keep his sullen peace. He was high-strung with impatience. "Why, had Lisi already been wounded when your husband arrived?"

"One better than that, Inspector. My husband was still driving there when who should come screaming down the road but the cripple's maid. He braked not to run her over, and she went on screaming and crying and asking for help, that her master had been killed or something, and would he get help."

"I hope he didn't," Bora said impulsively.

"You're damn right. He drove her to the state route and left her there. She could flag down someone else, he said. As if cars were plentiful! See, he only wanted her out of his way to get to the villa on his own, which he did. But the cripple was dead already, or almost dead, the swine." The hard calloused hands unclasped. "We're not such animals that we don't understand it's useless to get angry at the dead. But my man said he just stood there laughing, watching the swine lie with his back all twisted up. It was too late to do much else, but by God he said he kicked him in the mug, as a reminder of our dead child."

Bora was startled, a reaction that was not lost on Guidi. "And then?" he urged.

"The Devil's got him in his belly now, that's what. And God bless who sent him there. My husband returned the car to the depot the same day, and at the beginning of the following week you Germans came to pick him up for labour."

Bora straightened himself by the window, searching his tunic for cigarettes. "The decision was unrelated, you can count on that. What was your husband planning to use to kill Lisi?"

The woman held up her hands, squaring them in the air. "These. It's easy to kill cripples, don't you know?"

Bora remembered he'd left his cigarettes in the car, and he was desperate to smoke just now. He said, "Not always."

Notebook in his lap, Guidi had been scribbling at a furious pace. "Did your husband say if he struck the gate on his way in or out?"

The woman glowered at him. "My husband *never* had an accident. He used to race in mountain rallies when he was young."

"Did he say if he met any cars on the way to the villa, or back?"

"He didn't say and I didn't ask. But with all their trying to keep the rotten swine's death a secret, it'll come out sooner or later. First they said it was an accident, and now they're saying the wife killed him for money. The rich don't kill for money. That, I know. Power's what they want. With all the lives the cripple ruined, you'll be searching until doomsday for the one who might have done him in."

When Guidi stood to join Bora, who'd walked to the door and was leaving, she remained in her chair. "If you want to arrest me," she called out, "you go right ahead. Jail can't be worse than what I've got."

"I'm not going to arrest you," Guidi said.

Mud had overflowed into Guidi's shoes when they reached the car. Bora smirked at his own soiled boots. "There's an affecting proletarian wisdom in her, isn't there?" he said lightly. "'The rich don't kill for money.' Neither do the poor, apparently."

"There's nothing to smile about, Major. We can hardly check all the vehicles in the army depot."

"Especially considering we sent the lot to Germany. Don't worry, the old woman is telling the truth. It's another blind alley we've got ourselves into."

"Thanks to De Rosa! And you still listen to him."

Bora ordered the driver to start the car. "Guidi, Guidi, what am I going to do with you? You have an inquisitor's lack of humour, and none of the ruthlessness that goes with it. I don't *listen* to De Rosa. De Rosa is the garbage we'll leave behind when we're done with Italy. His companions might have tried to blackmail Clara Lisi, and failed at that. They might have killed Enrica Salviati, who knows. As for me, I keep in mind what Mussolini wrote about you Italians: it's not impossible to talk to you. It's plain useless."

"So, if Zanella didn't do it and Gardini didn't do it and De Rosa didn't do it, Claretta gets the rap so that we can close the case."

"I never said any of those people are off the suspect list. The only one among them who has a shaky alibi is De Rosa. Gardini would be the easiest to charge, but it's unlikely he'd borrow a car to do what he could do by shooting."

"Well, there's one more trail. If Lisi lent money to the Verona Fascists, as you said—"

"Don't put words in my mouth."

"It could be a conspiracy, not just a cover-up."

Bora seemed mildly intrigued. "I've ridden De Rosa's rear about this as much as I could. It'd be interesting if it turned out that *he* did it, though. Colonel Habermehl would have a drink or two over the revelation."

"What if the letters on Lisi's calendar do indicate the names of his debtors?"

"Then we'll have to pick at half the alphabet, because there's no 'C' among them."

Guidi found it irritating that Bora should open his book and start to read from it while they were talking. "We can't give up now!"

Carelessly Bora turned a page. "To be perfectly frank with you, Guidi, I have had enough of this case. It may be the fever, but I'm starting to dream about it at night, and it's not the kind of dreams I'd prefer. This morning I woke up with the idea that I ought to mind the meaning of the Immaculate Conception in this affair. What does the Immaculate Conception have to do with it, other than that it starts with 'C'? No, Guidi, we've done all we could for today. Kindly let me read. If you need me after today, I'll be in and out. Mostly out. Leave a message with Wenzel. He can't stand you, but he religiously passes all of your notes on to me."

With all of this, Guidi knew Bora was being defensive. More than disappointed, he might be avoiding an argument in order to cultivate some troubling thoughts of his own. It was a prudent distancing of his mind, which kept others from following a parallel path.

10

Guidi could not get in touch with Bora in the days that followed.

Lieutenant Wenzel acted as hostile as ever; the BMW was not parked by the kerb. Messages left were not returned. Once more, Bora estranged himself, using his responsibilities to isolate himself from others.

It occurred to Guidi that he had become oddly used to relating to Bora in their tense confrontational way, a chafing of personalities that functioned at some level. He didn't need Bora pulling away from the collaboration now that Claretta was about to go on trial.

After the tears she had listened to him wide-eyed during their last meeting, protesting that she didn't deserve to be sacrificed. For the first time Guidi had noticed dark hair showing at the roots of her curls when she ran her fingers through them. And, too, there had been that bit of bread crust stuck between her front teeth, sacrilegious to him like the marring of a beautiful portrait. Warily, Guidi kept out of mind the scene that followed Claretta's tears, unprofessional on his part as it'd been. Kissing had turned into mindless and groggy touching about, until they'd accidentally knocked the chair over, and the racket turned the interlude into embarrassment. Now Guidi felt guilty, and furious with Bora for seeing through him. But that bit of bread – that bit of bread lodged between Claretta's teeth was even more disturbing, a reminder of mortal vanity. A signal that spoke of tedium, banality and the unflattering physical facts: because fetishes do not show dark roots and do not need to brush their teeth. Guidi was amazed at how abstract his image of Claretta had been before the kiss. Even her beautiful high breasts had been graceful asexual bulges to his eyes, let alone what else there was under pink clothes, sheathed in pink underwear. What did Bora know about a bigoted upbringing? He looked like a man who kept religion out of his bed. All Guidi knew was that his mother was in a sulk, and that damned Bora was nowhere to be found.

Then, on Wednesday, 22 December, a telephone call arrived from the warden, and Sandro Guidi's world came crashing down.

On Thursday afternoon he was still recovering from the news. Morosely sitting in his office, with his feet propped on a small stool by the stove, he stared at his woollen socks, trying to distract himself by thinking of other things. One image after another broke like the surf against his discontent, until he thought of Valenki. He imagined him tall and ragged, like the madman Bora's men had shot in the hills, for whom Bora had tacitly bought a grave. Poor, desperate, with the curse and blessing of a sixth sense. No doubt Bora had asked Valenki about himself. He was the man to do it, and in a spiteful, self-punishing way, too. Guidi was maliciously curious to know whether Valenki's answer was ever legible on Bora's clean-shaven face.

Warming his feet and digesting his mother's soup, he let himself doze by the stove. In the superficial sleep that comes with being uncomfortable in a chair, the craziest dreams floated to him. He dreamed of Russian prisoners shooting German dogs and of submarine sailors in the fields of Sagràte. And he dreamed of Bora kissing Claretta on the bed of the command post, at which point he awoke startled and in a rage.

Turco was in the room, standing by the desk as he spoke into the telephone. "*Sissignuri, sissignuri.* Yes, sir. I will report to him. Good day to you."

"Who is it, Turco?"

"It was Major Bora, Inspector. He left word that he will meet you in Lago at thirteen hundred hours to go with you to Verona."

Guidi tried to disentangle himself from sleep, but not from his irritation toward Bora. "That's twenty minutes from now! To do what, did he say?" As if Bora were one to discuss issues with the lower ranks.

Turco's answer surprised him. "*Quannu mai*, Inspector. He said something about a church."

"A church?" Guidi sat up in his chair. "What does a church have to do with anything? What the devil does he mean?"

"A church is all he said."

Bora was still uncommunicative when they met. He led Guidi to the BMW, and started the engine. "We're going to Saint Zeno's," he merely informed him.

251

"I see. What's the occasion?"

"Other than the day after tomorrow is Christmas Day? It's a Benedictine abbey."

"I know. But why?"

"Zeno's main theological concern was the Virgin Birth."

"You're speaking in riddles, Major Bora."

"Vittorio Lisi would appreciate that, wouldn't he?"

Guidi made an effort not to raise his voice. "I hope the visit is related to the job at hand. I'm not in the mood for sightseeing."

"All you have to do is listen. In keeping with wartime, *in tempore belli*, they'll perform Mozart's *Requiem* instead of Christmas music. His wonderful last piece; you'll like it even if you're not familiar with it. It helps me to think, Mozart does. His original family name was Motzert, did you know that?"

"Major, let's not play around. Did you hear about Claretta?"

"No. What?"

"She's pregnant."

Bora jerked the car to an unnecessary halt. "I knew it. Holy Christ, I *knew* it!"

"She took ill on Tuesday evening. They called a physician, and it became clear that's what it was. She'd said nothing to anyone."

"How many months?"

"Four."

"Ha! At least for the law, the child might figure to be Lisi's after all."

"I don't know how you can laugh about any of this."

"I'm not laughing, it's a legal question."

Guidi looked down. "Anyway, she told me she was not with Gardini on the day of the murder, so her alibi is no better than it was."

"Here you're mistaken. I've known where she was for the past week. Look in my briefcase. There's a sheet with the address of a physician's office where Clara Lisi spent the afternoon of 19 November. Thanks to my impartiality, I had the stroke of genius to contact the best gynaecologists in Verona. There was always a chance she might have gone out of town, but it was worth trying."

Guidi did not bother to look for the address. "Forgive me, but I have a hard time believing that a physician would share the names of his clients, and by phone besides."

"I didn't ask for a name. My question" – Bora did not specify that Sister Elisabetta had been the actual caller – "was simply whether anyone found the purse *Signora* Lisi had left in the waiting room on Friday, 19 November. As I expected, all answers were negative. But a nurse at the right address said she remembered seeing *Signora* Lisi that day."

Guidi fumed. "And why didn't you tell me all this? Why didn't you show up at all for a week?"

"Because not all women who visit a gynaecologist are pregnant. I know that well. I didn't want to disillusion you if there was no need."

The words infuriated Guidi. "As if you gave a damn."

The church of Saint Zeno's rose from an open space at the western periphery of Verona. A monumental structure of alternating brick and limestone, it loomed alongside the slender tower of its ancient abbey. Bora parked the BMW in the alley that separated the two buildings, out of sight. The day was overcast; a wind had risen to curl the wispy clouds into tendrils of icy crystals.

Bora went directly in. Guidi, who had cooled down considerably, lagged behind. At the entrance, he stopped to look at the reliefs on the bronze door. Set off by disquieting, open-mouthed masks, the panels told the story of Saint Zeno, whose symbol seemed to be a fishing cane with a perch-like thing at the end of it.

Inside the church, the nave was cut short by stairs that descended to a deep crypt below; beyond this, a higher balcony with statues edged another level, and past it a third one reached the apse, where the long main altar stretched. Chairs had been lined on the ground floor, and some of the singers were already assembled on the floor above. Hardly any of the public had assembled. Bora sat in the first pew, where Guidi joined him. Within minutes people began to trickle in, bundled in the sombre hodge-podge clothes of wartime. The orchestra came last.

The *Requiem*'s opening strains were low, but at once mounted into a rich chorus, from which the soprano voice bloomed in *There shall be singing unto God in Zion*.

No one after Guidi came to sit in the first pew. Everyone except Bora seemed aware of how misplaced his uniform was here. Eagle-studded cap on his knees, he listened with an unusual, intent humility, as though music and words alike were in earnest and he should take warning.

When they came to the ominous *Dies Irae*, Guidi recognized the words and glumly let his mind drift, eyes now on the keel-shaped vault, now on the statues of the

254

baluster above the crypt. If he cast an occasional glance at Bora, it was to learn the reason for his being here, through observation if by no other means. But Bora's face revealed nothing, except that the music moved him.

And when Guidi had resigned himself to sit through the performance, at the strophe, *Weeping day shall be the day / When from ash where sinners lay / They will rise to judgement,* Bora unexpectedly stood and without a word to him crossed the nave under the scrutiny of the audience, aiming for a side door. Guidi uneasily waited for the next "Amen" before following through the same exit.

The side door led to the cloister. And there Bora sat with his back to a hazy swatch of sky framed by thin red columns. Thorny links of climbing roses festooned the archways between them. From the church, music rose and fell in waves as if the great flank of the building were breathing pure sounds. Bora sat, and held his face low.

Guidi did not attempt to draw close. Something in Bora was untouchable at this moment, a loneliness different from that of a soldier, although the soldier was responsible for it. Beyond the arches, an intimation of evening already dimmed the afternoon. The sky seemed to swoon in its hazy light, but the night would be clear, and the moon would shine.

"Well, Major. What is it?"

Bora looked up without lifting his face. "I left because I understood what I had to understand. But also because this, the last part of the *Requiem,* isn't Mozart's."

"Do you mean you found out who the killer is?"

Whether in denial or in refusing to answer, Bora shook his head. "I was listening to the music and thinking of Zeno and his pious tracts. How the Virgin Birth – the

Immaculate Conception – stands for lack of dependency, the *ultimate absence of bias*. It's all my fault, Guidi. I've known, and still remained prejudiced. Now I deserve what comes."

For a moment, no more, Guidi grasped what Bora's mind tossed at him, but not so well that he could hold on to it and feel its shape. He chose to let it go. "If you have no solution, what good are these *feelings* of yours?"

"No good. But now you see how fortunate Valenki was, that madness made everything fit neatly in his mind." Bora stood. Heading for a doorway at the end of the cloister, which likely led to living quarters, he said, "Kindly wait for me here, I have to check on someone."

Guidi watched Bora reach the doorway, and knock. For a moment he thought he'd recognized Monsignor Lai in the tall figure that came to open, but it couldn't be. How would Monsignor Lai?… No, it couldn't be.

By the time Guidi and Bora left Saint Zeno's, the countryside appeared sunken in blue dimness. A fat, waxing moon had risen ahead of them, a memory of the scythe it had been and would be again, reaping stars in the circle of its wide halo.

Bora had scarcely spoken a word since they had left the darkened city of Verona. Whether he had lost interest in the case or simply had nothing more to contribute to it, Guidi sensed that meaningful things had shifted in the German's mind, and he was not talking about them.

Guidi said, "If we call tonight, we could still keep them from transferring Claretta for the trial."

Bora kept quiet. From the dusk, as the car drove up to them, slack curves emerged one after another, faintly aglow with icy moisture. The gravelly shoulders bristled with brushwood and collapsed bundles of wild grasses. The season folded upon itself; only the wind would keep the snow at bay.

Guidi had sunk back into his own sad consideration of things when Bora slammed on the brakes, so without warning that Guidi would have rammed his face on the windshield had he not braced himself with both arms on the dashboard. The car, which had been travelling at sustained speed, came to a screeching, complete halt.

Still Bora said nothing.

"What is it, what's happening?" Guidi asked with heart in mouth, expecting an ambush.

Bora had let go of the wheel and was turning the engine off. Silence was instantly made, a darkness and silence that were wide and eerie. Guidi steadied himself.

"Look outside," Bora said. Guidi did so, trying to see in the bushes along the road, and Bora corrected him. "No, ahead. Look ahead of us. Look at the moon. All the useless thinking about letters and names in the appointment book, and trying to match the sign in the gravel with someone's name. We had the answer in front of us all along. Look at the moon."

Guidi stared up through the windshield. Soft clicks came from the engine as it cooled. Now that they had stopped, the wind braided around the car in whispers. Only now did his mind travel so close to Bora's path that, finding no resistance, it nearly coalesced with it. In rapid succession ideas fashioned themselves into a mosaic, piece by piece. Guidi turned to Bora, who had gone silent again.

"The crescent moon. Why, sure! The letter 'C' has nothing to do with it, and neither does Claretta, or Carlo Gardini. The mark in the gravel is a half-moon. The villa of the Ottoman crescent, with its semicircular colonnade – Mozart's forgotten *Halbmond* sonata. Lisi drew a crescent to indicate Moser's house! This is what was on your mind in the cloister of Saint Zeno's, isn't it?"

"No."

Guidi reasoned himself out of hope. "No, Major, it's a stretch. A coincidence. Moser's car is badly dented and scuffed, but you rode with him. You'd have noticed…"

Bora wouldn't look at him. "I noticed a long scrape on the left side of the Mercedes on the morning he drove me to Verona."

"It doesn't prove murder."

"No? I thank you for being so gracious, Guidi, but it all fits together. Moser's difficulty in keeping his fine house, the electricity cut off from most of it, the unkempt garden – the good times being over. Then there's Lisi's acquisition of historical properties, and his interest in the restoration of interiors. It's true, Guidi."

"So, Moser was one of Lisi's debtors."

"I'm certain he was. That he should run into us, of all people." Uneasily, Bora stroked the wheel with his gloved right hand, back and forth. "Naturally on Lisi's papers he would appear as 'M'. But in Lisi's last moments of lucidity the house of the half-moon stood for its owner, and besides it's easier to scribble a crescent than the letter 'M'. *Halbmond*, half-moon, the crescent. Moser. It's a final pun from him." Bora let go of the wheel. "*Luna mendax*, after all. Why didn't I think of it when you asked me what the proverb meant?"

"I still don't know what it means."

"It means that the moon draws a 'C' in the sky, but *lies* about it. According to folklore, when you see the moon form a 'C' in the night sky, you'd think she's a *crescent*, waxing moon. But it isn't. It is a actually a waning moon. When its hump faces the other way and forms a 'D', you'd think it is *decreasing*, while it is not. Why didn't I think that 'C' stood for the moon all along?" Bora sighed deeply. "The anguish I felt at Saint Zeno's was well founded. The biases I criticized in you, I was myself guilty of, and for the most shamefully inexcusable reason: because Moser looked harmless and spoke my language. Christ, because he *understood* me."

Guidi felt almost sorry for him. "There's a chance we're wrong, you know."

"No. You haven't spoken with him as I did when we drove to town. What he unsuspectingly said troubled me, but I didn't know why. Or didn't want to know. People say all kinds of things. And you're right, Guidi, it seemed too much of a coincidence. A damning one at that. When you suggested that Lisi might have been a usurer, I knew Moser was probably one of his debtors; still, I had no proof. Worse, I kept the suspicion to myself. I could *see*, as Valenki did in Russia, or like the madman who stole his victims' shoes for reasons we'll never know. I could see, and decided I was not seeing." Bora turned the key in the ignition, reawakening the engine. "We have a long call to pay in the morning."

"He'll deny everything."

"No. I'm afraid it will be all too easy speaking to him."

Bora did not say another word for the rest of the trip. After dropping Guidi at his house in Sagràte he drove on to Lago, followed by the waxing moon.

It sickened Guidi that Moser would not even try to argue the point, as though he expected this to happen, and he was relieved that it had come through Bora and himself after all. By the steady and defensive bent of Bora's lips, Guidi felt how it strained him to address the old man.

Moser said, "Well, Major, it is hardly the case of denying the truth at this point. I was brought up not to lie." His round, mild face showed overt sympathy for the young men facing him. "Killing is one thing, and lying about it quite another. As a good soldier, Major, you know that murder can be rationalized. You are welcome to take a look at the car. It's parked in the back."

"We've already done it," Guidi said.

The cruel light of early morning filtered with a mute, rosy hue through drapes and dusty window glass. Up in the domed vault, nascent sunbeams were just starting to criss-cross through opaque bull's heads. From the awakening glory of painted clouds, the crescent-bearing Turkish flags flashed to Guidi as he looked.

Moser caught his attention. "Life has ways of gaining on us, Inspector. The night I happened upon you, I would have treated you no differently had I known you were investigating Lisi's death. Had *you* known about me, I trust both of you would have accepted my hospitality all the same." He took a step toward Bora, whose emotions were not so safely checked. "It was very clever of you to understand Lisi's pun. Who'd have supposed he would draw a crescent to point to me and my house? It made my house into a liar moon. But when all is said, even doing away with that usurer would not save this place. It was merely time I was borrowing, in hopes I would die before the day of reckoning. *Dies Irae*, Major Bora." Moser walked to the piano, and sat facing the keys. "I want you to know that only after Lisi told me he'd turn this house into a hotel did I make up my mind. My house, a hotel! The soldiers' haven, where Mozart had played the Silbermann as a child! He *had* to die." Moser seemed himself surprised by the logic of the argument. "Who'd ever think that the last of the Mosers would summon the criminal courage to commit murder? Murder, it was. Yes. And I rationalized it much as you explain your own career, Major Bora. After all, I had a gun. My father's, last used to hunt boars in Serbia, but how appropriate. I planned to drive to Lisi's country house, let myself in and shoot him. The plan changed when I saw him alone in his wheelchair by the flower beds. God, that tawdry house of his, pink as a harlot and horribly furnished! I knew what to do, Major. I careened through the open gate and struck him at full speed. Then I put the car in reverse. But in driving out I miscalculated the width of the gate, and grazed one of the pillars. All in all, the deed was easy. Morally reprehensible, but easy."

Guidi said, "The fender of your car is also damaged."

"Good Lord, Inspector, it should be! I struck Lisi with all the bitterness of poverty and solitude in the face of his ill-gained wealth and abominable poor taste!" Because Bora had drawn close to the piano, Moser turned a friendly face to him. "*Na, Herr Major* – I hope for your own good that you never stand to lose your dear house as I did."

Bora was amazingly candid, considering that Guidi was present. "I think of it often, with the War going the way it is. If *my Turks* defeat me, I'll lose much more than my house. I may lose my country."

"You understand, then."

"No. I understand the necessity to kill, not to commit murder. And for my sanity, as a soldier I must be able to differentiate between the two."

Moser smiled a little. "My ancestors must have reasoned in the same way, but there's no difference really. Look at the ceiling, and tell me if it isn't fancy butchery that built this house, crescents trodden underfoot and all, the portico laid as a Turkish crescent in a flag of land. War is a great homicide, Major."

Sad, but thank God it's over, Guidi thought. He stepped toward the door to fetch the notebook, which he'd left in Bora's car. At that moment, Bora – looking at the ivories on the keyboard, not at the old man – posed another question.

"*Herr* Moser, when did *Signora* Lisi ask you to do it?"

An immediate, perfect silence came over the hall, suspended and intricate like a spider's web. Delicate and difficult to break, but Bora was not done asking.

"When did you talk to her, *Herr* Moser?"

Moser took a long, resigned breath before answering. He looked caught for the first time since Bora and Guidi had walked in. "That, too, you understood. By telephone, Major, in mid-November. By accident. You see, I was late for my payment that month, by no means an unusual event. But Lisi insisted that debtors call and set up a time to see him in Verona. Usually he added something to the dues, you know. So they were always hard calls to make, and from a public phone, too. That day his wife Clara answered, and we got to talking. I must tell you, Major, a good woman such as she, abused in spite of all she did for him – it revolted me."

Guidi was stunned. He watched, rather than heard, Bora calmly say to Moser, "Indeed. How much did *Signora* Lisi tell you about herself?"

"Not much, reserved as she is. She mentioned the children she bore him, her hard work as an actress before he forced her to leave the stage. Her parents' tragic death in the Spanish flu. She mentioned – no, I really understood it, from her reticence – how Lisi dared lay hands on her, despite her illness."

While Guidi was rooted midway between the foot of the stairs and the door, Bora kept absolute control on his words, and the situation. "Really. How ill do you think Clara Lisi is?"

"I take it you haven't met her, Major. I haven't either, but we spoke again by phone, two or three times. Poor Clara, confined to bed ever since their last child was born months ago. When she *asked*, Major…" Moser straightened his shoulders. "This, you must understand. It was suddenly like a knightly deed, for me. My crass desire to see him dead was ennobled by her request. There was now something sacred in bringing that monstrous human being down. Not only would I and God knows how many others be free of our debts, but a pure and good woman would be avenged for her years of suffering. I'd hoped to go up to her small bedroom after the shooting, and tell *Signora* Clara that her troubles were over. But the monster was in the driveway, and the rest, you know. The gun, Inspector, you'll find in the cellar."

Guidi said a mechanical yes. For some reason, what he feared most at this time was Bora's telling the truth about Claretta. But Bora said nothing more about her. "*Herr* Moser, is there anything I can do for you?"

As one suffocating, Guidi had to get out of the house. The few steps to fetch his notebook from the car exposed him to the chill of an astonishingly clear day, filling the ample semicircle of the colonnade. Only minutes ago, the thought of being able to tell Claretta that she was free had made him euphoric. Now – he didn't know what he felt now, other than confusion. What would happen next was so different from what he had envisioned, it took more than he had in him to make plans. When he walked back inside, Moser was standing at the centre of the hall and Bora several paces away from him, still facing the piano.

"Are we almost ready, Inspector?"

"Yes. I expect I could book you in the car."

With old-fashioned courtesy Moser bowed his head. "I thank you. Just the time to gather my change, then." Slowly but straight-backed, Moser walked to the beautiful stairway. Once at the top of the ramp, again he bowed to the men. "With your permission."

"Major," Guidi began, "I can't begin to say..." But Bora gave no sign of listening. Turned away from the stairs, he stood fixed to the honey-coloured silhouette of the Silbermann. Keeping watch, it seemed. For what, Guidi could not tell. "I'll phone the Verona police as soon as we reach a public phone." Oblivious to him, Bora stared at the beautiful length of the piano. "Of course you'll want to phone De Rosa as well, and Colonel Habermehl—"

The loud report from upstairs sent a burst of echoes through the vault. Guidi was so unprepared for it, it took him a moment to react. Then, "Damn, no, no!" He scrambled to the stairs, flinging the unlit cigarette over his shoulder. Past Bora, he reached and bounded up the steps. Bora let him go. His tense face flashed pale and was left behind.

Guidi shouted at him, "You gave him your gun! I stepped out for a moment and you gave him your gun!"

Bora unlatched his empty holster. At a deliberate pace, he followed up the stairs. In the bedroom, Guidi was kneeling by Moser's body. Blood had soaked the threadbare carpet under his head in a dark semicircle. Bora stayed only long enough to retrieve the P38, which without wiping he returned to the holster, and walked downstairs again.

When Guidi joined him in the garden, Bora had gone beyond the colonnade. There, pedestals overgrown with vines held statues of the four seasons. The time-worn statues resembled much-nibbled sugar, and the field-grey uniform stood like a shadow among them.

"I'll have to report this, Major." Guidi forced himself to sound unaffected.

Bora gave him an outraged, brief glance. "Go ahead."

Stone benches connected the pedestals. Guidi went to sit on one of the pitted, eroded surfaces and stayed there, drinking in the raw, cold sunshine of year's end with his eyes closed, so that a floating red-and-blue darkness surrounded him. "At least tell me why you did it."

"Why shouldn't I? He asked me to."

"You could have said no."

"I had no intention of saying no. It would benefit no one to keep him alive for the trial. All Moser wanted was to die in his house, and I gave him a chance to do it. It was a small concession."

"Except that you are an accessory to his death."

"So be it."

"While Enrica Salviati…"

"Enrica Salviati? Oh, please. It's a matter of cultural habits, Guidi: we Germans fire bullets into our own heads. In Fascist Italy people *stumble* on the tracks while a train is coming. Or a tramway. What if the comrades had decided to silence her, so that no more gossip could come out about the *departed saint*, Lisi? It could be, couldn't it? It's up to you to look into the matter, although I doubt you'll get very far."

Guidi opened his eyes, and saw Bora only a few steps away, standing with his head low in the winter sun. "With Moser dead, Major, Claretta is the only one who must answer for her husband's death. You'll have to testify in that regard."

"No. *You* will."

"From the start, this has been your game. Why should I take it over now?"

"Because I can't."

"And why not?"

"I'm being transferred from Lago." Bora unexpectedly seemed very young to Guidi, younger than himself and, despite his uniform and rank, more vulnerable, more endangered.

"Transferred? For no reason?"

"There are reasons."

Guidi swallowed. He was, more than ever, aware that Bora shared nothing with him but the filings of his mind, jealously guarding the rest. Only it might not be out of haughtiness, but out of prudence, or decency. Or courage. It came to his mind – a quick thought he chased away at once – that perhaps it had been Monsignor Lai, in Saint Zeno's cloister. That turning Gardini in to the SS was perhaps the price Bora paid to his military conscience in order to justify what he did for others, to save others, quietly, at the risk of his own life.

"It is up to you to make of this case what you must, Guidi. I have run out of time."

Guidi was tempted to detect a suggestion in Bora's words, and was careful not to jeopardize it by sounding impulsive. "So, where will you go?" he asked.

"I hope to be able to get an assignment to Rome."

"And if you don't?"

"If I don't, I don't know what will happen."

Guidi closed his eyes again. He knew Bora was walking away by the crunch of gravel under his measured, limping step.

The two of them could never be friends. Even though Bora had called him *mein Freund*, it meant nothing. Unwilling to look around, Guidi felt the wind rising to whisper incomprehensible words in his ears. Snow would soon follow on the north wind's back as on an invisible saddle. Today or tomorrow Claretta would act once more, according to how he decided to handle her role in Lisi's death. Would she deny everything? She would, lamb-eyed in her providential pregnancy. She'd either cry or smile at him, and he'd look away from her tears, or her smile. *Tomorrow, Christmas Day,*

1943. November is a short and cruel month, and December kills the year.

Soon he could no longer hear Bora's step. When he looked, he saw that he'd walked back to the BMW. Still Sandro Guidi remained on the bench, tasting the wind from the bitter north. He had to weigh in his heart the truth that Bora and he had, despite all odds, become what in other circumstances anyone would call *friends*. He had to, whatever it meant for their souls.

Beyond the garden, paling over the unruly crest of overgrown boxwood, the moon sank back into the sky. Guidi left the bench, and walked to join Martin Bora in the army car.

LUMEN

Ben Pastor

The first in the Martin Bora series

October 1939, Cracow, Nazi-occupied Poland.

Wehrmacht Captain Martin Bora discovers the abbess, Mother Kazimierza, shot dead in her convent garden. Her alleged power to see the future has brought her a devoted following. But her work and motto, "Lumen Christi Adiuva Nos", appear also, it transpires, to have brought her some enemies.

Father Malecki had come to Cracow from Chicago at the Pope's bidding, to investigate Mother Kazimierza's powers. Now the Vatican orders him to stay and assist in the inquiry into her killing.

Stunned by the violence of the occupation and the ideology of his colleagues, Bora's sense of Prussian duty is tested to breaking point. The interference of seductive actress Ewa Kowalska does not help matters.

PRAISE FOR *LUMEN*

"Pastor's plot is well crafted, her prose sharp...a disturbing mix of detection and reflection" *Publishers Weekly*

'And don't miss LUMEN by Ben Pastor. When an abbess thought to have supernatural powers is murdered in Nazi-occupied Cracow, the Wehrmacht captain's investigation is complicated by his compatriots' cruelty and the Catholic Church's secrecy. An interesting, original and melancholy tale.' *Literary Review*

"A mystery, it rivets the reader until the end and beyond, with its twist of historical realities. A historical piece, it faithfully reproduces the grim canvas of war. A character study, it captures the thoughts and actions of real people, not stereotypes."
The Fredericksburg Free Lance Star

www.bitterlemonpress.com